Praise for Michael Kun

"A truly interesting new voice."

—*Publisher's Weekly*

"A writer in the vein of J.D. Salinger."

—*The Richmond Times-Dispatch*

"Once readers sample Kun's hilariously off-kilter world view, they're frequently hooked for life."

—*The Baltimore Sun*

More Books from Michael Kun

More Books from The Sager Group

Mandela was Late: Odd Things & Essays From the Seinfeld Writer Who Coined Yada, Yada and Made Spongeworthy a Compliment
by Peter Mehlman

#MeAsWell, A Novel
by Peter Mehlman

The Orphan's Daughter, A Novel
by Jan Cherubin

*Words to Repair the World:
Stories of Life, Humor and Everyday Miracles*
by Mike Levine

Miss Havilland, A Novel
by Gay Daly

*Revenge of the Donut Boys:
True Stories of Lust, Fame, Survival and Multiple Personality*
By Mike Sager

Lifeboat No. 8: Surviving the Titanic
by Elizabeth Kaye

Eat Wheaties!, A Novel
By Michael Kun

See our entire library at TheSagerGroup.net

THE
ALLERGIC BOY
VERSUS THE
LEFT-HANDED
GIRL

By Michael Kun

A Novel

The Allergic Boy Versus the Left-Handed Girl: A Novel

Copyright © 2021 Michael Kun
Published in the United States of America.

Cover and Interior Designed by Siori Kitajima, SF AppWorks LLC

Cataloging-in-Publication data for this book is available from the Library of Congress
ISBN-13:
eBook: 978-1-950154-50-0
Paperback: 978-1-950154-51-7
Hardcover: 978-1-950154-52-4

Published by The Sager Group LLC
TheSagerGroup.net

THE
ALLERGIC BOY
═══ VERSUS THE ═══
LEFT-HANDED
GIRL

By Michael Kun

A Novel

THE SAGER GROUP

Artifex Te Adiuva

"Aaaah-chooo!"
—*The Allergic Boy*

"Cough! Cough!"
—*The Left-Handed Girl*

For my daughter Paige

Table Of Contents

PUBLISHER'S NOTE

The original, typed manuscript of this strange volume you hold in your hands was discovered among the personal effects of one James Edgar Nail of Baltimore, Maryland and delivered to this publisher by his daughter in a shirt box. It is being published here verbatim, including its unwieldy and inflammatory title, as well as several purposeful misspellings of words not often misspelled by men and women of letters ("dictation," "ascot," etc.). Any substantive errors or misstatements that remain within the text are Mr. Nail's, not this publisher's, and have not been remedied so as to preserve evidence of Mr. Nail's state of mind and to allow it to be conveyed to the reader without any editorial filter. In short, you will find no corrections and no apologies herein.

It appears, but cannot be verified, that the original manuscript of this book was written by Mr. Nail at different times between the calendar years 1982 and 2006, that conclusion being based upon the handwritten dates on several well-worn notebooks discovered among Mr. Nail's effects, as well as his references to historical events that occurred during that 24-year span of years and the absence of references to any events that transpired thereafter. There are, for instance, no references whatsoever to any historical events occurring after 2006 (such as presidential elections), or to any technology that was available thereafter (smartphones or electric cars), and several individuals long deceased are referred to in the present tense in the manuscript as if they were still among the living, including noted filmmaker Orson Welles (d. October 10, 1985) and professional basketball player Wilt Chamberlain (d. October 12, 1999). Additionally, Mr. Nail makes reference in one passage to being "62 years old, soon to be 63." Given his March 27, 1944 birthdate, as verified by a birth certificate issued on that date by Union Memorial Hospital in Baltimore, Maryland, that statement presumably would have been written sometime in calendar year 2006 unless Mr. Nail was confused about his own date of birth, the possibility of which is more than slim.

Although on occasion Mr. Nail refers to his "publisher," and several passages suggest that his manuscript was soon to be published in some form, those references do not refer to this publisher, which only first received an unsolicited, typewritten copy of the manuscript in the United States mail from Mr. Nail's daughter after Mr. Nail succumbed to a heart attack on a United Airlines flight headed toward Portland, Oregon; he was dead before the plane touched the ground, we have been told. To the extent Mr. Nail's statements about a forthcoming publication suggest that he had contracted with a different publisher to distribute this book, this publisher's legal representatives researched that possibility with considerable diligence in order to ensure that there would be no dispute with another publisher about the legal right to publish this work. No records were located that would indicate that any North American publisher had, in fact, purchased the rights to Mr. Nail's manuscript or had otherwise planned to release it for general sale to the public.

Intriguingly, the Autumn 1997 catalog for the publisher Advanced Medical Media includes a reference to a nonfiction book entitled "Allergies and Handedness," attributed to an author with the name Tomas Verdi, M.D. and scheduled to be published in hardcover edition in November 1997. It does not appear that book was ever published by Advanced Medical Media or by any other publisher, for that matter. No copies of that book have been located, nor does the Library of Congress have any record of such a book, and efforts to find one Dr. Tomas Verdi proved similarly fruitless, suggesting the name was a pseudonym or that he was a foreign author. Further, United States Bankruptcy Court records indicate that Advanced Medical Media filed for bankruptcy protection in 1998 under Chapter 11 of the United States Bankruptcy Code, and other records indicate that the company ceased all operations in 2002. Moreover, the very brief description of the book that appeared in Advanced Medical Media's Autumn 1997 catalog — "An analysis of recent studies regarding the correlation between allergies and left- (or right-) handedness" — confirms that it indeed was not the same book as Mr. Nail's and that the similarity of the titles is coincidental and nothing more. Accordingly, if any publication of the book that the reader holds was planned, it may well have been self-publication by Mr. Nail through one of the many "vanity presses" that were operating at that time. It is just as likely, if not more likely, that any anticipated publication was imagined by a man with a large scar on the side of his head.

At the request of Mr. Nail's estate, any author's royalties for this volume, after first being credited against the small advance payment made to the estate, shall then be directed to settle Mr. Nail's unpaid medical bills and other outstanding debts, with any royalties thereafter to be distributed to several charities and nonprofit organizations identified by his estate, including the American Cancer Society and the Agazola (Oregon) Neighborhood Crime Watch.

For reasons that will become evident to the reader shortly, this publisher is obliged to present this volume as a work of fiction. Libraries and bookstores are requested to shelve volumes of this book with works of fiction.

They are not bound to do so.

—Jessica M. Cavanaugh
Senior Editor
May 19, 2008

THE ALLERGIC BOY VERSUS THE LEFT-HANDED GIRL

A Story of Grace and Mercy
(But Also of Theft, Injustice and a Fucking Scar on the Side of My Fucking Head)[1]

By Jimmy Nail

---

1   A note to the editor: I ask kindly that you not remove "fucking" from the fucking title. Except if you need to do so for copies sold through the Book of the Month Club. I understand they can be prickly and may have a distaste for profanities. The same for publications in any countries that have laws forbidding the use of profanities. Israel perhaps? Hong Kong? Nova Scotia? (Although Nova Scotia may not be a country. That is probably worth researching.)

DEDICATION

For Poppy Fowler.

Not Poppy Fahrenberg.

And certainly not Poppy Fahrenheit, which is an absurd name for any person, real or imagined.

If someone ever walked up to you at a social function or a business meeting, took your hand in her tiny hand, and introduced herself to you as Poppy Fahrenheit, you'd laugh until you were gasping for breath. (Gasp, gasp, gasp!)

But I am straying from the more important point, which is the dedication of this important book. This book is dedicated to Poppy Fowler, wherever she may be, with grace and mercy.

SUNDAY PAPERS

The newspaper from which I would someday learn that Peter John Darbin had a heart — *The Sun,* one of Baltimore's daily papers — was the very same newspaper that I had delivered to neighbors as a teenager, waking in darkness at five o'clock in the morning to the beeping of an alarm clock (beep-beep-beep), folding the papers into thirds and stuffing them into a burlap shoulder bag, wheeling my bicycle up and down the streets, tossing papers on the stoops of row house after row house, then returning home for a quick breakfast before school.[2] Most mornings, though, it was cold cereal with milk or, if we ran out of milk, water.

Sundays were different. I still rose at the same dark hour — five o'clock (beep-beep-beep) — but like most Sunday newspapers, the Sunday *Sun* was much larger than the weekday editions. More sections, more advertising inserts ("Luskins Appliances Big Spring Sale!"), more everything. The Sunday *Sun* was too heavy and too thick to fold, or to carry in a burlap bag, or to distribute by bicycle. Instead, I would load the Sunday papers onto the same red wagon that I had played with as a younger boy, then pull the wagon behind me on the sidewalks as I walked the streets, a process that took several times longer to complete than the weekday routine but, hopefully, would lead to generous tips from customers who peered out their living room windows and saw me struggling.

---

2   There were days when breakfast was cold spaghetti left over from the prior night's dinner. "It's what they do for breakfast in Italy!" my mother claimed. That sound you heard was my stomach protesting.

It was on one of those Sunday mornings in June, the beginning of the summer between my junior and senior years at Theodore Roosevelt Regional High School, while returning home with my empty red wagon, that a stray black dog the size of a pickle barrel appeared between me and our row house. I did not think much of it until, as I approached, I realized that it not only was not retreating, but it was baring its horrible, yellow teeth, the same sickly color one might associate with a colicky baby. When I stopped, the dog knew I was afraid; dogs, like lawyers, can sense fear, or so I have been informed about both. When I took a small step in retreat, confirming what the dog already knew, it was upon me in a snap, its beast's teeth digging into my bare left calf like my leg was a ribeye steak (I was wearing shorts in the early summer morning).[3]

Just then, I heard the shriek of a frightened little girl nearby. It was chilling, like something you would hear in a horror movie before someone in a mask buried an ax into some girl trying to escape a haunted house. Was the girl behind me? She shrieked again. Where was she? Only then did I realize that the shrieks were coming from my very own throat; my voice had not changed yet and would not deepen until I had made my way to New York University. The beast's sharp, wet teeth twisted into my leg, producing another shriek, then a sneeze (aaaah-chooo, my dog allergy). I twisted but could not break free. I could not imagine an end to the attack, or the shrieks, or now, the sneezing (aaaah-chooo, aaaah-chooo, aaaah-chooo!). But suddenly, there was a dull thump, the sound of a bag of sand landing on solid ground. My leg was free, and the dog was scurrying away. It might have been whimpering; let us say it was. Someone had

---

3   To the editor: The teeth marks are still there many years later to remind me of the encounter. I could provide a photograph if you believe it would be helpful.

kicked it solidly in its pickle barrel ribs, and that someone now had a hand on my shoulder.

"You okay?"

"Yeah, it was a dog," I said, rubbing first the tip of my nose, then bending to touch my tender, bloody leg. I sneezed.

"I know it was a dog. I've seen dogs before."

"I was delivering the papers," I said, gesturing toward my wagon, "and then there was a dog." Again, I sneezed.

"Nice wagon."

"It's just for delivering newspapers," I said.

"I don't see any newspapers."

"That's because I was done delivering them, and I was headed home."

"Whatever you say."

"It's true. I deliver papers in the wagon on Sundays."

"Do you always sneeze when a dog is biting you?"

"I'm allergic to dogs," I said, then needlessly volunteered, "and cats and penicillin."

"That is such an interesting thing to share with a stranger. Which one is your house? I'll walk you home."

I pointed to our row house in the middle of the block and said, "Number 1336."

"That's funny. I'm living in number 1334 for the summer with my uncle."

"That's next door," I said.

"I know that's next door. That's why I said it. Jesus."

"Your uncle is Rob?" I said, suddenly recalling the name of the current tenant. He was an exceedingly thin, fragile-looking, black-haired man who worked as a teller at the bank (Maryland National Savings and Loan). He was always well dressed. Suit. Bowties. Pockets squares. He was, I was sure, a homosexual; I could hear him and his lover through the walls of our row house late, late at night ("Yes!" "Yes!" "Now!" "I'm close!").

"Yes, Uncle Rob."

"He seems like a nice guy."

"He's a jackass."

"Sorry."

"Is it your fault he's a jackass?"

"No."

"Then there's no reason for you to be sorry."

"He's a homosexual," I said.[4]

"That's what I hear, too."

"It doesn't bother you that he's homosexual?"

"Not as much as it bothers me that you're allergic to cats."

We were in front of our houses now — 1334 and 1336.

"I'm Jimmy Nail," I said, extending a hand far too formally. "Thanks for your help with the dog."

"Just doing my job keeping the neighborhood safe from dogs and homosexuals," my savior said. "I'm Poppy Fowler."

You're a smart one. You knew it was Poppy Fowler all along.

She extended her left hand first, then withdrew it and put her right hand in mine. I must have given her a strange look because she said, "What, you've never met a left-handed girl before?"

She squeezed my hand more firmly than I had expected, then released it. "You really need to work on your scream. You sound like a little girl. Try to scream like a man." Suddenly, she lowered her voice, mimicking that of a man, and patted her flat stomach. "A scream should come from here. From

---

4   I did not use the word "homosexual." I will not repeat here the word I used and will say nothing more about it other than that the word I used was commonly accepted at that time, more or less. You can probably guess the word if you'd like. It began with an "F." And if it helps make this account more complete for you, feel free to write the word here if you wish: _____. Just do not do that if you have borrowed this book from a library. Or from a homosexual friend. Neither will be pleased.

the diaphragm," she said gruffly. Then she screamed, loudly, from her diaphragm: "Jimmy Nail is allergic to cats!"

"Stop it," I pleaded, looking up and down the sidewalk, seeing no one.

"Fine," she said, before screaming, "Jimmy Nail is a homosexual!" from her diaphragm.

I thought I saw some curtains rustling in one of the row houses when she said that, maybe some eyes peering through a little crack in the curtains.

"Go get cleaned up," she instructed me. "I'll see you later, Jimmy Nail."

A SIMPLE TRUTH

Once in his life, every boy falls in love in an instant. In the time it takes to cough, the time it takes to sneeze.

He is powerless to do anything else.

He will be moved by irresistible impulses.

He will, suddenly, believe in the existence of God because, well, how else could this possibly be explained?

INTRODUCTION

I am not like you and you and you.

I do not look wistfully upon the asthmatic days of my youth, nor do I allow myself to change well-remembered details of those years to soothe an aching heart. Street lamps have not become cherry trees, nor rocks plums, or bruisings warm embraces. Solitary nights studying chess strategy manuals at the dining room table have not become Saturday afternoon triumphs on the football field.[5] The plump, acned girl who laughed at my earnest and stam-stam-stammering invitation to the winter formal ("A Winter's Brrrrr-eak") has not become a full-chested sweater girl who kissed, then bedded, me. My parents (Henry, June) have not, through magic (presto! chango!), become your parents: adoring, sweet, rah-rah-rah-ing my every little achievement. And so on and so on.

Let me be clear:

I am no pauper who became a titan of industry.

I am no hero who rose from a hardscrabble childhood, who bought a cape, who taught himself to fly.

I am no martyr.

And I am no liar, at least no more than you or you or you.

It is important that I remain accurate now, more important than ever. That is both my goal and my commitment: accuracy, painstaking accuracy. It is not my endeavor to catalog all of my shortcomings and a lifetime of

---

5   A note to the editor: Please do not change "football field" to "gridiron," the word often found in the sports pages to describe the field of play used in the game. Not only does the word not flow well, but I imagine that many potential readers (women, foreigners, homosexuals) may not know what a "gridiron" even is.

disappointments just for the sake of doing so, nor to create a long, humdrum account of silly sufferings best forgotten. No, I wish to be entirely forthright, to relate the good and the bad, successes (several) and failures (plentiful) in equally harsh and unforgiving light, because I understand that any inaccuracies, any hyperbole, any half-truths (or three-quarter truths or seven-eighths), could impeach my credibility on the larger matter to be addressed.

The larger matter, the nut in the proverbial nutshell, is this: In high school (Theodore Roosevelt Regional High School) and college (briefly, too briefly, New York University), when others played baseball or basketball or football, I played chess, and I read, but mostly I wrote stories (longhand, cursive, Palmer method). When my classmates went to parties and drank beer and spiked their drinks with whatever liquor they could put their greasy paws on, I stayed at home coughing (allergies), sniffing (more allergies) and writing. Always writing, a singular, solitary endeavor designed for lovestruck teenaged girls and skinny, shy teenaged boys, and, of course, for professionals who are paid to twist words around each other so that someone somewhere will keep turning the pages before reaching the revelation that occurs just before "The End." (The doctor was the boy's father all along! The murderer used an icicle, which explains the puddle of water surrounding the corpse! So *he* was the one she loved, not the other fellow!)

I will save you the time of turning the pages of this book to read the revelation that occurs just before "The End." Here is the revelation: I did it! Me! Your aging typist!

When my classmates at Theodore Roosevelt Regional High School danced or sang or cheered our school's athletic squads ("We stand tall and carry big sticks!"), I wrote, and I wrote, and I wrote. And coughed and sneezed and sniffed.

Then when I was done writing, I typed, and I typed, and I typed what I had written (clack-clack-clack-clack-clack.)[6]

I had, and still have, the calluses on my fingers to prove it. They do not go away. They are the telltale marks of a writer. (Or a seamstress, which I was not. I cannot darn worth a darn.)[7]

Mostly, I wrote short stories, a form that was popular at the time and published in many monthly magazines (*Colliers, Harpers*, etc.), less popular now. I wrote ghost stories (boo!). Cowboy stories (bang! bang!). Stories about gangsters or spaceships or professional athletes winning the big game or detectives solving unsolvable mysteries. They were stories about people and events I little understood, and, but for an occasional turn of a phrase, they were nothing to take much pride in, wastes of time and paper and ink, worthless clack-clacking. Upon the advice of a pretty red-haired girl I knew too briefly (see the "Dedication"), I put aside the ghosts and

---

6   The typewriter I used was a black Underwood that once belonged to my maternal grandmother (Helen, now deceased), who wrote an advice column for her local newspaper until it was forced out of business by a comparatively slick competitor. The typewriter was passed along to my mother (now deceased as well), who rarely used it, then to me on my twelfth birthday. (Do not think it to have been a disappointing gift; it was precisely what I had wanted. What would I do with a baseball mitt?) The typewriter is in safekeeping today, although I prefer not to divulge where it is stored for fear that someone might steal or wreck it and, in so doing, destroy a critical piece of evidence that supports my position both legally and ethically. (Do not think them to be the same: They may be related, but law and ethics are cousins, at best.)

7   A note to the editor: I recognize that this pun may be on the silly side of things, but I ask that you not remove it. It is important that readers find me charming as early as possible, and silly puns convey a certain non-threatening charm. That is particularly so for female, foreign or homosexual readers.

cowboys and spacemen and detectives, and I wrote instead about something I did understand, something I understood better than anyone. I wrote about a shy, asthmatic, allergy-ridden, broken-nosed teenage boy. I wrote about the pretty red-haired teenaged girl who briefly, too briefly, lived in the slender little house next door. I wrote, and it felt like flying. It was fiction, yes, but it was fiction with its toes dipped in fact.

I started writing that story before my senior year in high school. I put it aside, for reasons I will explain herein, and I would not finish it until my first semester of college. When I was finished transferring my words from handwritten to typed pages, I had written a short novel, a very impressive accomplishment for anyone, you must admit, let alone a college freshman, regardless of its literary merit. I handed the thin manuscript — two hundred pages or so of onion paper held together by sturdy rubber bands — to a similarly-minded college classmate to read over our Christmas break, and he gave me several of his short stories to read as well.[8] An even swap, more or less, at least from the standpoint of quantity. Two hundred pages (or thereabouts) for two hundred pages (or thereabouts).

But as mean luck would have it, I could not afford to return to college for the spring semester of my freshman year because of a sad reversal in my father's fortunes (horse racing, alcohol, no more need be said). Instead, I remained at my parents' modest three-bedroom Baltimore house, seemingly a continent away from my college classmate and

---

8   For younger readers, onion paper was exceedingly thin paper favored by writers for many years but largely unavailable at the time I am writing this footnote. It was close to transparent, like onion skin or the skin on your grandmother's arm. Given the choice of these two options to describe their product, the manufacturer wisely chose the former.

my thin manuscript, holding a series of uninspiring, nearly forgettable jobs (delicatessen, movie theater) to help my parents pay their mortgage and their bills, then joining the United States Army at a time when joining the Army seemed a thoughtful and reasonable choice for a young man looking to keep busy and maybe kill a few North Vietnamese.[9]

I would not see my typed manuscript again.[10] It remained in the possession of my sad-eyed, round-faced college classmate, who ignored my inelegant entreaties for its safe and immediate return, who hung up the receiver of the dormitory telephone whenever he heard my voice on the other end of the line, or shortly thereafter.

"Just listen to me for a minute," I would plead into my end of the telephone connection. "Peter, listen." I could hear the ruckus of the dormitory in the background on his end. Whooping, yelling, competing record players.[11]

---

9   Please note that I killed no North Vietnamese persons during my service to our great country. I want to make that plain so as not to impact sales of this book in North Vietnam. Mind you, I was more than willing to do so, if necessary, a point I hope that book buyers in South Vietnam will keep in mind.

10   Although I retained my original, handwritten notebooks! I did not make photocopies of the typed manuscript, as the smart-aleck lawyers suggested I should have done, for the simple reason that photocopy machines were not as readily available then as they are today.

11   Records were vinyl discs that somehow contained music within their circular grooves, and that music sprung to life when touched by the diamond needle of a machine that spun them around at different rates of speed depending upon the size of the vinyl disc. They were replaced by eight-track tapes, which somehow contained music on a thin brown strip of tape. Those were replaced by cassette tapes, which did the same thing, as far as I understand. Cassette tapes were then replaced by thin silver discs called compact

"Stop bothering me," Peter would respond. "I'm busy. I have no time to deal with people who failed out of school!"

"I didn't fail out," I would say.

"Well, I have even less time for dropouts."

"I didn't drop out," I would say, somewhat inaccurately. I would try to explain about my father, about the horse racing and alcohol, about how I was working at the delicatessen (or movie theater), but soon would only hear the click of the receiver, then the dial tone (bzzzzz!).

Eventually, someone else would answer my telephone calls to the dormitory, explaining that, like me, my classmate had also left school. (So you don't like dropouts, Peter? Hypocrite!) There was no forwarding address. He was gone, and my manuscript was gone with him.

I pictured my manuscript in the large metal trash bin outside the dormitory, pictured a burly, unshaved trashman snuffing out a fat cigar on the title page where the words *The Allergic Boy* were typed, pictured the ashy ring it left above my typed name (Jimmy Nail, no pen name or silly initials for me), pictured the same trashman hauling my manuscript off to the city dump, pictured the seagulls pecking at the letters like birdseed, and I resigned myself to retyping the novel again from my notebooks, which I did not do because, like you and you and you, I am sometimes lazy and often procrastinate. Plus, as you perhaps have experienced yourself, a task done twice is more tedious the second time. Imagine raking

---

discs that looked like metal drink coasters but somehow contained music. At the time I am writing this footnote, those compact discs are being replaced by some computerized technology that only a nuclear physicist could comprehend. I mention all of this because I can only assume that young readers of this book and future generations of readers will see my reference to "record players" and say, "What in the hell is he referring to?" Now you know, young readers. And please know that I was not the least bit offended by your use of the word "hell," but others might be.

fallen leaves into a pile only to have a brisk gust of autumn wind undo your work. Imagine your shoulders sagging as you commence the same task again.

Years later, returning from not killing any North Vietnamese, I would see the words from my manuscript in type, but not by my own hands. I would see them, stylishly edited and published, with the title and character names changed — no longer *The Allergic Boy*, but now *The Left-Handed Girl*, and Poppy Fahrenberg was now Poppy Fahrenheit (an absurd fucking name!) — and with my classmate's name on the dust jacket, his brooding photograph on the inside back flap.

His name on my book, his fat potato face where mine should have been.

His name: Peter John Darbin.

P.J., for short.

CONFIRMATION

Yes, *that* P.J. Darbin.

I can practically hear an army of eighth graders squealing at the mere mention of their idol's name.

Let me say it again: P.J. Darbin.

Squeal, children, squeal!

You will stop squealing soon enough, once you read my sad, entirely truthful story about your villainous hero. You will never think of him the same way again.[12]

---

12   A note to the editor: I believe there are several black-and-white photographs of P.J. Darbin that are in the public domain such that they can be reproduced at no cost to you. If I am correct, please insert one here. And use a black Magic Marker to give him a fat Hitler mustache and a villainous scar on his cheek that winds like a river through rocky terrain. Beneath, please print these words: "The world was shocked to learn that renowned writer P.J. Darbin in fact was an illiterate thief who was missing at least one chromosome. He may have also been the leader of the Third Reich."

A SIMPLE, HUMANE REQUEST TO P.J. DARBIN

Peter, you must set the record straight, before we die! This is your last chance!

A CLARIFICATION

Stop.

Please do not misconstrue the previous section. It was in no way meant to be a threat of harm but instead, nothing more than an acknowledgment of a truism: Time is running out on each of us. Death snakes closer each day.

You will not be able to set the record straight from your grave, Peter, or from a genie's bottle of your ashes sitting on someone's mantelpiece. Nor will it do any good if you wait until I am in the grave or in my own genie's bottle on my daughter's mantel.[13]

You must do it now.

Today!

Tomorrow!

Soon!

Please, Peter, I know you do not have a black heart. I know that you did what you did out of youthful indiscretion, that you never intended what occurred. I know that now. You probably thought I had died in Vietnam. I almost did. You should see the fucking scar on the side of my fucking head, Peter.

But you are no longer young, Peter, nor am I. As I write this sentence, I am as gray-haired and saggy as my grandfather ever was. My bones scream bloody murder when I walk.

Confess, Peter.

There are only three of us who know the truth: you, me and Poppy.

Poppy Fowler.

Not Poppy *Fahrenberg*.

---

13 "Hello, Claire," I say if my daughter should read this. "You are the joy of my life."

And certainly not Poppy *Fahrenheit*.

Confess.

Confess, then we can meet again in heaven and shake hands, forgiven and friends again.

YOU MUST KNOW WHOM TO HATE

At the moment that I am typing this sentence (clack-clack-clack), the sun is brilliant, the sky is clement and unclouded, the calendar says that it is March, and I am 62 years of age, soon to be 63, older than my father and grandfather ever were, younger than I will be tomorrow.

Other sentences in the book you are holding were written at other ages, some when I was 50, some when I was 60, and so on and so on.

This book you are holding has been written, then revised, then revised again for many years, but that will come to an end soon when (finally!) it will be published (hurrah!), and the truth will finally be told. Were you the first person to purchase this book? The hundredth? The *millionth*? No matter. You bought it, and I thank you warmly for your purchase and for embracing the unsettling truth this book sets forth.[14] You have made an old man happy. Today, I am like a sad little boy confined to a hospital on Christmas Eve. Tomorrow, I am going home to open my gifts, still wrapped and shiny under the tree!

From time to time, I have revised a sentence in this book if a detail returned to me or an error needed correcting, such that a single paragraph has become a Frankenstein's monster of words, composed of words written when I was 46, followed by words written when I was 52, then 61, then 48, and so on and so on.[15]

---

14   If you checked this book out from your local public library, you have made me a little less happy. I will receive no royalties in connection with your enjoyment of this book. Not that I am complaining, mind you. But still.

15   A note to the editor: Please do not change "Frankenstein's

Take the following sentence: "I harbor no animosity toward my old friend Peter (or little animosity, which appears occasionally, as bright and as fleeting as Fourth of July fireworks), because I understand that, in this world, you must know whom to hate."[16]

That sentence was written by three different men, all of them answering to my name if called, including one who is 62 years old, soon to be 63.

Whom do I hate, you may ask, if I do not, in fact, hate Peter John Darbin. Well, I hate Pol Pot, and Adolph Hitler, and Lee Harvey Oswald, like any right-thinking American would. And I hate a certain judge in Baltimore, Maryland.

---

monster" to "Frankenstein." Frankenstein was the name of the doctor, not of his creation. It is a common error and one I do not wish to repeat.

16   "Whom," of course, is the proper word here, not "who," even though "who" would strike the ear more pleasingly in this case. "Whom" sounds contrived in this context. It sounds pretentious and stuffy. But "whom" is the object of the clause and, thus, proper. I have no doubt that Messrs. Strunk and White would agree with me, unless they are drinking buddies of Peter John Darbin.

DISCLAIMER

Pursuant to a court order entered by Judge Miles C. Levy of the Superior Court for the County of Baltimore, Maryland, which was subsequently affirmed by the Maryland Court of Special Appeals (request for review denied by the Maryland Court of Appeals), in order that I be permitted to publish this book, which has been delayed for more than a full decade by a variety of legal wrangling the likes of which have not been seen since Al Capone was tried and convicted for tax evasion, I am required to issue the following disclaimer in English, in bold letters, in a standard type size and font, on this precise page and no other:[17]

All persons and events depicted in this book are entirely fictitious. Any resemblance to any real persons, living or dead, or to any actual events, is entirely unintentional. This includes, but is not limited to, a character referred to herein as "P.J. Darbin." While there, in fact, is a revered American author named "P.J. Darbin," author of the American classic *The Left-Handed Girl*, the character in this book named "P.J. Darbin" is not intended to be the real author "P.J. Darbin." The use of the same name

---

17   As astute readers know, disclaimers are normally found in small print the size of picnic ants on the page directly across from a book's title page, in the vicinity of the Library of Congress number that has been assigned to the book. Few persons ever read a book's disclaimer unless required to do so (the editor of the book, for instance, or its proofreader) or unless they have run out of all other reading material due to unusual circumstances (a prolonged flight or a travel mishap). Putting aside those extreme circumstances, you are likely the first persons since the Peloponnesian Wars to actually read a disclaimer. Lucky you. Lucky, lucky you.

is entirely unintentional. The fact that the fictional "P.J. Darbin" in this book is himself an author is also entirely unintentional, as is the fact that the fictional character named "P.J. Darbin" authored a book with precisely the same title as that which was actually authored by the real author "P.J. Darbin." The real author named "P.J. Darbin" did not author any portion of this book, and any portions of this book attributed to "P.J. Darbin" refer to the fictional "P.J. Darbin," not the real "P.J. Darbin." Any suggestions otherwise are unintentional.

So what you are about to read is just a great coincidence, as far as you know. As if a collection of spider monkeys sitting at a row of typewriters, striking keys at random with their furry digits, just happened to type "P.J. Darbin" not once, but over and over again (clack-clack-clack). As if they just happened to type, over and over, the words *The Left-Handed Girl* — that, of course, being the title of the novel for which P.J. Darbin is acclaimed, a well-worn copy of which is likely on your bookshelf if you are an American with any interest in literature.

Although, I actually wrote that book. Me, your aging typist.

Although, I actually wrote *this* book, the book you hold in your hands, not a collection of typing spider monkeys. Although, I pressed the keys and did not do so at random. I did not randomly type "Peter John Darbin" over and over. I pressed the "P" key with purpose, then I pressed the "E" key, and so on and so on.

Yet it's just an enormous coincidence.

As decreed by Judge Miles C. Levy, there is now a *real* "P.J. Darbin" and a *fictional* "P.J. Darbin." Coincidentally.

And there's a real me and a fictional one, too, I suppose. Just as coincidentally.

All I have to say about that is that Judge Miles C. Levy is a cocksucker.[18]

Not the fictional "Judge Miles C. Levy." The real one. There is no fictional one.

---

18   I would apologize for the use of this crass word, knowing that it is likely to be considered offensive by some readers. However, that apology would be insincere, at best, as words even more offensive appear throughout the pages of this book. For instance, the word "fucking" appears in the title. Twice. Perhaps you had not noticed, or the word was removed from the title to appease the Book of the Month Club. In any event, I would not want to trick you into believing that this is the only time you might be offended, only to have you later find yourself even more offended than you are now, such as when you came across the word "piss." Accordingly, if you find yourself disgusted by the statement that Judge Miles C. Levy is a "cocksucker," I would suggest that you return this book to your library or bookseller immediately. If it is the former (a library), they will be pleased if you return the book in one piece. But if it is the latter (a bookseller), please be careful not to break the spine of the book as most booksellers will not accept return of a book with a broken spine. You should trust me on this. I worked as a clerk in a bookstore after completing my service in the Army. Charm City Books was the name of the store, "Charm City" being Baltimore's longtime sobriquet, a reference not to the city's belief that it is charming but to charm bracelets that were sold here. That bookstore is where I first spotted my book with my classmate's name and photograph on the dust jacket. I was not charmed by the discovery.

ANOTHER COMMENT ABOUT JUDGE MILES C. LEVY

Please let me elaborate on my last comment by saying, without fear of contradiction, that Judge Miles C. Levy is a motherfucking, piece-of-shit cocksucker, and I would not cross the street to piss on him if he were on fire.[19]

Let me tell you what I would do if he were on fire, hypothetically speaking, as I am not threatening to set him on fire, only smiling at the hot fantasy.

If he were on fire, hypothetically speaking, I would cross the street and hover over him, like a crow over a carcass, like a mourner over the fresh mud before the headstone.

And when he said, "Please help me, I'm on fire," I would respond, "You didn't help me when I needed help, did you, Judge Cocksucker?"

Then, struggling for breath and finding only brown smoky air, he would say, "Who are you? I don't remember you."

And I would say, "I'm the one whose book P.J. Darbin stole." I would take off my hat and say, "Remember me now?" He would remember the fucking scar on the side of my fucking head, I am sure of it.

Then he would say, "Oh, yes, now I remember you. You're the one who claimed to have written the book about Poppy Fahrenheit. No hard feelings, I hope. Now please put out the fire. Oh, please, kind sir."

Then I would say, "Go blow yourself, you mother-fucking, piece-of-shit cocksucker. Do you have any idea

---

19   You were warned.

how much you cost me? I lost my fucking home because of you. I lost my wife. I lost my health insurance. My daughter counts boxes." Then I would walk away, laughing as the smell of burning flesh filled my nostrils like the smell of ground coffee. I would walk away — I'd *stroll* — and only turn back to yell, "And her name was Poppy Fowler. Not Fahrenberg. And certainly not Fahrenheit! What an absurd fucking name to assign to a beautiful girl!" Then I would whistle a happy tune, a hop in my step although my nostrils were burning.

The last thing I would hear from him would be the final sounds slipping past those lips that had enveloped so many swollen penises: "Cough! Cough!"[20]

---

20   Of course, this is pure hyperbole. Despite my occasional use of vulgarities, I am not a horrible person, and were Judge Miles C. Levy ever in such dire circumstances, burning and gasping, I would certainly rush to his aid and put the fire out. With a stream of my urine. I would gladly piss all over him to save his worthless life. But it is entirely true that I lost my house and my wife because of him. And my health insurance. I lost the shirt off my back, as they say, because of him. He drained me of everything that made me a man. That, friend, may be the definition of a "cocksucker."

MY DAUGHTER, THE BOX COUNTER

So why am I so troubled by Judge Miles C. Levy, flatulent, aging jurist and renowned fellatalist?[21] Why am I so troubled that I would resort to vulgarities and violent images?

Because it is as a result of his laziness, his biases, his arrogance, his ignorance and more that I am not recognized as having written one of the most popular novels of the twentieth century. You should know of me when I die. You will not, unless you read this book, of course.

Why?

Because he, Judge Miles C. Levy, dismissed my lawsuit against my former classmate and his almighty New York City publisher (Modern Day Publishing) for the theft of my book, of my "intellectual property" as it is known in legal parlance. It was he, Judge Miles C. Levy, who prohibited me from "taking any steps to harm the reputation of renowned American author P.J. Darbin" by contending that he did not, in fact, write the book he has been feted for writing. It was he, Judge Miles C. Levy, who entered what is known as an "injunction," prohibiting me for more than a decade from publishing an account (*this* account) of what transpired unless I included a ridiculous disclaimer (which you have recently read, likely with some bemusement) and unless the word "novel" was printed on the book's jacket to indicate to readers that the contents were pure invention rather than absolute fact, when they indeed are fact, fact, son-of-a-bitch

---

21   No need to consult Webster's for the definition of "fellatalist." It means "cocksucker." It just sounds less sloppy, like there was some sort of formal education on the subject. A night school class, perhaps.

fact. It was he, Judge Miles C. Levy, who prohibited me from proving my claim to you unless I acknowledged that my claim was fictional and that my book was written by the renowned author P.J. Darbin.

The real one, not the fictional one. There is no such thing as a fictional P.J. Darbin.

And there is no such thing as the "author" P.J. Darbin, unless you count the childish stories he indeed wrote in college, which I must attribute to a fictional P.J. Darbin when they, in fact, were written by the real P.J. Darbin.

There is but one P.J. Darbin.

There is only P.J. Darbin, the word thief.

P.J. Darbin, the scoundrel.

P.J. Darbin, the plagiarist.

P.J. Darbin, the reclusive millionaire, who at the moment that I type this sentence (clack-clack-clack) is reclusively counting *my* millions.

Instead of counting my millions myself, I wound up spending a small fortune on my lawsuit, only to have it dismissed with a shrug and a wink by Judge Miles C. Levy.

And now I do not have a house or a wife (Samantha) or health insurance, and our daughter (Claire) does not have a college education, unless you consider community college, which I do not believe you should consider.[22]

Instead of counting millions, I have $55 remaining in my wallet at the very moment that I am typing this sentence.

Fifty-five dollars.

---

22 My sincere apologies to those readers who attended community colleges and who believe themselves to have been insulted by my comments. But seeing as I had no formal higher education myself, save for that one semester at New York University, I have insulted myself even more, have I not? The answer: Yes.

Which is precisely what Judge Miles C. Levy charges for a blow job.[23]

Cocksucker.

Imagine that you are me.

Imagine that you completed a short novel before you had even completed your freshman year of college.

Imagine that the novel was something only you could have written, about someone only you could have written about, because it was based in no small part on your own life, your own memories.

Imagine that you shared that short novel with a fat-faced classmate named Peter to read over Christmas break.

Imagine that he would not return the manuscript to you.

Imagine that, several years later, after serving your country in the Army (but killing no one), after meeting then marrying a beautiful, black-haired, cornflower blue-eyed angel of a girl, you were working in a damp little bookstore called Charm City Books when a shipment of novels arrived with your college friend Peter's name on them, accompanied by a letter from the publisher exclaiming, "This is the 21st printing of a new American classic." Later, it read, "We have seen the future of American literature, and his name is P.J. Darbin!"

Twenty-one printings, and you have never heard of it because, again, you were busy serving your country on the other side of the globe.

Imagine that you delayed in reading the book for months out of jealousy, pure and simple. (Jealousy is a terrible thing. But I had no idea then that I was jealous of myself!)

---

23   Yes, another vulgarity. Again, apologies, apologies, a thousand apologies. And in the interests of accuracy — my goal and my commitment — I must admit that I have no idea how much Judge Miles C. Levy charges for blow jobs. They could be $20 each. They could be free. But whatever he charges, I'll bet he uses his teeth.

Imagine that your black-haired, cornflower blue-eyed angel of a wife began reading the book, unaware of your relationship to the presumed author. And imagine that your black-haired, cornflower blue-eyed angel of a wife turned to you one night in bed, the book propped up against her bare, freckled knees so you could see your former classmate's fat mug on the back flap, and said, "Does Poppy Fahrenheit sound like a made-up name to you?"

Imagine that the earth stopped spinning on its axis, screeching to a halt.

Imagine that you grabbed the book roughly from your wife's hands — too roughly, perhaps, because she jumped a bit — that you flipped to the first page and that, with the very first words ("Cough! Cough!"), you felt as if you were drowning. You were sinking, and each time you pulled your head above the churning waves, you were pulled down again, further each time until your feet were touching the pebbled bottom of the ocean floor as you looked up at a murky image of your wife's face above, her mouth opening and closing the way mouths do when someone is speaking, but her words were nearly soundless and entirely unintelligible.

Imagine that when you were finally able to pull yourself to the surface, gasping for air (gasp! gasp!), your heart in your mouth, you told your black-haired, cornflower blue-eyed angel of a wife about this grave injustice, your words coming out so fast that they bumped into each other, sometimes passing each other like Formula One race cars on a straightaway.[24]

Imagine that your black-haired, cornflower blue-eyed angel of a wife considered you as if she were considering a hungry dog yelping at her feet. The crazy husband! The addled

---

24 Apologies for the mixed metaphor.

war veteran with the head injury! He's finally snapped, just like the doctors predicted![25]

Imagine that calmly, so calmly, she said, "Jimmy, sweetie, you must be confused. You must have things jumbled in your mind again."

"Again," as if it had happened many times before, not just two or three times like anyone else. People forget where they put their car keys. People forget the names of their high school teachers.

Imagine that you could not say, "Remember, honey, I told you all about Poppy Fowler," because you had never told her about Poppy Fowler because how could you tell your black-haired, cornflower blue-eyed angel of a girlfriend (later, of a wife) about another girl you had loved more than her and always would?

Imagine that you informed the owners of Charm City Books (Stanley and Sarah Rubin) of the larceny that had been perpetrated, and imagine that they told you that your services were no longer needed, only to replace you with their niece (Diane) days later.

Imagine that you attempted to contact Peter to plead with him to correct this wrong.

Imagine that you discovered, as others have, that he is as reclusive as a mad bomber, hiding in a tiny, ramshackle house in a small, ramshackle town, photographed as often as Bigfoot, and nearly as hirsute, with a beard down to here.[26]

---

25   Hello to you, Drs. James Pellicane, Al Dodds and Donna Taffy. And fuck you for saying that to my wife.

26   A beard down to your chest, Peter, like a man who plays the washboard in a hillbilly band? Are you serious? You can afford a razor. You can afford millions of razors.

Imagine that you could not contact him by telephone and that your letters to him (longhand, cursive, Palmer method) went unanswered. Your telegrams, too.[27]

Imagine that you purchased an airline ticket and boarded an airplane, then rented a car to drive to his home with your reluctant, loving, black-haired, cornflower blue-eyed angel of a wife at your side, before finally knocking (knock-knock) — then pounding (BAM! BAM! BAM!) — on his front door. Your fist may not have bled, but it was quite red and sore.

Imagine that when you first announced yourself to him, his face became the face of a man who had forgotten his wife's birthday.

Imagine that after first claiming he had never heard of you — you, the person whose words he had stolen and for which he had accepted credit and riches! — he eventually and somewhat sheepishly acknowledged you and invited you and your reluctant, loving, black-haired, cornflower blue-eyed angel of a wife inside, only to pretend that you had never given him your manuscript in the first place. He knew nothing, he claimed, of onion paper and a thick rubber band. He remembered nothing of an exchange at a train station. "You must be thinking of someone else," he protested, "perhaps Charlie Root or his brother Calvin," which was not accurate and which would not explain how your book ended

---

27   For young and future readers, a telegram was how people once sent urgent messages to each other. The messages were typed in one location and transmitted through the airwaves to another location, then delivered on yellow pieces of paper by men or women in sharp, pressed uniforms and little caps. As crazy as that sounds, I assure you that I am not making that up. It was no crazier than attaching a message to the leg of a pigeon and expecting it to deliver it to the correct person, but people once did that, too. The history of the human race is a history of lunacy peppered by acts of genius or, sometimes, sanity.

up published under his name, not Charlie Root's name, not Calvin Root's. If it had been Charlie or Calvin, you would be pounding on one of their doors.

Imagine that you and your reluctant, loving, black-haired, cornflower blue-eyed angel of a wife spent several days in a tiny, paper-shades motel (The Family Inn) down the street from your old classmate's home, appearing at his door after breakfast each day and visiting with him, hoping that each day would be the day that he confessed his sins and promised to correct the damage he had caused, not only monetarily but to your status, acknowledging that it was you, not he, who deserved decades of accolades and fan letters and gifts.

Imagine that did not occur and that he eventually summoned the police to escort you and your reluctant, loving, black-haired, cornflower blue-eyed angel of a wife to the small regional airport that showcased his painted portrait near the café in the airport's lone terminal. "Cornwell, Home of P.J. Darbin," read the gold plaque beneath "Author Extraordinaire."

Imagine that as the police officers were pushing you into the back of their sparkling clean sedan, still wet and shiny from the car wash, you called out, "This means war, Peter! War! To the victor shall go the spoils!"

Imagine that you did not know if he heard your declaration of war but that you had bluish bruises to the skin on your neck and elbows from the police officers' unnecessarily rough treatment as they walked you to their car.

Imagine that, once home, you attempted to contact your former classmate's publisher, first by a handwritten note ("It appears you have been duped"), then by a typed one ("It appears you are an accomplice in a fraud"), finally by telephone ("Tell one of these motherfuckers to give me a motherfucking call!").[28]

Imagine that they ignored you.

Imagine that you rode a Greyhound bus from Baltimore to New York City.[29]

Imagine that, once there, you walked from the Port Authority building to the publisher's office, the sweat gathering at your neck and at the armpits of a shirt that had been freshly pressed when you had boarded the bus that morning, then sat in an overstuffed chair in the lobby for hours before a confident, well-dressed young woman in a tidy business suit led you to a conference room, where she nodded (but took no notes!) as you told her reasonably about the theft, looking at you with the big, sympathetic eyes of a nurse before promising to investigate the matter *fully* and contact you *promptly*.

Imagine that she never called. She never wrote. She never returned your messages ("Deborah, it's Jimmy Nail of Baltimore calling again").

Imagine that you arranged meetings with lawyer after lawyer after lawyer in Baltimore and its outskirts, each with a drearier suit and less appealing offices than the one who had preceded, pleading with each of them to take your case to court. "It's a dead-bang winner," you said. "We'll collect millions," you said. They rolled their eyes ceiling-ward as if at a noisy upstairs neighbor tap-dancing on bare wood floors.

---

28 I am not proud of my use of vulgarities, but I promised you accuracy.

29 The name of the bus company (Greyhound) is presumably meant to be ironic. Greyhounds are racing dogs. If a race dog ever moved as slowly as a Greyhound bus, or smelled as foul, its owner would surely take it out to the woods and give it an Old Yeller.

Imagine that you showed them your original, hand-written notebooks, and that they all said the same thing (more or less): "How do we know when you wrote this? You could have written it yesterday" even though the ink had faded, and the pages were yellowed and curling like the toenails of someone's drunken, unemployed Uncle Bob.

Imagine that you showed them the dates on the fronts of the notebooks, written in blue ink the color of a vein, dates that preceded by years the publication of your book by your former classmate and his publisher.

Imagine that they said, "But you could have written the dates yesterday, too," ignoring again the faded ink.

Imagine that you showed them stories that your former classmate in fact wrote and gave you to read over that long-ago Christmas break, stories that proved he did not have the skilled and dexterous mind to create the book he was credited with having written.[30] He had no humor. He had no panache. No grace. No mercy.

Imagine that they said, "But how do we know that you didn't write that horrid story yourself and type his name on it," accusing you of wasting all that paper and all those letters.

Imagine that they said, "If you can find this Poppy Fahrenheit, we might be able to do something to help you." Even though her name was Poppy Fowler. Not Fahrenberg. Not Fahrenheit, for god sakes. And even though they knew you couldn't find her because that was one of the first things you had told them upon meeting them. "I don't know where Poppy Fowler is," you had said, enunciating clearly. "She's disappeared like a magician's assistant," which was not entirely accurate because the magician's assistant always

---

30   Stories I do not have permission or legal authority to reprint here. But trust me.

reappears before the end of the show, except for that one in Cincinnati who was murdered. But still.

Imagine that you finally succeeded in finding a law firm that was willing to file your lawsuit for you, a law firm with offices directly above an unkempt convenience store, smelling always of frankfurters and burned coffee.[31] The store was called "Mr. Thrif-Tee." The firm, "Marcus, Marcus & O'Malley."

Imagine that you handed over a cashier's check representing most of your savings in advance for their questionable services, with monthly bills thereafter that, combined, resembled the gross national product of a small South American country.[32]

Imagine that your lawyers and their private investigators sent you occasional reports stating that they could not locate Poppy Fowler, the only person who could confirm that you, in fact, had written your own book, that your memories were your own, insisting that she had fallen off the face of the earth — if she had ever existed at all! Yes, your own convenience-store lawyers were questioning your integrity, your sanity or both — and charging you by the hour (or half-hour or one-tenth) for their insults!

Imagine that when they spoke to you, your own convenience-store lawyers invariably looked you not in the eyes but at the fucking scar on the side of your fucking head, a wound obtained in service of your country.

---

31 There was an advantage to the law firm being located over a convenience store: I could purchase a soda pop from that store after one of my meetings with the attorneys, along with boxes of cookies called Berger's Cookies, made only in Baltimore and sold only there. They were my daughter's favorites, little circles of shortbread covered with a dollop of sweet chocolate frosting. Try them; you will love them. Or not. Some people do not.

32 Hyperbole.

Imagine that noted fellatalist Judge Miles C. Levy dismissed your lawsuit. Dismissed it without even a trial before a jury of your peers as required by the United States Constitution!

Imagine that as he looked down at you, both physically and figuratively, Judge Miles C. Levy said, "If you cannot produce your star witness, Mr. Nail, then it seems as if your case is complete poppycock," emphasizing "poppy" and eliciting full-bellied laughter from much of the courtroom, including the chubby, middle-aged woman who was being paid to transcribe the proceedings on a little device the size of a toaster squeezed between her fat, mottled knees.

Imagine that Judge Miles C. Levy entered something known as a permanent injunction, preventing you from claiming to be the author of your own book — a violation of your rights under the First Amendment to the very same Constitution! — and from publishing your account (*this* account) unless you explicitly stated that your account was not true, unless you explicitly stated that the P.J. Darbin to whom you referred was fictional. (You have read that horse-shit disclaimer!)

Imagine that Judge Miles C. Levy would not allow you to tell the truth unless you acknowledged that the truth was a lie.

Let me ask you this: If you allow the truth to become a lie, then wouldn't a lie become something even worse?

Imagine that you paid the convenience-store lawyers another small fortune to appeal your case to a Court of Special Appeals (hello, second mortgage) and then to try to convince the Maryland Court of Appeals to listen to your plight (goodbye, health insurance).[33]

---

33 My lawyers charged me by the minute, like a payphone, except that telephone companies have a better understanding of time. I would talk to them for two minutes, only to get a bill charging

Imagine two years passing. Then five. Then eight. Ten. Imagine calendar pages flying like in old black-and-white movies starring actors with too-heavy makeup.

Imagine that, because of Judge Miles C. Levy, you lost your home and your loving, black-haired, cornflower blue-eyed angel of a wife (foreclosure, divorce, though in the opposite order chronologically).

Imagine that your smart and delightful daughter, born shortly after your discovery of this grand theft, grew up questioning your claim and your sanity, that she had to attend community college because of Judge Miles C. Levy, and that she had to find work as a part-time employee in the warehouse of a company that sold foam insulation, keeping inventory of the boxes shipped and received instead of attending medical school as she had intended.

Imagine all of that.

Do you think you would be happy?

No, you would not.

And if you said you would be happy, then you are a liar, just like the fleet of attorneys who represented P.J. Darbin.

"This is a travesty," they argued, and Judge Cocksucker nodded his head, a gesture he had obviously mastered from years of sucking on strangers' engorged penises in exchange for money, goods or services.[34] "This is a blatant attempt to

---

me for a 30-minute "teleconference with client." Then when I would call them to question the bill, I'd get another bill for *that* call. And so on and so on. It was a simple Ponzi scheme, based upon a succession of suckers paying for the previous sucker, only I was the sucker every time.

34   Please let me note here that the repeated references to Judge Levy performing fellatio on strangers should in no way be read to be an attack upon homosexuals, which could affect sales of this book, as I understand that homosexuals are avid readers. Yes, I would have made the same comments even if Judge Levy were female.

take advantage of an American icon. This is a blatant attempt to extort money from P.J. Darbin by someone who is not of sound mind."

Not of sound mind?

I will be the first to acknowledge that I suffered a broken skull in service of my country in wartime. The first to acknowledge that I have a fucking scar above one ear that curves over the top of my head, that looks like I ran sideways and drunk into an electric fan.

I have headaches at times. I am the first to acknowledge that tidbit, too. Headaches like buildings falling to their knees during an earthquake.

Is it a brain tumor? Maybe. Like others who served in Vietnam, I was exposed to a defoliant chemical called Agent Orange. It was part of an herbicidal warfare program that bore the too-cute name "Operation Ranch Hand." It melted everything in sight until it looked like chili, and it left us gagging and coughing (cough! cough!). It gave some soldiers lung cancer. Maybe it gave me cancer, too. Maybe it gave me a brain tumor.

But I don't know because I no longer have health insurance to get the treatment I need, and the Veterans Administration hospital is so backed up that I cannot even get an appointment to see a doctor for nine months. Nine! A couple could have intercourse in a cheap hotel and spit out a living, breathing, crapping baby while I wait for a doctor's appointment.

I need to see a doctor. But I can't.

I have a daughter who, on native intelligence alone, could have attended medical school and could have learned how to diagnose and remove brain tumors.

If anything, my comments could be construed as an indictment of prostitutes, whom I suspect buy very few books. Perhaps they check them out at the library.

She would treat me gratis, I know.

What if she determined that I did have a brain tumor?

What if my little Claire were the only person who could have removed my tumor?

And instead, because of P.J. Darbin and Judge Cocksucker, she was counting boxes in a warehouse. Part-time. One, two, three, four, five boxes.

While my tumor grew and grew and grew, sinking its tendrils deeper.

Six, seven, eight boxes.

Nine boxes.

Ten.

A COMPARISON OF ALLERGY HISTORIES

Putting aside all other issues large and not-so-large for the time being, and only for the time being, the main character in my novel *The Allergic Boy* was a teenage boy with a long history of allergies. The main character in *The Left-Handed Girl*, the novel stolen by my shifty, fat-faced, jowly college classmate, is also a teenage boy with a long history of allergies.[35]

Here is a complete inventory of the allergies suffered by the "authors" of these two books:

Jimmy Nail	P.J. Darbin
Shellfish	
Chlorine	
Dust	
Pollen	
Dog hair	
Cat hair	
Eggs	No known allergies
Mushrooms	
Penicillin	
Bee stings	
Chocolate	
Cut grass	
Weeds	
Agent Orange	

---

35   Please note that I typed "shifty" not "shitty." Not that a slip of the finger on the keyboard would have made a sliver of a difference.

My medicine cabinet looks like the wall of a big city pharmacy. His has nothing in it other than bandages (Band-Aids) and cotton swabs (Q-tips) and something for itchy skin patches called Itch-B-Gone with a drawing of a cheery, fat bee on the label. I know that for a fact: I peeked into his medicine cabinet when I used his restroom, and I snapped a photograph with my little camera.[36]

Now I ask you this, dear reader: Which man is more likely to write a novel about a teenage boy with multiple allergies? Someone who suffered from multiple allergies himself or someone who has only suffered from itchy skin patches perhaps caused by happy bees?

As my beautiful, black-haired, cornflower blue-eyed angel of a wife (or more accurately, my beautiful, black-haired, cornflower blue-eyed angel of an *ex*-wife) would say when asked such a silly question, "The answer, my friend, is blowing in the wind. The answer is blowing in the wind." Neither she nor I have ever taken credit for that phrase. It is actually a line from a song written by the popular American recording artist Bob Dylan, nee Robert Zimmerman.

Although, I would not be surprised if P.J. Darbin claimed that he wrote those words, too.

Now coincidentally, I should share with the reader that I just sneezed not once, but twice, in the midst of typing that last sentence.

Clack-clack.

Aaaah-chooo!

Clack-clack-clack-*clack*.

Aaaah-chooo!

---

36   A note to the editor: Please insert a reproduction of the photograph I have forwarded that has the words "Peter John Darbin Medicine Cabinet/Cornwell, Wis." handwritten on the back. Please have your legal team obtain the appropriate permissions from Band-Aid, Q-tips, and Itch-B-Gone.

Why do I mention this otherwise unremarkable event?

Because I have so many goddamned motherfucking allergies, that's why!

Every sneeze is proof of authorship.

Aaaah-chooo, aaaah-chooo, aaaah-chooo!

Proof, proof, proof!

P.J. DARBIN'S SKILL IN BOARD GAMES

When I was not snapping damning medicine cabinet photographs in his bathroom, my reluctant, loving wife and I played board games with Peter while we were discussing this extraordinarily serious matter at his home in Cornwell, Wisconsin. Monopoly, Life, Trouble, etc., etc.

There was one board game in particular that Peter favored. It was a popular game called Trivial Pursuit, devoted to questions about inconsequential information that sticks in your memory (like the name of the drummer in an old rock and roll band), taking the place of things you should remember (like your father-in-law's first name). The game's objective is rather simple to explain: Players answer questions in different categories (sports, movies, literature, science) to win small, colored pieces of plastic that resembled slivers of greasy fruit pie. If you were the first player to collect a sliver of greasy pie for each of the categories, you won. Hooray for you!

Peter and I wagered a six-pack of Michelob beer on each game. Why? Because that was what he liked to drink, and because I thought a drunken Peter John Darbin was more likely to spill the beans than a sober one. Peter won every time, drinking beer all the while, occasionally stumbling over to his restroom, the one with the near-bare medicine cabinet, but never spilling a single bean.[37]

---

37 This is an important detail: Peter John Darbin drank Michelob beer. Who would fabricate a detail like *that*? Who could? We bought the Michelob beer at the Cornwell General Store on North Parsonage Road, next to the Family Inn. Who would fabricate *that* detail?

Peter was a smart egg, I will give him that. Even a little tipsy, he knew everything. And I do mean *everything*. About *everything*. He knew it all. State capitals. Classical composers. Chemical compositions. Poets. Painters. Kings and queens. He even knew about professional wrestling.

One question read, "What was the name used by George Wagner when he wrestled professionally?"

Without hesitating, Peter blurted, "Gorgeous George." And he was right.[38]

Peter knew the answer to every question.[39] Or nearly every one. I only recall him answering one question incorrectly.

---

38 The truth is that I knew this answer, too. While I profess to be a fan of opera, of foreign movies, and of the fiction of John O'Hara and F. Scott Fitzgerald, I am also a fan of professional wrestling. When I was a child, I spent quite a bit of time alone (chess, writing, daydreaming about Nancy Hower and the rest of the cheerleading squad — rah, rah!). Pro wrestling proved to be a perfect hobby for a skinny, shy, broken-nosed teenaged boy with a rich fantasy life and time on his hands. Later, when I learned the outcomes were, ahem, pre-determined, I came to enjoy the characters the wrestler portrayed, the spectacle and the silly humor of it all. The idea that two grown men would agree to wrestle in something advertised as a "Chainsaw Match," whereby whoever reached the chainsaw in the middle of the ring first was allowed to use it on his opponent? That was priceless. That the wrestler who first reached the chainsaw would choose to smack his opponent over the head with it instead of revving it up and hacking away at limbs? Even more priceless. John O'Hara would not think of that on his best, drunken day. And Peter John Darbin could never think of that, drunk or sober. Never.

39 Now I acknowledge, as I must, that it is possible that he memorized all of the game cards during his many hours of solitude that he sat there in a stiff-backed chair and read the cards over and over again until he knew every question and every answer on each of the hundreds of tiny slips of cardboard.

The one question Peter answered incorrectly was this: "Name the author of *The Left-Handed Girl*." That question was not actually written on the card I held. I pretended that it was. I pretended I was reading that question directly from the little piece of cardboard in my hand.

My loving, reluctant, black-haired, cornflower blue-eyed angel of a wife let out a shriek.

Peter did not hesitate. When he said, "P.J. Darbin," I slammed my already-sore fist on the board, sending the tiny plastic slices of pie flying like bees confronted by a healthy dose of Itch-B-Gone.

"You are a liar, Peter. You are a goddam liar! You are a thief! You and I know it. And Poppy knows it, too. Don't forget that."

I pointed a finger at him. My finger did not frighten him one bit.

"You're a lunatic, Jimmy," he said. "There is no Poppy."

Suddenly, I found my fingers around his throat, squeezing gently at first, proving his point. "Tell the truth, Peter. Do it now. The truth shall set you free!"

My loving, reluctant, black-haired, cornflower blue-eyed angel of a wife was pulling at my shoulders, her efforts growing more forceful as I increased my own.

"Jimmy," she said. "Please, not like this. Remember what Dr. Dodds said."

"Listen to your wife," Peter spat out, his face turning pink and twisted, looking little like the photograph on the back flap of his book. I mean, my book. *My* book.

"Please, Jimmy," my loving, reluctant, black-haired, cornflower blue-eyed angel of a wife said. "Please, I'm pregnant."

And with that astonishing news, I released my hold on my tormentor's throat. He coughed, then stumbled across the room, over so many colorful plastic slivers of pie, then dialed the police station on his telephone. My loving, reluctant, black-haired, cornflower blue-eyed angel of a wife waited with me on a wooden bench on the front porch, my head on her lap. She stroked my back with her fingertips, and just as the police car pulled onto the gravel road leading to Peter's house, she said, "Jimmy, can I ask you a question? Why did you tell Peter that Poppy knows the truth? I thought you said she was someone you made up."

I answered, "I don't know why I said that, my mind must've gotten jumbled again," lying to her but telling you the truth.

Before I knew it, I was in the hands of a police officer who was squeezing my upper arms just as firmly as I had squeezed Peter's neck minutes earlier. His partner stood by the gleaming, freshly washed sedan, his hands on his hips like a Wild West gunslinger waiting for a reason to reach for his pistol.

"He was in the Army," my wife said to the police officer who was holding me, presumably to encourage him to loosen his hold, but her comment had the opposite effect. I will not be the first to write that those who served in World War II were treated as heroes; those of us who served in Vietnam were treated like escaped convicts.

"Baby killer," the police officer said.

"I didn't kill anyone," I protested, "much less babies."

It was true.

The police officer pushed me toward the patrol car. He grabbed one shoulder. The gunslinger grabbed the other. Something popped in my neck. I winced.

"Please," my wife said, "he was hurt in the war."

"Good," the first officer said, the one who had inaccurately called me a "baby killer."

My wife slid into the back of the police car next to me, rearranging the fabric of her plaid skirt. The police officers allowed her to stop at the motel to settle our account at the front desk and to gather our belongings into our bags; then we were off to the regional airport to sit outside the café near Peter's glorious portrait.[40]

Our beautiful, smart box counter arrived seven months later. As the gynecologist lifted her toward the ceiling, I was the first person that the box counter ever saw. I tell everyone she smiled at me, but of course, she did not. She screamed, as newborns do, and if she was looking at me at all, she was eyeing the scar on my head.

"Hello, Claire," I said. "You are the joy of my life."

And I say the same thing to her now if she is reading this book.

I will imagine that she will respond to that comment the same way she did when I would say that to her when she was a Baltimore schoolgirl: "And you are the boy of my life." Or should I say, I hope that is how she will respond when she reads that. If she reads that.

You are the joy of my life, Claire. You have been ever since that moment I imagine that you smiled at me.

---

40 Something just occurred to me all of these years later: We never returned our rental car! It may still be parked on the motel parking lot, covered in decades of leaves and dust! Our bill must be enormous. And yet it still would not match the millions that P.J. Darbin and his publisher owe *me*.

AN APOLOGY

At the outset of this book — indeed, in the "Introduction" itself — I assured both the publisher and you, the reader, of my painstaking commitment to accuracy. Should you not recall it, you will find it on the opening pages, unless that commitment was removed by the editor in the performance of his or her responsibilities.

Then in the section entitled "A Clarification," I wrote to Peter, "Confess, then we can meet again in heaven and shake hands, forgiven and friends again."

In honor of my commitment, I must tell you this: Peter John Darbin and I were never friends, at least not in the sense you or you or you would understand that word. A friend will call you on your birthday. A friend will maintain your secrets as if they were his own. A friend would not steal from you. I had no such relationship with Peter. But when I wrote that he and I could be "friends again," I was not misrepresenting anything to you, the reader of this book. No, I was misrepresenting something to *him*. Perhaps if he recalled us as friends, he would be more likely to confess, his heart suitably softened.

I offer my full-throated apology for any confusion my words might have created for you, the reader of this book.

As for my suggestion that Peter John Darbin and I would meet in heaven?

I have no idea if there is such a reward for the good and kind-hearted. Please do not take my word for it. You should believe what you believe. But if there is such a thing as heaven, do you really believe an unrepentant thief would be admitted? A liar? A plagiarist? A scoundrel? I think not.

AN EXPLANATION

Let me be very clear about a few other important matters now for the sake of accuracy (my goal, my commitment, etc., etc.).

I am not claiming to be P.J. Darbin.

Judge Cocksucker accused me of that at one point. He said, "We all know that *The Left-Handed Girl* was written by P.J. Darbin. And despite what you say, Mr. Nail, you plainly are not P.J. Darbin." Everyone in the courtroom laughed aloud when he said that. Everyone but me, to be accurate (my goal, my commitment, etc., etc.). I did not laugh. I boiled like a teapot.

But I did not assert then, nor have I ever asserted, that I am P.J. Darbin. I am asserting that I am me, Jimmy Nail, and that P.J. Darbin is P.J. Darbin, and that P.J. Darbin published *my* work under *his* name.

And I am also not asserting that I wrote *The Left-Handed Girl*.

I did not write a book with that particular title.

I wrote a novel entitled *The Allergic Boy.*

It was a novel based largely on my too-brief time with Poppy Fowler, whose last name I changed to "Fahrenberg" for the purposes of fiction but whose last name is truly "Fowler" for the purposes of truth.

That is the thin novel I handed over to P.J. Darbin to read over Christmas break (onion paper, rubber band), expecting that I would see him again when I returned for the spring semester, not knowing that I would not be able to do so (father, horse racing, alcohol). That is the manuscript that he put into his duffel bag and carried off with him.

He and his publisher edited the book. They rewrote it. They changed Poppy Fahrenberg to Poppy Fahrenheit. They changed names and places (but not all names and not all places). They changed details here and there. They changed the name of the novel from *The Allergic Boy* to *The Left-Handed Girl*.

I will gladly admit that *The Left-Handed Girl* is a far superior and more memorable title than the one I had selected. I wish I had thought of it myself. In my defense, I did not have a crafty, Ivy League-educated editor from a major New York City publishing house (Modern Day Publishing) to help me give the book a title; I was just a poor college freshman from Baltimore, New York's poor cousin. But that is a small and largely irrelevant point.

The large and largely relevant point, the *only* point, is the truth.

In the midst of my savings-draining lawsuit, I was required to sit for what is referred to as a deposition, answering under oath a seemingly endless stream of questions posed by P.J. Darbin's high-priced, sharp-dressed attorneys; I am sure their offices were miles away from the nearest convenience store.[41] Each question being nearly identical to the one that had preceded it, save for a slight change in one word or another, like the drawings on successive pages of a flipbook. As is my nature, I answered the questions truthfully. Thus, when P.J. Darbin's attorneys asked me if I had written a novel entitled *The Left-Handed Girl*, I answered, truthfully, that I had not.

---

41 Those attorneys were from a swanky New York City law firm called Blank & White. Their offices were located on Park Place. Even if you have never visited New York City, you would know how tony the neighborhood is if you have ever played Monopoly. I visited the offices of Blank & White on just one occasion. It was like visiting Tiffany's while you were wearing clothing from Goodwill. The floors were made of marble. *Marble.* They walked on the same substance that sculptures are carved from before they are hidden in museums.

Which was all Judge Cocksucker needed to hear.

"If you cannot produce your star witness," he announced (as I previously reported), "then it seems that your case is complete poppycock."

Laughter echoed off the courtroom walls.

Ho, ho, ho!

Ho, ho, ho!

A roomful of Santa Clauses.

"And if you admit that you did not write *The Left-Handed Girl*, then it appears that you have wasted my time and the taxpayers' money!"

"But," I stammered.

"One more word from you, Mr. Nail, and I will hold you in contempt of court!"

Imagine the sound produced by a gavel slamming against some hard wood.

But you understand the distinction I was making, do you not? It is a simple and clear distinction.

Let me present the evidence I should have been permitted to introduce at a public trial had I not been deprived of the constitutional right to that very trial, had I not been represented by convenience-store lawyers who smelled of frankfurters and burned coffee. Give me my day in court, and you will see. There will be no shadow of doubt in your minds, no Santa Clausing. When I am done, you will adore and respect me. And you will award me countless millions of dollars, enough that I could buy a slice of cake for everyone in the world were I so inclined.

EXHIBIT A

— The Allergic Boy

I wish to present to you, dear readers (my true judges and jury), my original handwritten notebook for *The Allergic Boy*, which may not be found in any bookstore or library, and of which there is but a single copy, which has been carefully safeguarded.[42] The faded handwriting on the cover and throughout the notebook is mine. There is no handwriting expert in this world who could conclude otherwise.[43]

---

42   It is stored in a separate location from the Underwood typewriter. I am no fool. Balding? Yes. Paranoid? Perhaps. Foolish? No, no, no.

43   A note to the editor: Please insert photographic reproductions of the cover and all pages of my notebook, which I will personally deliver to you at a mutually convenient time and place. While I appreciate that there will be substantial expense involved in reproducing the pages of my notebook, each handwritten page is as much proof of authorship as each "aaaah-chooo" that I aaaah-chooo.

EXHIBIT B

— The Left-Handed Girl

I also wish to present a copy of *The Left-Handed Girl*, which may be found in any bookstore or library of any repute, if one is not already filed away on your own bookshelf.

And if you do indeed own a copy, consider yourself lucky that you are not arrested and tossed in jail for possession of stolen property.

In some countries, they would cut off your hands at the wrists![44]

---

44   This is not a threat. I am merely making a point. But it is true. Chop, chop!

EXHIBIT C

— A Photograph

Next, I wish to present you, dear reader, with a photograph of one Poppy Fowler, age 18 (or 20 or 22, who knows?).[45] She is the thin, freckled girl with the mad spaghetti mess of hair, the one clutching the tennis racquet to her chest.[46]

Please also note who is standing beside her: It is me, your aging typist. While time has passed and I have aged, perhaps more poorly than most (I am 52 as I write this sentence, but I could easily pass for 70 if I wanted the senior discount at a restaurant), if you compare this photograph with the author's photograph on the back cover of this book, you cannot help but acknowledge that the boy in one and the man in the other share the identical twisted nose passed on to me by my father, and to him by his. Each is me. And each would dislike the other, the younger version finding the older one to be too angry and absent-minded (where are my eyeglasses?), the older version finding the younger one to be too meek and frightened of his own shadow (boo!). Such is life.

The photograph inserted here was taken at my request by one of the older, gray-haired women who was playing

---

45   Note to editor: Please insert a reproduction of the photograph I have forwarded that has the words "Jimmy/Poppy Summer" handwritten on the back. Below it, please type, "Photograph by Unknown." Please make sure to return the original to me.

46   I originally wrote "red hair," but it is a black-and-white photograph, so that detail would have been meaningless or misleading.

tennis on the court next to ours at the Baltimore public recreation center.[47] I did not ask the woman for her name and do not know it now. If I did, I would insist that she be given proper credit for her work in this book because people must be given credit for their work, don't you agree? All I can say now is "Photograph by Unknown."[48]

---

47 Do not look for it. It no longer exists. It is now a shopping center.

48 If the photographer should happen to read this book, I encourage her to contact my publisher to request fair compensation for her work. This is, after all, the only known photograph of Poppy Fowler.

EXHIBIT D

— A Letter to Peter John Darbin

For reasons that should require no explanation, I do not have copies of my handwritten letters to Peter.[49] However, I did make carbon copies of the few letters that I typed requesting that he return the manuscript I had entrusted to him.[50]

Here is one of those letters:

Dear Peter,

I hope this letter finds you well and enjoying the spring semester. I have written you several letters, but I have not received any response. Perhaps they did not reach you, or perhaps you have not had a free moment to respond given your presumably heavy classwork. In any event, I thought I would make another attempt.

As you know, before we departed for Christmas break, I gave you the manuscript for a novel I am writing called *The Allergic Boy*. I was looking forward to receiving your

---

49   If an explanation is needed, who in his right mind makes copies of the handwritten letters he sends? Answer: no one in the entire history of mankind.

50   Carbon paper was a sheet of inky black paper placed between two pieces of white paper. Anything written or typed on the top white sheet would be reproduced in slightly smudged lettering on the bottom white sheet. I have not seen carbon paper in a great many years. The Xerox machine was the beginning of the end for carbon paper. (The computer was the end of the end.) If you bought stock in a carbon paper company, I can only hope that you sold it off ten seconds after seeing your first Xerox machine.

comments when we returned to school, but as you know, I was unable to return.

Stupidly, I did not make a carbon copy of the manuscript. The copy I gave you is my only typed copy. (I still have my original, handwritten copy but would prefer not to have to retype the whole damned thing again, as I am sure you can understand. A task done twice is more tedious the second time.)

I know it's not a very good book. In fact, I suspect it's a piece of garbage. I probably should be embarrassed by it and likely will end up depositing it in the trash can where it belongs once I reread it. But I would like it back.

I am enclosing a check made out to you in the amount of two dollars, which should more than cover the cost of mailing the manuscript back to me at the above address. If you could put it in the mail sometime in the next week or two, I would owe you a favor.

Sincerely,

Your friend Jimmy Nail[51]

---

51   Again, the reference to "friend" is a lie to him but not to you.

A NOTE ABOUT THE CHECK

P.J. Darbin cashed the motherfucking check!

So to the millions of dollars that he already owes me, please add another two dollars![52]

---

52   Before you ask, let me answer: No, I do not have the cancelled check. It never occurred to me to retain it. I have made my stomach sick just thinking about that fact but have come to realize that the cancelled check would have proved nothing. So I sent Peter John Darbin a check for two dollars. Whoop-dee-doo! It could have been for anything. It could have been for beer. It could have been for Itch-B-Gone. It could have been for a blow job. No, wait, Judge Miles C. Levy is the one I said was a cocksucker, right? Sorry, I got confused for a moment.

EXHIBIT E

— Another Letter to Peter John Darbin

Dear Peter,

I thought I would give this one last try before I ship out. Yes, I have enlisted in the United States Army.

I leave in two weeks and would really like to get the manuscript back before I depart. I don't want to have to retype the goddamn thing.

I am enclosing another check for two dollars. Please — *please* — send the manuscript back right away. If you have discarded it, please let me know. No apology necessary — I'd just like to know.

Sincerely,

Private James Nail

P.S. Vietnam, here I come!

A NOTE ABOUT THE SECOND CHECK

Add another two dollars to the tab![53]

EXHIBIT F

— A Telegram to Peter John Darbin

COME ON PETER. SHIPPING OUT IN TWO DAYS.
JIMMY.

EXHIBIT G

— Another Telegram to Peter John Darbin

FINE. DO WHATEVER YOU WANT WITH IT. IT IS GARBAGE ANYWAY. AND YOU ARE A [REDACTED] JACKASS. JIMMY.[54]

---

54 The word redacted by the dumpy, pudding-faced representative of the Western Union telegraph company was "motherfucking." It would have violated company policy for the agent to have transmitted that word. He would have been fired on the spot. For an extra ten cents, though, he volunteered that he was willing to type "motherfudging." I kept my money.

WHOM NOT TO HATE

"Why do you not hate P.J. Darbin," you might ask. "You have every reason to, don't you? He stole your book. He stole Poppy Fahrenheit. How can you not hate him?"

It is a fair question, more than fair considering the circumstances.

He did steal my manuscript, as neatly as if he had ambled up to me with a black ski mask covering everything but his tar-black eyes and girl's mouth, shoved the business end of a pistol into my abdomen, and whispered, "Give me everything you have," before racing off into the darkness of night. And I have lost everything, or nearly everything, as a result.

But you are wrong about one thing: He did not steal Poppy Fahrenheit. She is mine.

And it's Fahrenberg, not Fahrenheit, anyway.

I mean, it's *Fowler*.

It is because of him and his stubby-fingered theft that I have thought of Poppy Fowler every single day without exception. It is because of him that I continue to carry her with me everywhere I go. It is because of him that I remember a summer from my boyhood when I was happy as a dog in kibble (bark! bark!), when I met every morning with a tiny whiff of hope, when I took a silk purse and turned it into a sow's ear.[55]

I cannot hate him for that.

But he is still a **[REDACTED]** piece of garbage. He still stole my book. He still took my memories and called them

---

55   I do not have that backwards, as those familiar with the ending of *The Left-Handed Girl* know.

his. He still owes me a house and a wife and a daughter, and millions of dollars — plus four more for postage!

And a few more for the telegrams. They weren't free.

EXHIBIT H

— A Story

As I mentioned at the very outset of this book, I devoted much of my coughing, wheezing, sneezing high school years to writing stories. Ghost stories (boo!). Cowboy stories (bang! bang!). I could share dozens of these stories with you to convince you that I had the skill to write the book that would become known as *The Left-Handed Girl*. Humor. The panache. There was one story called "A Great Day to Catch a Giraffe" that was quite nicely done, if I do say so myself, particularly the part about the giraffe.[56] There was another I like called "The Last Bolt," too.[57] Perhaps I will publish them in my next book, *The Last Bolt and Other Stories* by Jimmy Nail, acclaimed author of *The Allergic Boy*.

Instead, I wish to share a different story with you, not one of my best, not even close. It is a story that I wrote the summer before my senior year at Theodore Roosevelt Regional High School, the summer I turned a silk purse into a sow's ear. I present it here because it was the first of my stories that I ever shared with Poppy Fowler. (Not Fahrenberg. And certainly not Fahrenheit!) And I ask you, kind reader, to pay particular attention to the name of the

---

56   The giraffe escapes.

57   In "The Last Bolt," a carnival owner fires one of his workers. When he does, the worker silently hands him a single bolt and walks away, leaving the carnival owner to try to determine which ride is now short a bolt. In the end, the owner not only has to beg his former employee to return to work, but he has to give him an ownership interest in the carnival. You would read that story, wouldn't you?

young son in the story. Even if you choose not to read the story in its entirety, please run your fingers down the pages until you find his name. You will be rewarded. You will stick in your thumb and pull out a plum!

A note to the editor: Please insert here a complete copy of my short story entitled "The Way We Wash Our Clothes," which I will send to you via electronic mail transmission over the computer my daughter the box counter gave me for my birthday.

PULL OUT YOUR THUMB

That story you have just read, the authorship of which is entirely undisputed, can only be described as trash. Pure, stinking trash. I admit that. It was written by a boy of 16. In one night, no less. When he was entirely distracted by amorous thoughts about a red-haired girl who had moved in next door.

Rereading that story, I am reminded of the words shouted by my dear friend Private Frank Ditto as he lay in the mud in a clearing in Vietnam, a bullet having drilled a tunnel through his thigh, his blood seeping from the wound and mixing with the mud: "Jesus fucking Christ, you must be fucking kidding me!"[58]

A character named Skim?

Another named Pie?

Jesus fucking Christ, you must be fucking kidding me![59]

What immature, ham-handed hogwash.

What muck.

But I hope you noticed something. I hope you noticed that the name of one of the young boys is "Allie." The very same name as the narrator of *The Left-Handed Girl*.

I promised you a plum if you stuck in your thumb, didn't I?

---

58 Blasphemy, I know. But I am quoting for the sake of accuracy. Everyone knows you can say anything you want, no matter how grotesque or unsavory, so long as you are quoting someone else.

59 No excuse this time.

EXHIBIT I

The Allergic Boy versus *The Left-Handed Girl*

Here are the unassailable *facts*:

TITLE	
The Allergic Boy	*The Left-Handed Girl*
AUTHOR	
James Edgar Nail	P.J. Darbin, supposedly
PUBLISHER	
None, because of theft!	Modern Day Publishing Big Fancy Office New York, New York
MAIN CHARACTERS	
Allie Hester Poppy Fahrenberg Lou Moore	Allie Peller Poppy Fahrenheit Phil Campbell

A MESSAGE TO THE FAMILY OF PRIVATE FRANK DITTO

Although the years have passed like men racing by on bicycles, some years more swiftly than others, some forgotten, I still mourn the loss of your son and brother Frank, whom I am sure you loved and enjoyed. He was a good, well-mannered man. He believed in God, despite his final words. He told exquisitely bad jokes, and his winding, rambling stories would put you to sleep faster than a swig from a bottle of cough syrup. I trusted him, and in combat, that is the sweetest compliment you can pay to another soldier. We all trusted him. If trust were currency, Frank would have been a Rockefeller.

But as you surely know, one of the first lessons the Army teaches in boot camp (Fort Thomas, South Carolina) is to keep your mouth shut like a window against a storm if you are ever wounded. Shout, and you give away your position. Which, of course, is exactly what Frank did when a bullet buzzed through the air like a metal bee and found the meatiest part of his thigh. His last words on earth were "Jesus fucking Christ, you must be fucking kidding me!" He might as well have waved his arms over his head and shouted, "Here I am! Right here!" He might as well have tooted a trombone. The next metal bee that flew across the field found his nose.

I know. I was there. His nose landed on my chest or, more accurately, pieces of it.

In the grand scheme of things, "Jesus fucking Christ, you must be fucking kidding me!" would not be a bad choice for one's final words were one, in fact, to have such a choice. (I will try to make sure that they are my final words, too.)

Now your son and your brother's final words will be forever memorialized in this book. That is an honor normally reserved for statesmen like Washington and Lincoln.

Please know that even after all these years have passed (I am 46 as I write this sentence), just thinking of Frank can turn the corners of my mouth upward, even on the darkest of days when I am hungry and my reluctant, loving, black-haired, cornflower blue-eyed angel of a wife (or now, my ex-wife) and our little girl (who starts high school soon and hopes to go to medical school someday!) won't speak with me or return my telephone calls. Frank was a peculiar young man. He always will be. He will never be a peculiar old man, sadly. And if there is a heaven (I have no opinion), he is surely looking down fondly on all of us. On all of you.

FRANK DITTO'S FAVORITE JOKE

Frank Ditto, as I have just written, liked to tell jokes as much as you and you and you do. Joking is one of the things that makes us human. But not everyone has a sense of humor. Ask a thousand people if they have a good sense of humor, and all one thousand will say yes. Five hundred of them are lying.

But Frank had a splendid sense of humor.

There was one joke in particular that he would repeat. I heard him tell it at least a dozen times during our tour of duty together. I can hear it in my dreams if that is what I am dreaming of. I can hear him speaking in that sluggish voice of his, always as if he had just been awakened from a sound sleep.

Frank: "How do you make a hormone?"

Soldier: "I don't know."

Frank: "Don't pay her!"

The joke, in case you missed it (I suspect you did not), is a play upon the homonymous "hormone" and "whore moan." Wherever we were, the barracks or a trench or in mess or on patrol perhaps, the joke would typically spur a mild, half-hearted debate about the accuracy of the punchline. It would never elicit a genuine laugh, to my recollection.

"If you want to make a whore moan," someone would invariably argue, "shouldn't you pay her *more*? Not paying her won't result in her moaning. It will just piss her off."

"She's moaning because she's not getting paid," Frank would explain too emphatically. He had made the argument before. It did not improve with time.

"But people don't moan when they're angry," the soldier would say.

"Where I come from, they do."

"Wouldn't she yell and call her pimp if you didn't pay her?" the soldier would say. "Then the pimp would come running over and beat the living shit out of you with a baseball bat."

"Or maybe he'd shoot you," another soldier would add, helpfully, "if he had a gun."

"Exactly," the first soldier would say. "Either way, if you don't pay her, you're going to get fucked up."

"Then you'll be the one moaning," the second soldier would say.

"You're missing the fucking point of the fucking joke," Frank would say, his jaw tightening as if someone was tugging on a guy wire.

"No," another soldier would say, "we get the fucking point of the fucking joke, you dumb fuck. But if you pay her more, instead of less, she'll moan to make sure you enjoy yourself."[60]

"Exactly," another soldier would say, nodding in agreement. "You should pay her more if you want moaning."

"Has that been your experience?" Frank would ask.

Depending on the solider, he would respond by saying, "I've never had to pay for to get laid" or "Hell, yes." Whoever he was and whichever response he chose, he was probably lying. There were a lot of prostitutes in Vietnam and not enough condoms. Penicillin manufacturers made a fortune during the Vietnam War.[61]

---

60   In the Army, "dumb fuck" was a term of endearment. Or nearly so. Hundreds of soldiers have accidentally called their wives "dumb fucks," then spent the rest of the night apologizing.

61   True. Not a penny from me though. I'm allergic. It makes my blood run too hot, like a car engine overheating. Imagine steam coming out of my ears and nostrils.

It was during one of those silly debates that one of our compatriots (whom I shall not identify in order to avoid causing any humiliation for his widow and half-orphaned children) mentioned a one-armed prostitute to whom he had paid a visit in London. He tucked an arm behind his back to illustrate.

"I gave her an extra pound," he said, "and she moaned like her appendix was on fire." There was laughter, as you might imagine. I laughed, too, because I had once had an appendectomy and recalled the extraordinary pain I had been in prior.

I stopped laughing abruptly as another thought slipped into my mind.

"Wait, wait, wait," I said from across the barracks after a moment. "What did you just say?"

"I paid ten pounds for a one-armed hooker in London," the young private repeated matter-of-factly, as if every word in the sentence he spoke was as mundane as a list of ingredients for stew. She had one arm instead of two, which is the standard allotment, you dumb fuck. "I gave her an extra pound, and she moaned like she was having her appendix removed with a spoon."

"Ouch," someone shouted, laughing.

"Was she British?" I asked. I put my cup down with a clink (our cups were made of metal) and moved swiftly across the room as if I were on wheels.

"No," he said, "American."

My heart leaped, like a ballet dancer. "What color hair did she have?"

"What?"

"What color hair did she have?"

"Who gives two shits what color her hair was? Do you know what I called her? I called her Jackpot, because she had one arm like a slot machine."

He pantomimed pulling the arm of a slot machine, and the room filled with robust laughter. I was not laughing. There was nothing to laugh about any longer.

"Tell me what color her hair was," I demanded. "Now."

"What's wrong with you, Jimmy?"

"Nothing is wrong with me, just tell me what color hair she had."

"Red, you fucking weirdo."

It leaped again. "What was her name?"

The private gestured toward me with a thumb and, to our colleagues, said, "Get a load of this dumb fuck." Then to me, he said, "Her name was whatever your mother's name is."

Before either of us knew it, my fingers, which were accustomed to moving chess pieces and had never been used in a fight of any sort, were circling his throat, squeezing, squeezing, my fingertips sinking into his thick neck as if it were ice cream, as if he had stolen my book and published it under his name, but of course, I did not know about that yet. I only knew what I wanted to know, and I had decided (hastily) to squeeze the information out of him.

"What was her fucking name?" I demanded again. Then, more slowly enunciating each syllable, I said, "What was her motherfucking name, you motherfucking, cocksucking piece of shit?"

"I don't know," he coughed. "I swear, Jimmy, I don't know. Calm down."

"Think," I said.

"I don't know."

"Then think harder, you fucking moron."

"I swear, Jimmy," he said. "I don't know."

But I knew: Her name was Poppy.

Poppy Fowler.

Not Poppy Fahrenberg.

And certainly not Poppy Fahrenheit!

Later that night, that soldier and three of his imbecilic friends covered my mouth and tied my wrists and ankles to the posts of my cot, then beat my bony chest and my stomach with the heels of their boots. Thump, thump, thump! I could not blame them, and I did not report them. No, even battered, I was smiling inside.

"Someday," Poppy had once told me as we sat in the sun on her front stoop drinking soda and eating potato chips, "I'm going to live in Europe."

Just the thought of her in Europe had made me start to miss her.

"People in Europe are much more sophisticated than people here," she had added. "Smarter, more open-minded. If we lived there, this would be wine and cheese." She pointed to the soda bottles and the bag of potato chips.

"What will you there do for a living?" I had asked. "How will you make money to live on?"

"Wait tables in a coffee shop or sing songs at a night club," she'd said. "Or maybe, I'd charge men for this," she had added, moving both hands slowly across her body like a model in front of a new sedan at the car dealership. "I could be a millionaire and never even have to get out of bed."

"You're joking."

"Am I? Men have offered me a lot of money to get inside my shorts."

"Now I know you're joking."

She raised an eyebrow in a way that revealed that she had practiced raising her eyebrow. "You, I'd give a discount."

ONE MORE THING

You may be wondering how Frank Ditto was shot in the thigh in the first place, how some nameless, faceless North Vietnamese soldier even knew where to aim in the inky darkness of a summer night.

The American soldier who was on patrol with Frank sneezed. Aaaah-chooo! He was allergic to weeds. He had not shared that fact with the Army when he had enlisted. It had not seemed important at the time. He had just wanted to kill North Vietnamese, and he had not even done that.

ENOUGH BOOKS ALREADY!

This would appear to be as appropriate a time as any to tell you about "The Write Program." Or more accurately, to permit a woman named Ginger Seel to do so. This is the sworn affidavit that she submitted to Judge Cocksucker:

AFFIDAVIT OF MRS. GINGER SEEL

I, Mrs. Ginger Seel, being duly sworn and of sound mind, hereby declare, testify and affirm as follows:

1. I am over 18 years of age and am competent to testify to the matters contained herein.
2. I currently reside in Rochester, New York.
3. I served as a nurse in the United States Armed Forces from **[REDACTED]** to **[REDACTED]**, when I received an honorable discharge. Since that time, I have been employed as a registered nurse in several hospitals in New York. I am currently employed as a registered nurse specialist at Rochester Presbyterian Hospital in Rochester, New York.
4. From **[REDACTED]** to **[REDACTED]**, I was stationed at a military hospital in **[REDACTED]**, Vietnam. For a significant portion of that time, I was assigned to the trauma unit, providing care for soldiers who had sustained a wide variety of traumatic injuries in battle, including the loss of limbs or digits, severe burns, damage to (or loss of) hearing or eyesight, and brain injuries.
5. Many of the brain injuries sustained by soldiers whom we treated could not, in fact, be treated, and my role as nurse was to provide medication or comfort to the extent a soldier was even conscious. The treatment for other soldiers with brain injuries varied depending upon

the nature and severity of the injuries as well as the portion of the brain that was affected.

6. Soldiers suffering from relatively minor, non-invasive brain injuries to the frontal lobe were classified as "Grade 1, Class A, Type a." Soldiers so classified were normally given a significant chance of sustained improvement and of returning to their prior lives, barring other injuries, complications or resistance to treatment.

7. During the time that I was stationed at the military hospital in **[REDACTED]**, Vietnam, the protocol for the treatment of soldiers classified as "Grade 1, Class A, Type a" typically involved both a medical and a rehabilitative aspect. The medical aspect involved the administration of medication to reduce any cranial swelling, as well as painkillers, with dosages varying depending upon the circumstances. The rehabilitative aspect involved an experimental program known as "The Write Program," which was developed at Duke University and intended to rebuild the muscles of the brain and to retrigger synapses that may have been damaged through the initial trauma.

8. While not unpleasant, "The Write Program" was a time-intensive program for both the patients and the nursing staff. In essence, a nurse such as myself would read a sentence aloud to a soldier, who would then write down what he recalled of the sentence. In theory, a soldier would become increasingly adept at the process, gradually increasing the amount of information he could both recall and transcribe accurately. In fact, I observed more than a few soldiers classified as "Grade 1, Class A, Type a" who at first could only recall and accurately transcribe two or three words that were read to them, but who eventually were able to accurately transcribe lengthy sentences or multiple sentences. I also observed marked improvement over time in spelling and penmanship,

which signaled improved brain activity and brain-muscle coordination.

9. When we first began to implement "The Write Program" at the military hospital in **[REDACTED]**, Vietnam, we were instructed to employ the novel *The Great Gatsby* for such purposes. However, reading the same book aloud to multiple "Grade 1, Class A, Type a" patients, often in the same day, became tiring for the nurses and the patients. Accordingly, the nurses requested and were given permission to read other materials to these patients.

10. Because our hospital library was not extensive, we often relied upon magazines or books that were sent to us by friends or family members. One book in particular that I read to several patients was a new novel that my parents sent me for my 24th birthday, which fell on **[REDACTED]**. The novel was entitled *The Left-Handed Girl*. It was written by P.J. Darbin. I still own the copy that my parents gave me, which includes the inscription, "Sweetie — stay safe! Happy 24th! Love, Mum and Pop." "Mum and Pop" refers to my parents, Deborah and William Gilbert, now deceased.

11. Because of the number of patients we treated and the short duration that some remained at the hospital, I am afraid that I do not recall most of their names, save for Private Matthew Seel, whom I eventually married and who resides with me in Rochester, New York.

12. I do not recognize the name "James Nail," nor do I have a specific recollection of treating a soldier by that name. However, I do have a recollection of treating a "Grade 1, Class A, Type a" soldier from Baltimore, Maryland who told me that he had attended New York University briefly but had to leave because his father had suffered a financial reversal and had lost the barber shop he owned as a result.

13. The soldier from Baltimore had fractured his skull. He had an open wound on his head that was stitched closed. He was treated with medication for cranial swelling and pain, and he participated in "The Write Program."

14. I do not recall specifically which book or books that I and the other nurses employed with the soldier from Baltimore as part of "The Write Program." It may have been *The Left-Handed Girl*. However, I do recall that he asked for and received permission to keep the composition notebooks in which he had transcribed what had been read aloud to him. He indicated that he wished to keep the notebooks so he could read them on the flight home. The notebooks had black covers with a white square slightly above the middle of the page for one to insert a title and name.

15. "The Write Program" was discontinued at the military hospital after several suicide attempts by soldiers. Fortunately, none of the suicide attempts were successful. Each soldier left a similar note: "Enough books already!"

16. I do not recall if the soldier from Baltimore was one of the suicide attempts. He might have been.

17. One more thing: We could not give the soldier from Baltimore penicillin. He was allergic to penicillin. He was allergic to *everything*. That is only a slight exaggeration. To this day, I do not understand how he was not disqualified from service in the first place.

18. I declare under penalty of perjury under the laws of the United States of America that the foregoing is true and correct.

—————————————

Mrs. Ginger Seel

A RESPONSE TO THE AFFIDAVIT OF MRS. GINGER SEEL

Do not jump to any conclusions.

Yes, yes, yes, the affidavit of Mrs. Ginger Seel is troubling evidence.

Yes, I was treated at a military hospital in Vietnam after suffering head injuries in the service of my country. I did not hide that from you. The fucking scar on the side of my fucking head is right in the title of this book.[62]

Yes, I was classified as "Grade 1, Class A, Type a," and yes, my treatment included that program they called "The Write Program." Hours after hours after hours of transcribing the words read aloud by a series of young nurses, all kind, some kinder than others, all bored to the brink of tears by the tedious task of reading the same words over and over and over to a bunch of bandaged, medicated teenagers pretending to be grown men while hiding their erections.

While I cannot say so with certitude, I believe one of those nurses was named Ginger. Her last name at the time was Gilbert, which she pronounced "jill-BEAR," although she had no French blood in her veins. ("It's an affectation," she said sweetly, and as affectations go, a far better choice for a pretty, fresh-faced young woman than, say, a monocle or walking stick.)[63]

---

62   Except, perhaps, in Book of the Month Club editions. Or in countries where such language is prohibited.

63   No matter how comely she might be, a woman with a monocle and a walking stick could only bring to mind the Planters Peanut Man. Or his mother.

But you will note that in her sworn affidavit, Mrs. Ginger Seel stated, "I do not recall specifically which book or books that I and the other nurses used with the patient from Baltimore ... " I do. I do recall *specifically*. The book that the nurses read to me, over and over and over again, was, in fact, *The Great Gatsby*.

You are right to question how I would remember that.

You are right to question how I could make such a statement with such stone-faced certainty, particularly given that I had a brain injury at the time and may still have one. I may even have an undiagnosed brain tumor that only my box-counter daughter could have diagnosed. (The booming headaches! Boom!)

And you are just as right to question why you should believe me, given that I have substantial motivation to lie, as they say in the movies whenever actors pretending to be lawyers pretend to try to convince a jury of actors of another actor's make-believe guilt.

The answer to your question is not blowing in the wind. The answer is in my own handwriting in a set of black-covered composition books that I lugged home with me when I was discharged.[64] They begin thusly, "In my younger and more vulnerable years, my father gave me some advice that I've been turning over in my mind ever since. 'Whenever you feel like criticizing anyone,' he told me, 'just remember that all the people in this world haven't had the advantages that you've had.'"

Any remotely dedicated student of American literature will immediately recognize those words. Those words, of course, are the well-known, off-quoted first words of

---

64   They are stored at a separate location than the Underwood typewriter, which in turn is stored separately from my notebooks for *The Allergic Boy*. I told you: I am no fool.

The Great Gatsby, written by F. Scott Fitzgerald, a former Baltimorean no less.

Even after all these years, I can still close my eyes and hear those words read aloud in the soft, vaguely nasal voice of an Army nurse who hailed from upstate New York and had a French-sounding surname.

"In my younger and more vulnerable years," she would say.

"In my younger and more vulnerable years," I would write.

"My father gave me some advice."

"My father gave me some advice."

And so on.

And so on.

And so on until Jay Gatsby was no more. A gun, a bullet, bang-bang![65]

---

[65] My apologies if I have ruined the ending to that brilliant novel for any of the readers of this book (which, as you know, I am obliged to inform you is itself fiction). But if you have not already read that book by now, it is fair to assume you have made a conscious decision that you are not going to read it. In other words, if you had any interest in reading it, you would have done so already. Jay Gatsby dies at the end.

IN MY YOUNGER AND MORE VULNERABLE YEARS

My late father (Henry Alfred Nail) was a barber (snip, snip), trained and licensed by the State of Maryland, which actually requires training and licensing for such a vocation, along with physicians, lawyers and schoolteachers. He had his own creaky little barbershop called, unimaginatively, Henry's Barbershop, adorned with the very red-white-and-blue barber pole that you were already imagining in your own minds. Some of those readers who lived in our Baltimore neighborhood will likely remember my father's barbershop well, if only for the small painted sign that hung in the front window: "It'll Grow Back." My mother dreamed up that sign one night and painted it herself, and it brought a certain knowing smile to people's faces, as those were the words inevitably spoken by a consoling father or mother to the sobbing boy who had just lost his curly locks to my father's clippers: "It'll grow back."[66]

My father said that to me after many haircuts that had left me in tears or close to them: "It'll grow back." Perhaps your parents said it to you. We said it to Claire after her first haircut. The second one, too. Both times, the hair stylist cut her headful of curls so that she resembled a short clown.

---

66   My father did not cut girls' hair. Just boys and men. He would get sued for discrimination if he refused to cut girls' hair today. He also did not cut black people's hair. I try not to remember that because it makes me respect him even less. I know people whose parents participated in the Civil Rights marches at the same time my father refused to cut black people's hair. "I'll lose all my regular customers," he tried to explain. He might have been right. But still.

Henry's Barbershop did fine, as far as barbershops go. Steady business on afternoons after the local schools let out, booming business on Saturdays when businessmen waited their turn on the wall of fake leather chairs across from the barber's chairs (often perusing a poorly concealed stack of girlie magazines), closed by state law on Sundays because God wanted everyone in church, not out getting haircuts (and not perusing girlie magazines).[67]

My father usually earned enough from the shop to pay the mortgage and the bills, but then came the crushing losses at Pimlico Racetrack (run faster, you nag!) and the drinking (glug, glug, glug). No one wants to have his hair trimmed by a wobbly, acid-breathed barber. Bits and pieces of ears don't grow back. Any doctor worth his weight can confirm that in an instant.[68]

Business dwindled, the State of Maryland came knocking on the door (BAM, BAM, BAM!), my father's license to cut hair was revoked and the barbershop was soon closed for good, not just on Sundays, replaced, fittingly enough, by a liquor store. It was called Liquor World, its name screaming in pulsating red neon letters.

---

67   The magazines were in a far too-neat stack on the ledge beneath the cash register, and they bore names like *36D* and *Leg World*. There were others, many others. I never saw my father purchase them. They just appeared beneath the cash register, as if they were reproducing. It was not the best way for a boy to learn about girls.

68   Or "her weight," in recognition of the many female doctors who are likely to purchase this book, whom I do not wish to slight in any way. Except for the one who told my lovely, black-haired, cornflower blue-eyed angel of a wife that it was only a matter of time before I snapped. Hello again, Dr. Donna Taffy. I hope you have lost your license by now.

Without the barbershop, the barber's money was gone, like a magic trick. (Pffffft! Gone!) It would never come back, like that magician's assistant in Cincinnati.

Without money, the barber's boy couldn't return to college.

The barber's boy worked a series of meaningless jobs before going off to Vietnam.

There, in Vietnam, the barber's boy killed no one, hand on Bible.

There, in Vietnam, a man's nose was shot off and landed on the barber's boy's chest.

There, in Vietnam, the barber's boy's head was cracked open like a boiled egg.

There, the barber's boy's head was sewed up, and young nurses read *The Great Gatsby* to him, beginning, "In my younger and more vulnerable days ... ," ending when Jay Gatsby was dead.

When a nurse with a French-sounding surname unraveled the bandages that were wrapped around the barber's boy's head so he could inspect the scar in the tiny mirror of her compact case, the first thing he noticed was not the scar but that his head of brown hair was gone, reduced to stubble in most places and patches of smooth pink flesh in others, most notably around the curving scar itself, which looked like a pink creek. As he ran his palm over his head, both he and the nurse spoke the identical words, in slightly different tones: "It'll grow back."

The barber's boy and his nurse shared a sad, echoing laugh.

But his hair did not grow back, at least not around the scar. The hair there was gone for good, like earth that had been salted.

CLARIFICATION

In case there was any confusion about the previous section, the barber's boy was me, your author, your aging typist, your historian.

But you knew that, didn't you? You're a smart one.[69]

---

69   A note to the editor: Please insert here the photograph of me in the hospital bed with the turban of bandages around my head. Beneath it, please type, "Private James Nail, bearing wounds suffered in the service of his country (although he did not kill any North Vietnamese), unaware that his manuscript had been stolen and published by erstwhile college classmate P.J. Darbin, who never served his country because he was a motherfucking coward." Do not substitute "motherfudging."

EXHIBIT J

— The Great Gatsby

In a cramped, sunless courtroom in downtown Baltimore that smelled oddly of oil, I presented my original, black-covered, Army-issued composition books containing my handwritten transcription of *The Great Gatsby*.

Transcribed in a military hospital in Vietnam.

Transported back to the United States of America in a military-issue trunk via a military transport plane.

Stored in a very, very safe place, far away from the stubby fingers of P.J. Darbin's lawyers who might accidentally (wink, wink) drop them in an incinerator, where they would be turned to dust.

"So now you are claiming that you wrote *The Great Gatsby*, too!" one of those fancy-suited lawyers asked me when I presented the composition books.

"No," I answered, "you are twisting my words."

"Those are your words in these notebooks?"

"That's not what I said."

"Is that or is that not your handwriting in this notebook?" he asked, holding one of them aloft like a Southern preacher with a worn Bible. He was a slim, athletic-looking man with short, slick black hair and the look of wealth. I could picture a younger version of him wearing a crisp polo shirt and standing on the deck of a yacht.

"Yes, that is my handwriting, but — "

"And here, where it reads, 'In my younger and more vulnerable years,' is that your handwriting?"

"Yes."

The slick-haired lawyer turned to Judge Cocksucker. "Your Honor," he said, grinning, "it seems as if your courtroom has been graced with the presence of the one and only F. Scott Fitzgerald!"

Judge Cocksucker snorted. "Mr. Fitzgerald," he said to me, "it is quite an honor to have you before us, but I could have sworn you were dead!"

I said nothing.

"Well, are you dead?"

He waited for an answer. Everyone waited with him.

"No, sir," I answered.

"So who are you today?" Judge Cocksucker continued. "Are you P.J. Darbin or are you F. Scott Fitzgerald?"

I said nothing. I looked at my convenience-store lawyers. They were inspecting the ceiling.

"Answer me, goddamit!" He pounded a fist on a brown leather-bound book that rested in front of him. The booked jumped. His face had turned the color of a delicious apple. "I asked you a goddam question."

"I am neither," I said.

"That's right," Judge Cocksucker said. "You are neither. You are nobody."

Then, leaning over the bench, he addressed the court reporter. "Sweetheart," he said softly, honey practically dripping from his lips, "remove the word 'goddam' from the transcript." The woman nodded dutifully. You could tell she was not called "sweetheart" often.

SWEETHEART

Poppy, where are you, sweetheart?
    I need you, sweetheart.
    I need your help, sweetheart.
    No?
    Not here?
    Not ready to appear yet?
    That's fine, sweetheart. Take your time.
    Let me move on without you, sweetheart.

EXHIBIT K

— My Composition Books

I wish to present to you, dear reader, my black, Army-issued composition books containing my handwritten transcription of *The Great Gatsby*, starting with "In my younger and more vulnerable days ... " and ending with Jay Gatsby's death (bang! bang!). Unfortunately, I may not do so because the words contained in them are not my own and reproducing them here would violate the copyright owned by the estate of F. Scott Fitzgerald.

The real F. Scott Fitzgerald, not the fictional one.

There is no fictional one, to the best of my knowledge.

But you have that book on your bookshelf, do you not? Right there. See?

-

HAPPY BIRTHDAY TO ME

Today I celebrate my birthday. I am 40 years old, eating a leftover slice of birthday cake and watching the filmmaker Orson Welles tell some somewhat amusing stories to Johnny Carson on "The Tonight Show."

Today is my birthday. I am 46 years old and reading a thrilling book called *The Hunt for Red October*, a nice little present from the box counter.[70] She knows I love books.[71]

Today is my birthday. I am 58. As I celebrated my own birth, the television news reported that both Milton Berle and Dudley Moore had died, one after the other. They were both comedians. There was nothing funny about their deaths. I checked my pulse to confirm that I was not joining them. I am not, at least not today. I will someday. I will take my last breath, then blurt out, "Jesus fucking Christ, you must be fucking kidding me!"[72]

Today is my birthday. I am 61. I am 50. I am 47. I am 52.

---

70   The author of that thick novel, a man named Tom Clancy, is from Maryland, my home!

71   Except for one. Actually two. I do not like *Ulysses*, the one by James Joyce. It is unreadable. And most people who claim to love it never got past page 10. I got to page 300, or thereabouts, before I said, "Enough. Life is too short, and this is too long." Young readers, if you are ever assigned to read that book by one of your teachers, tell him to fuck off. Or her, as the case may be.

72   If there is an afterlife, I hope Frank Ditto is reading this. And if he is, I have this to say, "Hello, Frank. How are you? I may owe you quite a bit in royalties for using your final words so often in this book. Will you accept a check?" And I would also say to him: "You should pay her *more* if you want her to moan."

And on each of these birthdays, I am the author of *The Allergic Boy*, stolen from me and published as *The Left-Handed Girl*.

If I live to be 100, I will say the same, only more softly so you have to lean in to hear me, and perhaps with some cake crumbs at the corners of my mouth that I do not notice. Tell me about them, and I will lick them off.

A LETTER TO THE FORMER GINGER JILL-BEAR

Dear Mrs. Seel:

You do not remember me, at least not by name. I was a soldier from Baltimore, Maryland, one of the young men to whom you read while you were stationed at a military hospital in Vietnam. I am the one with the allergies, Private James Nail. Or I was Private James Nail then. I am no longer a Private. And I am no longer private (ha ha). My life is now an open book, as they say. An open book that will be published shortly in hardcover throughout the United States and (fingers crossed) worldwide. Your name will appear in that book several times, at least. All references to you will be positive, I assure you.

As you may recall, several years ago you submitted a sworn affidavit to Judge Miles C. Levy in a lawsuit in which I was involved. Perhaps that will ring the proverbial bell. (Ring, ring, ring!)

I do not wish to quarrel with you about the contents of your affidavit. I do not wish to debate whether you read *The Great Gatsby* to me or whether you read *The Left-Handed Girl*. (It was the former, but again, let's not quarrel.)

Instead, I wish to ask you about something else you read to me. I realize there is a million-to-one chance that you will remember this, but do you recall reading aloud a telegram that I had received? Not the one from my mother about the tornado. Do you recall the telegram you read to me from a young woman?

If you do, please contact me immediately. I assure you that I will reimburse you for any and all costs you might incur. And in exchange for your time, I will gladly send you an autographed, first edition copy of my book, which is titled *The Allergic Boy Versus The Left-Handed Girl: A Story of Grace and Mercy (but Also of Theft, Injustice and a [REDACTED] Scar on the Side of My [REDACTED] Head)*. A cumbersome title, true, but one that gets to the heart of the matter quite swiftly and effectively.

Whether you should recall that long-ago telegram or not, please let me thank you sincerely for your service to our country and to me in particular. I remain forever grateful.

Sincerely,

Jimmy Nail (nee Private James Nail)

P.S. How did I pass my Army physical with all of my allergies? That is not a long story, Mrs. Seel. I slipped a ten-dollar bill to the doctor who administered the physical. (If only I could tell you what those same ten dollars could have bought me in Europe!) Yes, while many boys were fleeing the country or concocting elaborate schemes to get *out* of the war, like eating a bar of soap before their physicals — the soap causes heart palpitations — I was bribing doctors to get *in*. And that was *before* I suffered a head injury.
P.P.S. It did not grow back.

AN ENTIRELY ACCURATE TRANSCRIPTION OF THE TELEGRAM

The following is taken verbatim from one of my black-covered, military-issued, Vietnam hospital composition books:

JIMMY. OH HONEY. I JUST HEARD YOUR NEWS. WHAT A PAIR WE WOULD MAKE. POPPY.

Even after all these years, I can still close my eyes and hear those words read aloud to me in the soft, vaguely nasal voice of an Army nurse who hailed from upstate New York and had a French-sounding surname.

"Jimmy stop," she would say. "I just heard your news stop."[73]

And so on until "Poppy stop."

"Poppy stop" was Poppy Fowler. It could be no one else but Poppy Fowler.

Not Fahrenberg.

And certainly not Fahrenheit!

She had found me years before I had to find her.

---

73   In the long-lost language of telegrams, "stop" was meant to indicate the end of a sentence. I must admit that I occasionally was amused at the thought of the confusion that would be created by a telegram that actually included the word "stop." A telegram that read, "I understand you have been screwing my wife and would like you to stop," for instance. There is probably a better, more humorous example to be made. I will leave it to the editor to make a suggestion. I am all ears.

THE SPAGHETTI YEARS

The home in which I was reared — and "reared" is the correct word, not "raised," because children are reared, cattle are raised — was a faded red-brick row house in a gritty old section of Baltimore known as Charles Village. It was blocks from the renowned Johns Hopkins University, then an all-male school, now coed, the breeding ground for many geniuses and thousands of clean-cut, well-fed lacrosse players, few of whom gave the time of day to any of us who had been reared in that neighborhood because, well, maybe you had to get a look at us. Poorly dressed, acned, noses running, buzz cut haircuts from a barber who may (or may not) have been drunk. But we did not give those fresh-faced, bright-eyed college boys the time of day either, so no feelings should have been bruised on either side of the equation.

For those readers unfamiliar with such architecture, row houses are extremely narrow homes, two or three stories tall, pressed against and connected to each other like the folds of an accordion, one home sharing a wall with the next, that home sharing a wall with the one next to it, and so on and so on until you reach the street corner, and it is that lucky home that only shares one wall with a neighbor, the other wall facing the street, the streetlights, the sun, the moon. We were not fortunate enough to live in one of the corner homes. A barber's income was not sufficient for such luxury. No, we lived in the middle of the block in a row house my father inherited from his, sharing north and south walls with a succession of lower middle-class families and young, single businessmen. It would bore you to salty tears were I to endeavor to list our next-door neighbors — the So-and-sos, the Whozzits, Mr. Whatshisname — and bore me to tears to try, so let us skip that pointless endeavor, shall we.[74]

You might ask how narrow our row house was. It would be only a slight exaggeration to suggest that Wilt Chamberlain, the great giant of a basketball player (Philadelphia 76ers, Los Angeles Lakers), could have stood in the center of our dining room, spread his wings and touched the north wall with the fingertips of one hand and the south wall with the fingertips of the other.

You might also ask how thin the walls were between adjacent row houses. Radio and television shows ("The Andy Griffith Show," "Gunsmoke"), birthday celebrations, quarrels and amorous adventures (I am, ahem, being polite for the moment) bled through those walls, muffled slightly, but only slightly. Whatever we may have heard of the lives of our neighbors north and south, they certainly heard of ours as well. My father (Henry, the drunken, gambling barber) and my mother (June, saint) nevertheless sometimes forgot about those acoustics, not understanding why the So-and-sos or the Whozzits could not meet their eyes the morning

---

74 I will mention that one was a dark-skinned man who played professional baseball for the Baltimore Orioles for a brief time before he was drafted and sent to Vietnam. He died there and never came back. I died there, too, over and over again. I died every day, sometimes two or three times in a day. I was not suited to be a soldier, not because I did not have the discipline, but because I did not have the makeup. I did not have the spine. I shit my pants at least a dozen times, once because I heard a twig snap in the distance, and I washed the shit out of my pants in the latrine in the middle of the night with a bar of soap. But I have digressed. I was talking about the black baseball player. He died just once and for good.

after they had loudly discussed our family finances, or the drinking, or the gambling.[75]

The finances, the drinking, the gambling. They were linked inseparably, as you likely imagined they would be. The drinking went hand in hand with the gambling, draining our family's already meager finances. The dwindling bank account led to more drinking and more gambling. It reached the sad point where my parents could hardly afford food for the three of us. As a result, for nearly two full years — my freshman and sophomore years at Theodore Roosevelt Regional High School — we ate spaghetti for dinner nearly every night, spaghetti being the cheapest and most filling meal my saintly mother could find at the market. Spaghetti with butter and cheese.[76] Spaghetti with tuna.[77] Spaghetti with buttered bread crumbs.[78] Spaghetti with broccoli and peppers.[79] Even 40-some-odd years later (I turn 55 next month!), my stomach grumbled as I typed this paragraph. It remembers.

---

75   A note to anyone who currently resides in one of those townhouses and suffers from those same problems: get some foam insulation. Call Charm City Insulation on Claremont Road. You can ask for my daughter, Claire Cleary (her married name), joy of my life. If you mention this book, maybe she'll try to get you a discount!

76   The recipe is self-explanatory.

77   Cook spaghetti. Add contents of a can of tuna after draining the fishy oil. Stir. Close your eyes while eating.

78   Melt butter in saucepan. Add bread crumbs. Stir until browned. Sprinkle on spaghetti. Pretend it is a meal that would be served in Rome.

79   Self-explanatory.

One evening, while recuperating from my wounds in a stiff hospital bed in a town apparently now known as Redacted, Vietnam, my head encased in a turban of bandages, an Army-issued composition book by my bedside filled with the elegant words of one-time Baltimorean F. Scott Fitzgerald ("In my younger and more vulnerable days"), a young shiny-haired nurse brought me a special treat for dinner, something other than the thin broth I had eaten most nights as I recuperated in that uncomfortable bed.

"Voila," she announced, dramatically removing the gray cloth napkin that had concealed my dinner. "A solid meal! Spaghetti with marinara sauce!"

She was so pleased. She was so proud. She had the look on her face of a small girl who had just delivered breakfast in bed to her adoring father on Father's Day.[80] I couldn't disappoint her. I would not learn how to disappoint women until I met Samantha, my black-haired, blue-eyed angel of a wife (now ex-wife); Lord knows she could have done better. I tried to swallow a few bites of the spaghetti but soon found myself gagging, coughing, wheezing. My stomach remembered.

"Oh my gosh," the shiny-haired nurse said. "Is it another allergy, Jimmy?"

"Yes," I lied. "Tomatoes." Tomatoes, for those of you who recall the exhaustive list I presented as evidence earlier, are not among my allergies. But I did not want to share the embarrassment of the spaghetti years or tell this fine young woman who was serving her country (and me) that I had not been able to eat spaghetti since.

Pity was written on her pink forehead and in her wet eyes. I did not mind. I was pitiful (a fucking scar on the side

---

80 "Hello, Claire," I say. "Thank you again for all of my Father's Day breakfasts. They were as fine as anything they serve in a five-star restaurant."

of my fucking head, a turban, naked and too skinny beneath a thin hospital gown).

She apologized, then dabbed my lips with the napkin and took the metal tray away, returning minutes later with a simple bologna sandwich on white bread.

"Not allergic to bologna, are you?" she smiled.

"No, ma'am."

"Or white bread?"

"No, ma'am."

"You shouldn't call a woman 'ma'am' if she's younger than you."

"Sorry."

"It's okay. I thought it was sweet." She said nothing more while watching me eat the sandwich, then wiped my lips with a napkin and said, "Why don't we return to the adventures of Mr. Jay Gatsby," picking up where we had left off before the spaghetti incident.

I wish I could say that kind nurse was Ginger Seel (nee jill-BEAR). It would make for a better story if it had been her, but I promised you accuracy. I practically raised my hand and gave you the Boy Scout's word of honor that I would tell you the truth.[81] That nurse was not Ginger Seel (nee jill-BEAR). It was a different nurse whose name I do not recall at all, not her first, not her last. She was dark-skinned; she would have been called colored then but black today when I wrote this sentence. Or Afro-American when I wrote this one. Or African-American when I wrote this one.[82] I only

---

81   I was not a Boy Scout, so giving that oath would have had no meaning to me.

82   Although my father had refused to cut their hair and sometimes referred to them by a heinous slur that I will not repeat here other than to note that it started with the letter "N" (yes, that one), I harbor no prejudice against colored people, or blacks, or Afro-Americans, or African-Americans. As I have said, our

say she was dark-skinned so that you can picture her in your mind, or try to.

If that dear nurse should stumble upon this book, I beg her forgiveness for not recalling her name. (Stephanie? No. Christine? Hmm, maybe. Christine sounds right.) But it is the nature of the work of a nurse to render a valuable service and then be forgotten. Just as it is the nature of the work of a writer to wish to be remembered by everyone, always and forever, but usually end up just as forgotten, his name washed away as if he had written it in the sand at low tide.

---

neighbor who played baseball before losing his life in Vietnam was colored, or black, or Afro-American, or African-American. And my dear friend, the late Frank Ditto, who also lost his life in Vietnam, was colored, or black, or Afro-American, or African-American, although I suppose saying that he was my dear friend proves nothing if you are scouring these words to see if I am (or was) a bigot. The first thing a bigot will tell you is that he's not a bigot. And he will preface his comments by saying, "I'm not a bigot, but," followed by something that is undeniably offensive. No one has ever said something innocuous like, "I'm not a bigot, but I like iceberg lettuce." Let me be the first: "I'm not a bigot, but I like iceberg lettuce." There. Done.

THIS IS POPPY FOWLER

This is Poppy Fowler. I could paint her portrait from memory. And I did before the memory of her face could be washed away. I took a night school painting class at the high school in Towson, Maryland several years ago just so I could learn how to paint, just so I could paint this portrait. The only other painting I have ever created was of the box counter, my little Claire, the joy of my life. You should only paint that which you love. That might be a quote from someone famous like da Vinci. It is possible I just made it up.[83]

---

83   A note to editor: Please insert here a reproduction of my original oil painting of Poppy Fowler, the one that is hung above my desk when I am alone, or stored in the bedroom closet when I have company, replaced by a framed Salvador Dali print, the one with the melting clocks. You have my permission.

GRACE AND MERCY

I saw Poppy Fowler (love of my life, ghost in my dreams) later the same day that she saved me from the pickle barrel dog, the encounter I described near the beginning of the book you are now reading. From an upstairs window in the empty bedroom where my mother stored her sewing machine and her sewing supplies, through the thin curtains, I spotted Poppy sitting on the marble stoop of the row house next to ours, the one she was inhabiting with her homosexual Uncle Rob.[84] She was dressed in an oversized navy-blue polo shirt and cream-colored shorts, and she was shaving her long, tanned legs under the heat of the June sun. She had a metal wash basin and a flat razor like the one my father used to shave customers' necks smooth. She rubbed soapy water from the metal basin on her right leg, then ran the razor from her ankle to her thigh, leaving a smooth, brown highway behind. Then she started at her ankle again and pulled the razor up again, widening the path. She was humming or singing something as she shaved, words I could not decipher even with the window of the empty bedroom (except for the sewing machine and sewing supplies) open against the heat.

Finally, without taking her eyes off her work, she yelled, "Hey, allergic boy!"

---

84   You can do your own research to confirm it if you would like, but most row houses had stoops made of marble, the same material artists use for famous sculptures, the same one that fancy New York lawyers walk on in their fancy New York law offices. The stoops were often the nicest part of the house. On Saturday mornings, you could look up and down the street and see dozens of women on their knees scrubbing the marble clean, buckets of steaming hot water beside each.

I jumped back from the window, tripping over the sewing machine and nearly falling to the ground.

She yelled again. "Hey, allergic boy, do your parents know?"

I said nothing, ducking out of sight.

"Do your parents know?" she repeated.

"Know what?" I called back after a moment, my body still concealed.

"Do they know that you're a pervert?" She laughed. "It's okay," she said. "All boys your age are perverts. It's a biological fact. Their penises are growing and starting to take over their lives."

I leaned a bit out the window. "I wasn't staring," I said. I was not convincing.

"All boys your age are liars, too," she said. She continued to shave her leg, running her fingers over the freshly shaved skin. Then she took a small powder-blue towel and patted her leg dry.

"I have one more leg to go," she called out blindly to me. "If you want to watch me shave it, you'd better get down here in a hurry."

"What?"

"You heard me, pervert. Run!"

By the time I made it outside — my injured leg, a bandage covering the dog's teeth marks, slowed me down slightly, and I counted to 20 Mississippi before I opened our front door — she had already soaped up her left leg and was holding the razor suspended over her ankle, waiting for me. Her long red curls covered her face like an awning. Silently, I took a seat on the step by her feet, and she began.

She swept the mess of red hair from her eyes. Her eyes were green, the color of summer grapes.

"Now don't get too excited," she teased.

"I won't."

"From the diaphragm," she reminded me.

I lowered my voice a little and said, "I won't," and she laughed. It sounded like a hiccup.

"Shaving your legs is a perfectly normal activity performed by every woman in the Western world."

"I know."

"Your mother does this. Your grandmother does this. Your teachers do this."

"I guess."

"Although they probably don't have legs like these, do they, Jimmy Nail?"

"I don't think so."

"You pervert, have you been checking out your mother's legs, and your grandmother's, and your teachers'?"

"No!"

She smiled with those magnificent green eyes. I can close my eyes now and picture hers. I can see them in a painting over my desk, a color fashioned from green, yellow and white paints mixed carefully.

She focused on her work for a moment or two, exposing ribbons of fresh, tanned skin with each stroke.

"Tell me about yourself, Jimmy Nail," she said. My heart skipped whenever she said my name, which would be often.

"What do you mean?"

"I mean, tell me something interesting about yourself. Pretend we just met, and I know nothing about you."

"We just did meet."

"Then it should be easy. Tell me the most interesting thing about you, Jimmy Nail. And it better not be about how you're allergic to cats and goldfish because that will bore me shitless." She smiled. "Yes, I said 'shitless.' Are you going to tell your mom?"

"No."

"Then say it yourself."

"Say what?"

"Say 'shitless' so I know you're okay with me talking like that."

"Shitless," I said.

"Diaphragm."

"Shitless," I said in a deeper voice.

"Use it in a sentence, Jimmy Nail."

"No."

"Yes."

I did not hesitate for long. "After I am done shitting, I am shitless."

She laughed very, very loudly, then wiped her nose with the back of her hand. "Nicely done, Jimmy Nail. Bravo. Now tell me something about you that won't bore me like I'm done shitting."

"I play chess."

"Yawn."

"I'm on the chess team at school."

"Tell me something else, anything else, Jimmy Nail. I'm begging you."

"I'm very good at math."

"Double yawn."

"I like to read."

"Triple yawn. You're going to put me to sleep. I'm struggling to keep my eyes open. It feels like I've been drugged."

"I like to write stories."

She stopped shaving and waved her razor at me. "Now *that*," she said, "that's interesting, Jimmy Nail. That's the type of thing that would get a girl's attention. That's the type of thing that would get a girl all hot and bothered. What kind of stories do you write?"

"All kinds," I said. "Stories about cowboys, stories about spaceships."

"And *that's* what will lose a girl's attention. Cowboys and spaceships? Jesus Christ! A girl wants stories about love, about hearts breaking, about romance, about people overcoming their circumstances. Girls want stories about grace and mercy, Jimmy Nail. Got any of those, or are they all cowboy and spaceship crap?"

"Plenty," I said. It was a lie. I had no stories about grace and mercy. I knew nothing about grace and mercy. I knew about cowboys and spaceships, mostly because I had read about cowboys and spaceships, and I knew about chess and math.

She gave me an exaggerated, toothy smile. "Look," she said, "you've got my attention again. My chest is heaving with desire. My loins are starting to boil. Can I read one of your grace-and-mercy stories?"

I nodded.

"Now," she said, her voice adopting a singsong quality, "seeing as I saved your life from a tiger this morning — "

"It was a dog."

"Tell people it was a tiger, okay? It's a better story. If you're a writer, as you say you are, you're allowed to embellish your stories. It's a law, I think. People will expect you to embellish your stories to make them more entertaining. It's called artistic license, okay?"

I nodded.

"So as I was saying, seeing as I saved your life from a tiger this morning, I want to ask you a question, and you have to answer honestly. Okay? One hundred percent honesty?"

"Okay."

"Do you think I'm pretty?" asked the prettiest girl I had ever seen. Of course, she already knew the answer. Waiting for my response, she waved a hand at nothing, then she breathed in the air she had just displaced.

"Yes," I said. "You are very pretty."

"I thought so."

"I have nice legs, don't I, Jimmy Nail?"

"Yes."

She put a hand on her chest and said, "Not much upstairs, though."

"That's okay," I said, and she laughed.

"I wasn't asking for your approval, dummy," she replied, "but thanks anyway. Some boys only care about what a girl has upstairs. If a girl isn't stacked, they won't give her a second look. A real man, a romantic man, one who cares about grace and mercy, would love a woman even if she was as flat as an ironing board. Love and boobs are two different things. Three actually."

I was nodding.

"Is that something you care about, Jimmy Nail? How big a girl's boobs are?"

"No," I answered, although I must admit that suddenly I was thinking about the stack of girlie magazines at Henry's Barbershop; most of the girls in those magazines were, ahem, healthy in that department.

"Good answer, Jimmy Nail. Very good answer. Do you like my hair?"

I confirmed that I did, and she combed it with her fingers.

"My father is Irish," she said. "All the men have red hair. The women — well, our hair is aided and abetted a bit."

I assume she meant that she dyed it.

"You'd like to kiss me wouldn't you, Jimmy Nail?"

I hesitated.

"You don't have to answer. I know you'd like to kiss me. I can tell by the way you're looking at me. It's not going to happen today. It may never happen."

My heart sank more than a little. I am sure it showed in my face.

"But it probably will," she added. "Writers are good kissers. At least that's my experience. Writers and drummers. Athletes are the worst. They think kissing is a sport."

She was finished shaving her leg, and she tossed her blue towel to me.

"I'm too tired to dry my leg off," she said. "You do it."

And so I did. I took my time, running the towel from her ankle to her thigh, then back down, before pushing it up again. She leaned back on her elbows and closed her eyes against the sun. Finally, she said, "Jimmy Nail?"

"Yes."

"I don't think my leg can get any drier."

That was how our friendship was born, on a marble stoop outside a row house in Baltimore, a young boy saved from a tiger by a slightly older girl, then that young boy drying off that slightly older girl's freshly shaved leg, every second committed to memory and, now, to paper. The boy gave the girl her blue towel, then returned home to his bedroom and to his Underwood typewriter and to his stack of onion paper, and he remained in his room until the late evening, ignoring the moaning of the girl's homosexual uncle and his lover that seeped through the wall like the odor of someone frying bacon ("Yes!" "Yes!" "Oh, God!"), pressing little keys non-randomly until he had completed a story he called "The Way We Wash Our Clothes," which he placed in a manila envelope and delivered to the girl's stoop with the next morning's newspaper. On the envelope, he wrote: "FOR A PERFECT GIRL, WITH GRACE AND MERCY." Then he watched from the upstairs window of an empty bedroom (except for a sewing machine and sewing supplies) as the girl's uncle retrieved it, read the message, tucked the package under his arm and disappeared back into the house he was renting. Through the wall, he heard the uncle yell, "Who have you been screwing, you whore?" Then he heard a thump that sounded oddly like a wet newspaper dropped on a marble stoop. Then a cry or something that sounded like a cry.

A REMINDER

I told you before.

I told you in the "Introduction."

I am no hero.

I did not buy a cape.

I did learn how to fly.

I could not punch my way through a wall, no matter how thin.

A DETAIL YOU MAY CONSIDER IMPORTANT

In which hand did Poppy hold her razor as she shaved her leg?

Her left.

ONE MORE THING

There is one detail I omitted from the description of that encounter on the stoop, not with any ill intent, but merely because I have struggled with how to convey it in writing without either misspelling words on having it appear entirely nonsensical. It involved a slight pause that Poppy inserted between the syllables of several words. It could be conveyed easily if I were to tell you aloud. I will try my best to do so by using misspellings and ellipses.

Do you remember when Poppy said, "I don't think my leg could get any drier"?

When she did, I stopped drying her leg, handed her the blue towel, and said goodbye, then walked toward our house so I could write her a story about grace and mercy. Just as I reached for the doorknob, Poppy called, "Hey, Jimmy Nail."

I turned toward her.

"Want to see my dick ... tation pad?"

I was confused. "What?"

"Yes or no?

"Do you want to see my dick" — she paused for a second or more — "tation pad?"

I did not know what to say, but Poppy was laughing so hard that it would not have mattered what I said.

"Or would you rather hold my ass ... cot?"

THE FIRST CHAPTER

The first story I gave Poppy was the one I shared with you earlier, the one called "How We Wash Our Clothes," the one with the character named Allie.

Later, much later that summer, just days before the accident, Poppy sat with me on the front stoop of her uncle's row house while I read her the first chapter of the novel I had begun to write for her, with a character named after her. She sat beside me, her head on my shoulder, as I tried to hold the thin stack of onion paper steady. I was distracted, very distracted.

I began, "Aaaah-chooo!"

Ten minutes later, I ended, "Neither does God, according to the bishop."

I would write no more of the novel until I had reached New York University.

EXHIBIT L

— *The Allergic Boy* versus *The Left-Handed Girl*

Let me now present you, dear reader, with select excerpts of *The Allergic Boy*, presented side by side with select excerpts of *The Left-Handed Girl* for ease of comparison. Are they identical? No, not identical per se. I never once said they were identical. But, inspecting them side by side, you do not need to be an expert in letters to recognize that they tell the same story, or nearly the same story. You know the story. You read the book. You saw the movie.

No amount of rewriting, no amount of editing by some skillful New York editor wearing tortoise-shell eyeglasses and his striped college tie, can disguise the fact that the book in the right-hand column is stolen from the one in the left-hand.

That pun was not intended.

TEXT

The Allergic Boy

Aaaah-chooo!

Excuse me. I just sneezed. I do that a lot. Why? Allergies. I have a lot of them.

Let me introduce myself. They called me Allie, and I answered to it, but my real name is Alexander, and someday, that's what everyone would call me that or Alex. At least I hoped so. Allie's a pretty silly name if you ask me, especially for a boy. It sounds like a girl's name, like a nickname for someone named Allison.

Even Poppy called me Allie, and I must have told her at least once a day that I preferred Alex. But that's the way girls are sometimes. They like to find something that bothers you, and then they keep doing it time after time until you start to like it. Then — boom! — they stop.

Allie was my father's idea. He was a drunk, and I suppose you want to know all about it, what alcohol he drank and

The Left-Handed Girl

[A note to the editor: Pursuant to the "fair use doctrine," which has been acknowledged by the United States Supreme Court and which allows the use of copyrighted material for "transformative" purposes, such as to comment upon, criticize, or parody a copyrighted work, please insert here the entire first chapter of *The Left-Handed Girl*, which I am commenting upon and criticizing.]

what alcohol he smelled like, but I'll tell you that stuff later, if I feel like it. Anyway, there was this shortstop for the Baltimore Orioles named Allie Meacham — his real name was Alexander Floyd Meacham — and my father was taken to him, his quickness, and his hard-nosed style of play. And his nickname. So that's how I got stuck with Allie.

"It makes your father happy," my mother said. "You can call yourself whatever you want when you go off to college. Just be thankful that it isn't your given name."

But it might as well have been. My parents called me Allie. Teachers, neighbors and friends called me Allie. And as I've mentioned, even Poppy called me Allie.

Everyone called me Allie.

But call me Alex, okay?

The first time I ever met Poppy, she saved me from a tiger that attacked me while I was delivering newspapers. I'll tell you all about that later, if I feel like it.

The second time I met her, I watched her shave her legs, and she told me she might kiss me someday. I'll tell you about that later, too. Maybe. If I'm in the mood.

Poppy thought I was some kind of genius or something or, if not one already, that I would be someday, and I think that's what she liked about me. It's funny because most teenage girls seem to want nothing more than to be seen with some popular athlete, and here was Poppy who wanted to be seen with a genius. A genius who happened to be allergic to everything: shellfish, dust, pollen, dogs, cats, penicillin, you name it. I wasn't about to question her taste or her values, but it was pretty confusing, let me tell you, even more so since she was an athlete herself with athletic good looks and that certain charm that's peculiar to athletes. Actually, I guess it's only charm if you like the person. I can't think of a word to describe it if you don't; all

I know is that it's the
sort of thing that might make
you want to walk up to that
person and just belt him in the
mouth really hard. You know
what I mean.

I never wanted to belt
Poppy in the mouth. I did
want to kiss her, though.

Anyway, I'm convinced
that Poppy got the idea that
I was a genius about a week
after we'd met, that afternoon
when we sat on the stoop
of the row house where she
lived and looked through her
photograph album. I absolutely
hate photograph albums, the
way people point out things
from their stupid lives and
laugh and make really weird
faces and everything. And the
whole time you're supposed
to sit there and act like you're
really interested in seeing
pictures of wrinkly, old
relatives and summer camps
and junk like that. But when
you like someone, you pretend
that you like the same things
that they do, and I liked
Poppy, so I just sat there and
nodded like I had half-a-brain
or something.

Poppy showed me one picture of her standing on a dock, and you couldn't see anything behind her except for water. She was wearing a golfing cap, a loose shirt that was ten times too big for her and probably one of her father's discarded dress shirts, Bermuda shorts, and these milk-white boat sneakers that looked like she'd just taken them out of the box. She looked like a *boy*. Her skin was also white, just like linen, and there was this really crazy expression on her face. It was hard to tell — she was either sick or bored, possibly both. There was a fish dangling from a string she pinched between her thumb and index finger, and somehow, it seemed as if she were holding the fish more than an arm's length away. No kidding. I know that's not possible, so don't go thinking that there's something wrong with my mind or something, but it really did seem that way.

"That looks like a trout," I said. You should always say something when you're looking through someone's stupid photograph album just so they'll know that you're still awake. And you should definitely say something if it's a girl you really want to kiss.

"It is a trout," she grinned, and she leaned over and kissed me on the cheek. It was the first time she kissed me, and it was just one of those little ones that your grandma gives you on your birthday or something, but it was still nice. "Do you know everything, Allie?"

See what I mean about her calling me Allie? See what I mean about her thinking I was a genius? But the funny thing is that it was just a guess. I don't know anything about fish except for what they taste like, and trout tastes pretty good. Even now, I'm not sure if they live in fresh or salt water. Really. I'm not making that up.

"No, I don't know everything," I said.

"What don't you know?"

"Well, for one, I don't know how to drive a car."

"So I'll teach you."

I knew she'd say that. In fact, I'd planned it. Sometimes, I can be a pretty sneaky guy, let me tell you that now. I just figured that here was this girl who drove a little red convertible, and if I told her that I didn't know how to drive, there was absolutely no way that she wouldn't offer to help me. Like if someone tells you you're really good at poker or cooking or something like that, you can't *help* but teach them. That way you can show them that they were right, that you really *do* know a lot about poker or cooking or whatever. Do you know what I mean?

So I'd pretty much just tricked Poppy into spending several hours a day with me in her car, driving around town.

I told you I was sneaky, and that's not even the best one. Not even close. The best one was way back when I was in second grade or something. There was this girl who went to my church named Katy Lynch who always made fun of my name. She used to say,

"Allie, Allie — is your
real name Allison?" and all
the other kids would laugh.
So at First Holy Communion,
I put this slimy little garden
snake down the back of her
dress. No kidding. I really did
that. It didn't wreck the dress,
but it completely ruined the
ceremony. You had to be there.
She started wiggling around
like one of those belly-dancers,
and then she yelled out,
"Shit!" in front of the bishop
and God and everyone. And
if you don't think that's a big
deal, there's something wrong
with you.

The bishop doesn't like the
word "shit." Neither does God,
according to the bishop.

MY DRIVING LESSONS

Most boys are taught how to drive a car by their fathers or their older brothers. How to pop the clutch, how to shift gears. Me, I was taught by a beautiful red-haired girl, just as Allie was in *The Allergic Boy* and just as Allie was in *The Left-Handed Girl*.

It was several days after I first encountered Poppy Fowler — Wednesday? Thursday? — that I returned from delivering the newspaper to see her sitting in the driver's seat of her uncle's red convertible. Her head was tipped back, exposing her long thin neck, and her eyes were pressed closed as if she were sunbathing. The skin around her left eye was a little swollen and a little discolored. Makeup had not concealed it.

I approached the car, not sure what I would say to her. Without lifting her head or opening her eyes, she said, "Your story was very melancholy."

"Sorry," I said.

"Nothing to say you're sorry about. I like melancholy. It was a nice story."

"Thanks." I was standing behind the driver's side door of the car. She had not moved.

"Nice title, too — 'The Way We Wash Our Clothes.'"

"Thanks."

"Why did you set the story during the Depression?"

"We studied it during school last year."

"Good thing you didn't study the Spanish Inquisition."

When I did not respond, she said, "It was a joke, Jimmy Nail. No one wants to read a story set during the Spanish Inquisition."

"Oh, okay."

"Apparently, it was not a very funny joke." She rubbed her pretty nose with her pretty fist. "Anyway, it was a very nice story, Jimmy Nail. Thank you for sharing it with me."

"You're welcome," I said. I was suppressing a small smile, or trying to. "I'm glad you liked it."

"Can I ask you a question?"

"Yes."

"Did you write it for me?"

"Yes."

"I thought so. That was very sweet of you. Boys do nice things for me, but I think you're the first boy to ever write me a story."

"Really?"

"I'm pretty sure. One boy wrote me a song once. It wasn't especially good. Remind me to give you a kiss on the cheek later."

"Okay."

"You won't forget?"

"No, I won't forget."

"I figure a short story is worth a kiss on the cheek, don't you?"

"Yes, that sounds fair."

"I won't tell you what you'll get if you write a whole book for me."

When I didn't respond, she tilted her pretty head and opened her eyes. "Jesus Christ, that was another joke. You know, some people think I'm pretty funny. That was actually a very funny joke."

"I agree."

"Well, you didn't laugh. That's what normal people do when they hear something funny."

"I'll remember that."

"Here, let me try again. Let me tell you a joke." She rearranged her pretty face so that it appeared extremely solemn, almost sad, but still pretty. "Did I tell you that I just started a new diet?"

"No, you didn't."

"I only eat things that begin with the letter A." She paused. "A piece of pie. A piece of cake."

I laughed a genuine laugh, and she smiled with pride.

"There you go," she said. "That's what normal people do when they hear something funny."

"I should be taking notes. That was a good one. Did you make that up yourself?"

"No, I heard it on TV."

"Oh. Well, it was still a good one."

She inhaled deeply, and when she exhaled, she said, "Let's go for a drive." She slid over to the passenger seat and held out her car keys — her uncle's car keys — for me to take, but I didn't.

"I don't know how to drive," I said.

"Really?"

"Really."

She raised her thin eyebrows as if she'd thought of something fascinating, then slid back to the driver's side and cocked her head to signal me to walk around to the passenger side. "I'll teach you," she said. "I've got nothing better to do this morning."

"Seriously?"

"Seriously."

I stepped into the car. "Are you sure your uncle won't mind if we take his car?"

"Who cares? He's an asshole."

I did not disagree. I had heard. I had seen. I closed the door and she started the engine.

"One thing first," she said, and she leaned over and kissed my cheek lightly. "Thanks for the story."

I am sure I blushed (it was the first time a girl had kissed me), but Poppy did not mention it. She then began my driving lessons. I was not paying close attention. I saw movement of her body, I heard sounds coming from her lips, but I learned little that morning. I recall the sounds of metal gears crunching, the feel of the car lurching and stopping, and a wet mark on my left cheek.

When we were done with the lessons, Poppy drove to a small, green park not far from our homes. She produced a blanket from the trunk of her uncle's car, spread it out on the uncut grass, then fell back on it and patted the ground beside her in invitation. I sat next to her and watched her as she breathed, her bony chest rising and falling like a wave.

"You're a terrible driver," she whispered. "Terrible with a capital 'T.'"

"I told you it was my first time."

"Well, it was a pleasure being your first," she said. Soon, she fell asleep, her head resting in the crack of her doomed arm. When I was sure she was asleep, I ran my fingertips over the bruise beneath her eye, then pressed my lips against it. She awoke just for a second, smiled, and then shut her eyes again.

"I'll kill him," I whispered into the air above her face.

"Who?"

"Your uncle the homosexual. I'll kill him."

"Shhh," she said, "don't talk like that, Jimmy Nail. You don't need to do a thing."

THE MANY WAYS I PLANNED TO KILL UNCLE ROB

Knife in the stomach.
Knife in the chest.
Knife across the throat.
Shoot him with a gun.
Run him over with his own car.
Push him off a cliff.
Push him off a building.
Poison his coffee.
Baseball bat.

Whatever the method, fast or slow, bloody or bloodless, painless or excruciating, as Uncle Rob took his last breath on this earth, I would say, "You don't mess with Jimmy Nail's girl."

MARYLAND VERSUS VIRGINIA

Peter and his fancy New York City publisher altered the beginning of the book — *my* book — as you saw for yourself. But you can still see it is mine, right?

In the book I wrote, Allie met Poppy when she saved him when he was delivering newspapers. That, of course, is precisely how Poppy Fowler and I met.

In the book I wrote, the second time that they met, Poppy was shaving her legs on the stoop. That, of course, was the second time I met Poppy Fowler.

In the book I wrote, Allie explained that he was named after a shortstop who played professional baseball for the Baltimore Orioles. Why did I write that? Because I was reared in Baltimore, and the Orioles were the team my father (and, to a significantly lesser extent, I) rooted for.[85] They played ball in Memorial Stadium, a short stroll from our row house in Charles Village. The stadium was dedicated to the men and women who had died in the service of the United States of America, and you could hear the cheers of the crowd from my bedroom. My father named me James after his favorite ballplayer on the Orioles squad, a shortstop by the name of Jimmy Pearce.

In publishing my book in his name, Peter changed the setting from Maryland to Virginia, and instead of referring to the Baltimore Orioles, he referred to the Washington Senators. Why? Because Peter was reared (not "raised") in Virginia, the state just south of Washington, D.C. It was a

---

85   We briefly had a neighbor who played for them before going to Vietnam and not coming back. I mentioned that, did I not? That might be in my other notebook. A note to the editor: If I have already mentioned that, please delete this footnote. No need to tell the same story twice.

clever change, too clever by half. Why? Because the other towns that are referenced throughout the book are all small towns in *Maryland*, not Virginia. Peter and his fancy New York City publisher must have thought I had concocted the names of those little towns and never took the time to see if they actually existed.

They do. Every last motherfucking one of them!

Anyone who takes a moment to inspect the maps of Maryland and Virginia could not help but notice this. There is a Darryton in Maryland, my home state, where *The Allergic Boy* takes place. There is no Darryton in Virginia, Peter's home state, where the purloined *The Left-Handed Girl* takes place. The same for Elliot, and Tariffville, and Winchester Falls, and Harper's Square. They are all small, rural Maryland towns that our high school chess team played and (somewhat regularly) defeated, due in no small part to your aging typist's prowess moving bishops and knights and pawns until some other boy threw up his hands in defeat. All those nights at the dining room table pouring over chess strategy manuals, many not having won any girl's heart, but they spelled defeat for the small-town high schools in Maryland.

Explain that, Peter. Explain how the names of the towns in your book are actually in Maryland, not Virginia.

I am waiting.

It is simple geography, Peter. It is Maryland versus Virginia.[86]

---

86   I cannot tell you how many times I have turned on the television set and heard those very words — "Maryland versus Virginia" — each time a reminder of what Peter John Darbin had done. "Tonight in college basketball," an announcer will say, "it's Maryland versus Virginia." Or, "This afternoon's football contest is a doozy — Maryland versus Virginia." It happened frequently because the two schools — the University of Maryland and the University of Virginia — were both part of a confederation of schools named the Atlantic Coast Conference that engaged in athletic contests

In this case, Maryland will win, because although it may take some time (decades?), the righteous shall always prevail over evil.

In this case, Maryland will prevail over Virginia.

Just as I will prevail over you, Peter.

Just as I was once certain that I (small, weak, allergic) would prevail over a man who would strike the girl who made my heart beat.

---

against each other. Oh, I will not turn off the television when I hear those words "Maryland versus Virginia." I will sit close to the television set and root until I am hoarse for the Maryland boys. They're playing for me, Peter! "Touchdown, Maryland!" Did you see that, Peter? That's me beating you!

EXHIBIT M

— *The Allergic Boy* versus *The Left-Handed Girl*

TEXT	
The Allergic Boy While Poppy may have thought I was a genius, I'm pretty sure I'm not one. I mean, I am a good guesser, and it really does take some intelligence to do some of the sneaky things I did, but I don't think I'm a genius. I could be if I wanted, though. Really. A doctor told me that once. That was when I was a freshman at Highlands, I guess. My parents made me go see him because I wasn't doing too great in school, and he said that I was an underachiever. You probably know what that means, but in case you don't, it means that I don't apply myself, that I could do much better if I really tried. It's just that I don't try. He's probably right, but I just wasn't interested in school, and if you're not interested in something, it's next to impossible to be good at it.	*The Left-Handed Girl* [A note to the editor: Pursuant to the "fair use doctrine," please insert here the entire second chapter of *The Left-Handed Girl*, which I am commenting upon and criticizing.]

My biggest problem with
school was that everything they
taught us was so goddam corny
that I just wanted to laugh right
out loud, and I would have if
I didn't want to get stuck in
detention hall every afternoon
with all the creepy, sweaty guys
from woodshop class who seemed
to get detention every day. Things
like the speed of blocks sliding
down inclines and square roots
and the history of the Civil War
just don't seem like they're too
useful to know. And if they're
not useful, then there's no point
in breaking your neck learning
them, not if you ask me, at least.
I'm not just saying this because I
didn't like studying either. I mean,
I seriously doubt that anyone is
ever going to walk up to me in my
entire lousy life and ask me to tell
him the square root of thirty-six
or something. And if someone
ever does, boy am I going to laugh
at him pretty hard.

You know what was really
bad — and you're probably going
to hate me for saying this if you're
one of those literary types who
takes books out of the library all
the time and would rather read

Charles Dickens than go see a brand new movie with a load of pretty girls in it. What was really bad was English class. English teachers always make you read tons of pages of old novels and stuff, and it seems to me the older it is, the cornier it is. Take that story "The Gift of the Magi," for instance. I apologize if the guy who wrote it is related to you or something, but that one was so corny that I had to laugh. This guy sells his pocket watch so he can buy a hairbrush for his wife because she's got really long, beautiful hair. But she sells her hair so she can buy him a gold chain for his pocket watch. So you end up with a bald lady with a hairbrush and some sap with a watch chain but no watch. You've got to be kidding. The worst part is that we're supposed to believe that there are guys just walking the streets buying other people's hair. Give me a break. I'll bet that happens about as often as people walk up to you and ask you what the square root of thirty-six is. And when I say that, I mean it's not too often.

But at least that was better than poetry since it could really make you laugh. Poetry I could never understand. It was just sentences that rhymed and didn't even tell a story. I remember some graffiti that was written on the wall in one of the boys' bathrooms at Highlands. It said, "POETRY IS THE FLATULENCE OF FRUSTRATED FICTION WRITERS." I thought that was pretty hysterical, especially when I looked up "flatulence." Highlands really was a good high school — the guys there were so smart that they'd say "flatulence" when they could have said "farts." I would have said "farts." But I wouldn't have said that in the first place.

Boy, I'm really rambling about this school stuff, aren't I? Sorry. I didn't mean to. I really just wanted to explain why I never did that hot in school. Although, I could have if I'd wanted to. I just didn't want to because I'm an underachiever. A doctor diagnosed that.

But I can fake being smart if I have to. Like when I first met Poppy's uncle. Boy was that ever a great one.

Poppy was living with her uncle because her parents were really mean to her. Not that her uncle was much better. He was a cretin with a capital "C."

Anyway, we were sitting at dinner in their dining room. Poppy's uncle made this pot roast that was absolutely horrible, and I really wanted to spit it out in my napkin or something. I'm not joking. It really was that bad. But like I said, when you like someone, you pretend you like the same things they do, even if it means eating their uncle's crumby cooking.

Anyway, we were sitting there at the table, and I had my mouth filled with this piece of meat that was like a hunk of hot fat, and Poppy's uncle started asking me a lot of serious questions.

"Well, son, what are your intentions after you graduate from high school?" I hate it when people call you "son," even if you really are their son. I don't know why, I just do.

So I really turned on the smarts. "My ultimate goal, sir, is to practice the law." Guys love it

when you call them "sir." I don't
know why. Guys also love it
when you tell them you want to
be a doctor or a lawyer. "I hope
to enter a highly competitive
college. I feel that only under such
an atmosphere can I truly excel
and build those skills that will be
needed in law school as well as in
my career as a lawyer."

"The law certainly is a fine
profession."

"Yes, sir, I realize that. I
truly feel that there is no more
important role in our society
than that of maintaining justice.
I can think of no field that I'd be
prouder to enter, and I can only
hope that I'll do well enough to be
accepted into it."

Poppy had this big smile on
her face, and I could tell she was
just as impressed as her uncle the
cretin.

"It sounds like you've got
some head on your shoulders,"
he said. "I'm sure you'll be a
success, a fine addition to the legal
profession." Then he started eating
again. What a cornball.

If you knew how much I hate
lawyers, you'd understand just

how good I am at shoveling the
old crap. There's absolutely *no way*
I'd ever want to be a lawyer. All
they do is take money from poor
people, or put people in jail, or get
guys who are supposed to be in
jail out of jail. I once read in the
newspaper about this guy who
went into a liquor store and got
a six-pack of beer. And when the
owner asked him for the money
for the beer, the guy pulled out
a pistol and said, "Here's your
money," and shot him right in
the face. Right in the goddam
face! And do you know what —
the guy's lawyer got it so that he
didn't have to go to jail because
the policemen asked him if he'd
done it before they read him his
constitutional rights. They're
not supposed to do that, I guess.
This guy *admitted* that he blew
the other guy's goddam face off,
and he's not even in jail now. Just
because of lawyers. I'd rather be a
bum and wear old rags and never
shave and have to pick through
other people's garbage than be a
lawyer. I really would. But it sure
impressed the heck out of Poppy's
pain-in-the-ass uncle.

I can talk about just about anything if I wanted to, even if I don't know anything about it. Sometimes, I can get on such a roll that even I don't understand what I'm talking about anymore. The key is knowing a lot of impressive words, the more syllables the better, and knowing what it is the person you're talking to wants to hear. The easiest way to do this is to wait until the person you're talking to says something and then say *the exact same thing*, only rephrase it a little. That way, you can talk about anything, even politics. Take my word for it.

POPPY'S PARENTS

Let me be clear: I never had dinner with Poppy's Uncle Rob, the homosexual bank teller, the man who had left the soft skin around her eye swollen and purple-blue. I just imagined it, and when I imagined it, he invariably ended up dead on the floor (knife, gun, poison, baseball bat, you name it). But I did not include that in *The Allergic Boy*.

Everything in the book about Allie meeting Poppy's uncle, the pot roast, the nonsense about Allie wanting to be a lawyer, it is all fiction, something I imagined, then scribbled into a notebook before transcribing it on an Underwood typewriter (clack! clack! clack!) and giving it to a college classmate to read before he boarded a train for Christmas break. That is what writers do. I made up a scene where Allie had dinner with Poppy's uncle. Or do you believe that P.J. Darbin also made up a scene where Allie had dinner with Poppy's uncle? Are you fooled by the uncle serving fish in his house instead of pot roast in mine? Are you fooled by Allie talking about how he would like to be a doctor in his book rather than a lawyer in mine?

You know there is only one person who could write about Poppy Fowler and that he is yours truly? You can see that P.J. Darbin stole from me, right? You can see that he is a thief, that he is absolutely heartless, right?

MAY YOU ROT IN HELL

But Peter John Darbin was not heartless.

Peter John Darbin has a heart.

Or had one, to be accurate.

That was confirmed by the sickening headline on the front page of this morning's *Sun*, which read, "P.J. DARBIN, ACCLAIMED NOVELIST, DEAD OF HEART ATTACK" in the thick, bold letters usually reserved for a declaration that a war had ended or a new president had been elected.

I read that headline no fewer than three times and studied the accompanying photograph — it was the same brooding photograph that appeared on the jacket of *The Left-Handed Girl* where my own photograph should have appeared — then shook my head side to side as if rattling my noggin might rearrange the letters on the page to form some different sentence. I wondered if I might be dreaming.

But it was no dream, was it? It was a nightmare. Or rather, a nightmare within another nightmare, like Russian nesting nightmares.

P.J. Darbin had stopped breathing and had become a dead person, just like that, and now he is being praised to the high heavens in the *Sun*. Every newspaper I inspected at the newsstand published similar articles, and every television news show eulogized him, too. Soon, *Time* and *Newsweek* magazines will publish their lengthy obituaries.

"The great P.J. Darbin."

"The master storyteller P.J. Darbin."

"The award-winning P.J. Darbin."

"The reclusive genius P.J. Darbin."

Had he pulled children out of a burning building? No.

Had he cured a dreaded disease? No.

All he had done was write a little novel decades earlier. And he had not even done that.

When reporters on the television news shows approached pedestrians like me and you and you and you (or more accurately, just you and you and you, not me) and asked them for their reactions to the great P.J. Darbin's sudden demise, many of those people cried or appeared on the verge of crying, so much had *The Left-Handed Girl* touched them. They wept like they had lost a relative, not a parent or sibling perhaps, but a much-loved uncle or aunt who had brought them candies and expensive birthday gifts. And I wept, too, for entirely different, entirely selfish reasons.

Please understand that I never wished Peter dead, not like I did Uncle Rob, the homosexual bastard. Never. True, I may have said so in anger once or one hundred times, but I am no idiot. I have always, always understood that a dead Peter John Darbin was of no use to me or my pure pursuits. Only a living, breathing Peter John Darbin could help a living, breathing, coughing, sneezing Jimmy Nail. Only a living, breathing Peter John Darbin could confess and, in so doing, return to me everything that was rightly mine (family, home, acclaim, riches, in no order).

A dead, decaying, bug-riddled Peter John Darbin cannot confess, can he? And I am wise enough to know that, now that he is dead and decaying and soon to be riddled with bugs, my claim to authorship of *The Left-Handed Girl* will only seem more far-fetched, more bewildering, more crazed, more crass, more opportunistic. Yes, his death has transformed him already. But it has transformed me as well and just as swiftly. When his heart quit doing its simple job (ba-BUMP, ba-BUMP, ba-BUMP), I became a man trying to steal from the dead. I became a grave robber, just one without a pickaxe or shovel.

Damn you, Peter.

Damn you, you motherfucking piece of garbage.

You could have fixed this. You could have given back to me what is rightly mine (family, home, acclaim, riches, in no order). Instead, you chose to take them with you into the afterlife, if there is one, into the ground if there is not.

May you rot in hell, Peter. Rot in hell with all of your riches, Peter, and your bottles of Michelob, and your shiny, little board game pie slices. Perhaps I will join you there someday. If there is a hell, and if it is all it is cracked up to be, a place where a soul faces its worst imaginings every moment for all of eternity, perhaps you and I will be room-mates, rotting together, torturing each other, playing board games, and watching the unwatchable movie version of *The Left-Handed Girl* over and over again as it is projected on the wall of our cell. Day after day, we can poke at each other with tridents and drown each other in a river of refuse, shit-ting on each other until we are shitless, then awake in the morning fresh and eager to do it all over again.

Today's news that you died of a heart attack may have confirmed that you, in fact, had a heart, but I have every confidence that an autopsy will show that it was a very small one. The size of a peanut. The size of a pea. Black as an anvil.

You have turned me into a grave robber, Peter.

All I can say now is, prepare to have your grave robbed.

I KNOW WHAT LOVE IS

The purple-blue bruise beneath Poppy's eye healed, quickly and fairly well, but not perfectly. If you had not known that her Uncle Rob had struck her, you likely would not have noticed a thing. But of course, I knew, and it was difficult not to picture that whenever I saw her. (Fucking Uncle Rob.) It was difficult not to notice the tiny scar near the corner of her eye, smaller than a grain of rice, that had not been there before. (Motherfucking Uncle Rob.)

I was inspecting that little scar as we lay on beach towels on the grassy patch of land behind our row houses after I had finished delivering my newspapers.[87]

She was propped up on her (beautiful) elbows, her (beautiful) red hair pulled back into a (beautiful) ponytail, her (beautiful) eyes concealed (mostly) by a large pair of pink sunglasses the color of bubble gum. You could still see the little scar if you looked at her in profile. (Mother-fucking son-of-a-bitch Uncle Rob.)

"Jimmy Nail?" Poppy said quietly.

"Yes."

"Are you looking at my fucking eye right now?"

"Yes."

"Well, I wish you'd stop because you're making me really fucking uncomfortable."

"I'm sorry."

"It's fine, sweetheart." (That was the first time she called me "sweetheart.") "Okay?"

---

87   The headline that day: "Toddler Rescued From Well." The headline explained it all. The fire department extracted the little boy only hours after he fell into the well. He was fine: filthy, thirsty, but fine.

"It's not okay," I protested. "What part of him hitting you is okay? He's your uncle. That doesn't give him the right to hit you. And what kind of guy hits a girl anyway?"

"I never said he had the right to hit me, sweetheart." (Twice.) "I'm just saying that I don't care. I've been hit before. I have an older brother. It's not like he never hit me. It's no big whoop. And if I don't care, why should you?"

"Because."

"Because why?"

I almost said, "Because I love you, Poppy. I've loved you from the moment you saved me from that tiger. Everything feels different since that moment."

But before I answered, she said, "Please don't tell me you love me, Jimmy Nail. At least, not now. Boys tell me that all the time, and they don't mean it. They usually mean that they want to have sex with me, because they confuse sex and love."

"I know the difference," I said.

"You know the difference?"

"Yes."

"Because you've had sex before with girls at your school?"

"No."

"Because you've been in love before?"

"No, but I know what love is."

She turned to face me, resting on one elbow. Our faces were inches apart.

"Sweetheart," (three) she said, "love is about knowing everything about someone. The good, the bad and horrible. It's about knowing their secrets and not giving a shit."

"That's what you say."

"So tell me, Jimmy Nail, where did I grow up?"

"Baltimore." There was more than a hint of a question in my answer.

"No."

I started to ask her where she had grown up, and she pressed a (beautiful) fingertip against my lips to stop me. I kissed it, which she pretended not to notice.

"Elliot. I grew up in Elliot, Maryland." She paused only to inhale through her nose.

"We beat Elliot in chess last year," I said before I could help myself. Poppy shook her head.

"What are my parents' names?" she said.

"I don't know."

"Stanley and Margaret Fowler of Elliot, Maryland."

"What is my brother's name? Where is he now?"

"I don't know."

"I know you don't know. I never told you. I never even told you I had a brother until two minutes ago. His name is Scott. Scott Fowler. He works in a grocery store. What's the name of the grocery store?"

"I don't know."

"It's called Kitchener's Market. It's the biggest grocery store in Elliot."

"Okay. You have a brother named Scott who works in a grocery store called Kitchener's Market. Big deal."

"It is a big deal, shithead. It's a huge deal. You don't even know me."

"I don't think you need to know someone's family history to love them."

"Fine," she said, "then let's talk about me. Am I on any teams at school?"

"I don't know."

"I'm on the swim team, sweetheart." (Four.)

"Okay, I'll remember that."

"Jesus Christ, Jimmy Nail. It's not about memorizing facts about someone." She fell onto her back, exasperated with me but not finished making her point.

"What job did I have last summer?" she asked.

"I don't know."

"I was a lifeguard at the municipal pool."

"Okay."

"You could have guessed that. I just told you I was on the swim team. It wouldn't have been hard to guess that I worked as a lifeguard."

That was true.

"When is my birthday?" she asked.

"I don't know."

"November second. Do you see what I'm saying, Jimmy Nail? You may want me, you may want to fuck me until I scream your name, but you don't know me. And if you don't know me, you can't love me. And if you can't love me, then you don't love me. And if you don't love me, please, please, please don't tell me that you do."

Her logic was sound. But still. But still.

"Whatever you're thinking," she said, "please stop."

"I was just thinking that I would like to hold you right now," I lied. "I wasn't thinking about whether I love you, and I wasn't thinking about having sex with you. I was just thinking about how nice it would be to hold you."

"Oh," she laughed, "that's all? That's fine." She shimmied over a little and put her head on my chest, and I wrapped my arm around her waist. My fingertips were touching her bare stomach.

"Jimmy Nail?" she said after a moment. "You're not thinking about having sex with me?"

"No."

Her hand was on the inseam of my bathing suit.

"You're such a goddam liar," she smiled. "You need to roll over onto your side before your mother looks out the window and sees that thing."

"I can't control it," I said. "It has a mind of its own."

I rolled on my side.

"You're not in love with me Jimmy Nail," she said. "Trust me."

"But — "

"But nothing."

"Let me finish," I said.

"Fine."

"But don't you want to see my dick ... tation pad?"

Poppy laughed loudly. "Not yet, sweetheart." (Five.) "Not yet."

EXHIBIT N

— The Allergic Boy versus The Left-Handed Girl

TEXT	
The Allergic Boy I met Poppy during the summer I was 16, after she saved me from a tiger, which I still haven't told you about, have I? It was the summer between the year of being a junior and the year of being a senior. I know that sounds pretty corny, but that's the way I remember events, by their relationship to my age or my schooling. I think that's the way a lot of kids are. Years began in September, not January, and ended in June, and the weeks between the end of one of my years and the beginning of the next were considered neither a part of the year passed nor of the year upcoming. You're probably thinking that that's silly, but they were the summers, plain and simple, and it almost wouldn't be fair to include them as part of the school years. You know how I feel about school. So there were the summers, and there were the years.	**The Left-Handed Girl** [A note to the editor: Pursuant to the "fair use doctrine," please insert here the entire third chapter of *The Left-Handed Girl*, which I am commenting upon and criticizing.]

It's funny, but I don't remember Maryland summers being too horrible before that summer. But they've been a regular pain-in-the-ass since then, believe me. That summer was the time that the tar from the roof shingles melted and dripped onto the patio just like maple syrup. I'm exaggerating — I do that a lot — but it really was hot that summer. Our front lawn got all brown and then just sort of burned away, and my mother even soaked my sheets in cold water so I could sleep more comfortably. And it was the time that my father's face turned red like one of those Macintosh apples as he dug the new well in the backyard. He collapsed and fell in. The heat did something to the dogs and the vegetable gardens, too, but I don't remember what. If I did, I would tell you.

My father died during the summer of being 16. My summer of being 16, his of being 46. It happened a little more than a week after he fell. His heart never got better, and he never even came home from the hospital. I don't understand much of that doctor stuff anyway, because if I did, I would explain better. He just died while his sister was in the room visiting. Some neighbors and relatives carried the casket at his funeral. They wouldn't let me help. They kept saying that I was too small, but it's really just that they all wanted to be big shots. You know how people are with stuff like that.

I'd gotten a job over at Kitchener's Market just for the summer. That's a grocery store over in the shopping center, and it was my first job. The manager said he liked to hire schoolboys to work during their breaks, that they worked hard, but that was really a pretty stupid thing to say if you ask me because they really didn't have us doing much. It just seemed that they had us doing it forever. I did a lot of worthless things, like stocking shelves and collecting shopping carts from the parking lot and stacking fruit and mopping the aisles and a bunch of other things that are too corny to mention. All of this for eight to 10 hours a day. It seemed as if I were always there, and I might have been, too, because I don't trust any of those managers enough to think that they might not have fooled around with the clock or something. Some people do that, you know.

Anyway, I was there at Kitchener's when all of my friends were at the beach. I was there when everyone else was playing football behind the grammar school. I was there when positively *everyone* was over in Winchester Falls watching the Fourth of July fireworks. I was there when my father dropped into the well, too.

I saw the ambulance and the fire truck speed by the front window at Kitchener's and then back again half an hour later, but I didn't know that they had gone to our house until I went home for supper. It's funny how stuff like that happens — I mean how I remember seeing them drive by and everything, and I didn't even know that they were going to our stupid house.

Mrs. Corrigan was waiting for me when I got home, and she drove me straight over to the hospital. She was our next-door neighbor and a nice lady. Really. Her air conditioner was on full the whole way, and I kept shifting the vents so the air would blow right on my face and chest. It was hot that summer. Stinking hot.

Usually, I came straight home and ate, and when the sun had gone away, Dad and I would start up on the well. We were going to dig the whole stupid thing at night by porch light, a few hours each evening, but after two or three weeks, we were way behind schedule. The nights were getting shorter, and they were starting later. You know how it is in the summer. Anyway, my dad didn't think we'd finish at that rate, so he started digging on weekends. He dug like a maniac most of the day, even when it got unbelievably hot out, and Mom brought him big pitchers of iced tea and bottles of cola. I helped as soon as I was finished at Kitchener's.

Poppy worked over at the pool. She was a lifeguard there, and I guess I saw her practically every day after the funeral. My mother said that I should give up my job at Kitchener's and rest, that it was a bad summer to start working. It was a stupid job anyhow — I told you that, didn't I? So I quit, and I spent most of my time just sitting by the pool instead, at first to watch the water, later to watch Poppy. I know that sounds like a pretty dumb thing for a guy to do — just sit by the pool all day, I mean — but I really didn't feel like doing anything else. I just wasn't in the mood to do anything else. Does that make any sense?

I have an incredible imagination. Incredible. I can think of the most amazing things if I have a lot of time

to think about them. Like if I'm in a
fancy restaurant or something, and
I'm waiting for my meal, my mind
just goes berserk, absolutely berserk. I
might think that the chef has an open
wound on his arm, and he's getting
all this blood and stuff in my food.
Or maybe the parking lot attendant is
going through our glove compartment.
Or the waitress just had an argument
with her boyfriend and is in a really
nasty mood, so she decides to put little
dog hairs in my soup or something. Or
maybe the coat check girl is trying on
my coat and stretching it out of shape
and making it smell all funny.

Well, my mind was going
absolutely crazy when Poppy came
over to talk to me at the pool. You see,
there were these two little kids, a boy
and a girl, right across the pool from
me. They were sitting on towels next
to their mother, or at least a lady who
looked like she was probably their
mother or something. She was lying
back in one of those beach chairs with
these funny black things covering her
eyes that looked like little sunglasses.
But they weren't sunglasses at all.
They were just these black things. So
she really couldn't pay attention to
her kids at all because she couldn't see
them at all through the black things.

The boy opened up her beach bag
and pulled out a chocolate bar. Not
a regular one, but one of those giant
size ones. He took off the wrapper,
broke the candy in half, and gave one
piece to his sister or whoever she was,
and I thought that that was really
nice. Sometimes, kids are really nice,
a million times nicer than grown-ups.
Then they started eating, and since
it was so stinking hot out, they got
chocolate all over them. I mean *all*
over them — their faces, their hands,
their bathing suits. This is where my
mind started going crazy on me. I
started thinking what if everyone were
allergic to chocolate like I was. Did you
ever think of that? If everyone were
allergic to chocolate, I'll bet people
wouldn't eat so much of it. So I was
thinking pretty hard about that, and
then I started thinking that there were
these two innocent kids who were
about to *die* because they were eating
so much chocolate.

Then I started sneezing. Why?
Because I'm allergic to chocolate. I'm
allergic to *everything*.

"Drop that chocolate!" I yelled
across the pool. "Drop that goddam
chocolate!" The lady sat upright and
pulled off those black things, and then

she grabbed her children by their wrists and screamed about how the chocolate was for later. Both of the kids started crying all over the place, and I was sneezing like crazy.

"What did you do that for?" It was Poppy. I hadn't seen her since I'd watched her shave her legs after she'd saved me from a tiger. Anyway, she just knelt down beside me.

"No reason, really." I was pretty embarrassed, let me tell you.

"Hey, I'm sorry about your father."

"Thank you."

"Are you and your mother okay?"

"We're both fine, thanks." I didn't say anything else, which was pretty dumb of me, but she really did catch me by surprise. Really. So she just got up and returned to her chair. I had only intended to stay for a little while, but I stayed until she was finished with her shift. I watched her put on shorts and a shirt and sneakers, walk over to her bike, and ride away. Then I went home myself. My shoulders and cheeks had been burned by the sun, and when I got home, my mom said it made me look healthy. It only hurt when I slept, and even then, not much.

Poppy swam often and well, and I liked going to the pool to watch.

She went back and forth across the pool seemingly a thousand times an afternoon. Her arms and legs stirred the water, and her head turned every fourth stroke or so, and it was all just so lovely. That's a word I don't use very often, but it really was. Lovely, that is.

So I just sat there and watched, like some kind of jerk or something. Sometimes, I pretended she was in the Olympics. Sometimes, she was in the middle of the ocean. I told you about my imagination, remember?

"How did you know about my father?" I asked her once. She had just pulled herself out of the pool and was shaking her hair dry. Believe me, it really took a lot of courage to go and talk to her. She really was pretty, and I always get sort of nervous around pretty girls. My dad always told me that I shouldn't get all nervous, but I always did. You can't just stop something like that because your dad tells you to.

Poppy had these tiny freckles on the bridge of her nose and under these huge, green eyes. They were the color of grapes. She had really long, wavy hair that my mother said was auburn, but I'd just call it red. And she had a very pretty shape, too, but I don't like talking about stuff like that. Poppy really was beautiful, and if you ever saw a picture of her, you'd go positively nuts. No kidding. She'd knock you right out of your tree.

"It was in the newspapers." She didn't seem surprised that I was talking to her. Attractive people don't get all nervous when someone starts talking to them like normal people do.

She smiled and said, "Won't you come sit with me and talk. I get pretty lonely sometimes sitting there by myself."

Now I've got to admit that that's a pretty corny thing for a girl to say. It's like something someone says in a movie or something. You know what I mean. This pretty girl will be sitting by herself in a bar or something, and then this guy who's dressed sharp will pass by. Then she says something to him like Poppy said to me, and she wrinkles up her face, and then she and the guy get up and leave. Anyway, it was okay for Poppy to say that. Now if some girl who wasn't pretty came up to me and said that, I would have laughed my head off. Sometimes, I feel guilty about stuff like that.

So we both walked over to her chair. She sat in it, and I sat beside it, pulling my knees up close to me. I really was nervous, let me tell you that.

"Seen any tigers lately, Allie?" she asked.

"It's Alexander."

"Everyone calls you Allie," she said. "That's what I'm going to call you. Is it because you have allergies?"

"No," I protested. "They call me Allie after a guy who played shortstop for the Orioles named Allie Meacham." It was the same lie I told you at the beginning of this book.

"Okay, Allie Meacham, whatever you say. It's not like I have the greatest name. Poppy Fahrenberg. Who has a name like that?"

I smiled, and I know she saw it. I didn't want her to, but I couldn't help it. I was starting to like her already, and I even liked her name. Poppy Fahrenberg. I think it sounds nice when you say it out loud. Did you ever notice that it's a lot easier to like someone if they have a name that sounds nice? Yeah, I feel guilty about that once in a while, too. It's not like people can help what their name is or anything.

Poppy smiled back, and then she tried to lower her head so I couldn't see it, but I did, and that made me feel less stupid about smiling in the first place.

"You don't go to Highlands, do you?"

"No, I go to a private school up in Elliot."

"Why?" I told you I can get pretty nosey.

"I used to go to public schools until I started swimming. They don't have a swim team at Highlands. They've got a terrific swim team up in Elliot, and the coach is great. So I go up there."

This had never been of any concern to me before, but suddenly, the absence of a swim team at Highlands really got me teed. Think about it. What if there are kids in town who are really good swimmers. Well, they should be able to compete, right? Just like football players get to play football, and wrestlers get to wrestle. And if you ask me, swimming's not nearly as stupid as football or wrestling. A high school *should* have a swim team. It's absolutely absurd not to. I'm dead serious about this.

"Tell me about your father," she asked me in a quiet voice, and it was then that I noticed that I was beginning to like that, too. I don't usually think about things like people's voices, but hers was very nice. It was soft and charming in an old-fashioned sort of way. Very ladylike. Really.

"What do you want to know?"

"I don't know, just tell me something. Anything."

"He fell in our well and died."

"I know that. Tell me something else. What was he like?"

"I don't really know what to say, Poppy. Could we talk about you instead?"

"But will you tell me about your father later?"

"Promise."

She talked for a while about her swimming and then some about her school and friends. She told me how her parents were mean to her, so she was living with her uncle. It was interesting. It really was. I listened to her and stared at the freckles on her nose. They were great. You really would go nuts if you ever saw them.

I hadn't noticed, but a blond boy about our age was standing behind Poppy. He said hello to her and started talking, and I was about ready to get mad. I hate it when you're talking to a girl, and some other guy decides it's okay for him to cut in. And then I started thinking that maybe he was Poppy's boyfriend, and that made me sort of depressed. Then I thought that if he was Poppy's boyfriend, he just might beat the hell out of me. Some guys are like that. They don't like it if you even *talk* to their girlfriend. They just beat you up for it. It would be pretty easy, too. I'm not a big person. In fact, I'm pretty small. I don't think it's a big deal being small except that it makes it a million times easier for guys to beat you up. But it ended up that he was just another lifeguard, and Poppy just pointed out a couple things in the pool to him.

"Look, I have to head home now," she said. "Are you going to be back tomorrow?"

"I guess so." Sometimes, I'm so smooth it's unbelievable. I mean, of course, I was going back, but you can't let a girl know something like that. That's what smooth is.

And I went back the next day to talk with her. I told her all about my father. Everything, even stupid things like what his favorite color was. And I told her a lot about me, too. It's great when you meet someone who's interested in everything about your lousy life. Most people just want to talk about sports and junk like that, and if you ever try to talk to them about real stuff, they give you a look like you're absolutely out of your mind. But Poppy liked talking about things like that. She was a fantastic girl. You'll just have to take my word for it, I guess.

And I never would have met her if it hadn't been for that goddam tiger.

AN APOLOGY OF SORTS

I imagine that some unsophisticated readers might try to impugn my integrity because in the excerpts I have just presented, Allie lied about a tiger and about the origins of his nickname. Of course, a more sophisticated reader will understand the critical distinction between an author and a character. An author (me) can write about an untruthful character (Allie) without being untruthful himself.

I did not lie about the tiger. *Allie* did.

And I did not lie about the origins of Allie's nickname. *Allie* did.

I apologize if that is confusing in any way. I do not imagine that it is except, again, for an unsophisticated reader or someone with a limp noodle for a brain. Like Judge Cocksucker.

At the hearing in Judge Cocksucker's oily courtroom, one of Peter John Darbin's attorneys — the larger one, the one with ears the size of spinnakers (exaggeration) — read portions of that prior section aloud, then asked me, "Are you contending that you wrote those passages, Mr. Nail?"

"I certainly did," I responded without hesitation.

"They were not written by P.J. Darbin?"

"No."

"They were not written by F. Scott Fitzgerald?"

Laughter ensued, at my expense, of course.

"No."

"They were written by you?" He spoke deliberately, seeming to inspect each word that came out of his mouth, holding it up to the light to admire it.

"Yes."

"James Edgar Nail?"

"Yes."

"And you admit those words are not true?"

"What?"

"You admit there was no tiger roaming the streets of Baltimore, Maryland?"

"Of course."

"Good. I am glad you are willing to admit that lie."

"It's a story."

"And you admit that Allie did not get his nickname from a shortstop from the Washington Senators named Allie Meacham?"

"What? I wrote Baltimore Orioles. Peter changed it to Washington Senators."

"Fine, Mr. Nail, I'll play your game. There never was a shortstop for the Baltimore Orioles *or* the Washington Senators named Allie Meacham, correct?"

"Correct."

"So it is a lie to say that Allie got his nickname from a shortstop named Allie Meacham because there was never such a person?"

"It's fiction."

"In other words, a lie. A lie you admit to writing?"

"What?"

That was when Judge Cocksucker turned to me and said, "Answer the question, Mr. Nail. Did you write that lie?"

I could only answer in the affirmative.

"Then let the record reflect that Mr. Nail is an admitted liar," said Judge Cocksucker.

That is what the record reflects. According to the official transcript of the legal proceedings in the case known as *James Edgar Nail v. Peter John Darbin and Modern Day Publishing, Inc.*, I, one James Edgar Nail, am an admitted liar.

A COMMENT ABOUT MARCUS, MARCUS AND O'MALLEY

Readers with even limited interactions with the United States legal system are likely asking the same question right now: "What were your lawyers doing, Jimmy? Why weren't they defending you? Were their heads wedged in their over-sized buttocks?"

My lawyers, the Marcus brothers and their partner O'Malley, were seated at a courtroom table, silently counting the minutes that ticked off, more time that they could add to the bill that they would send me. They twirled their pens, they whispered in each other's hairy ears, they picked their fat noses when they thought no one was looking (I was), and they counted those minutes. When I looked to them for help, pleading with them with wide eyes, they would look to the ceiling as if distracted by a complicated math problem they were each trying to solve without scrap paper.

When asked a particularly tricky question, I looked to them for a signal of some sort, but the fat one only grinned at the short one, who grinned in turn at the judge.

"I object," I finally said after Judge Cocksucker stated, for the record, that I was an admitted liar.

You would have thought I was Milton Berle or Jackie Gleason, so loud and so long was the laughter that filled the courtroom.

"So now you're a lawyer, too, Mr. Nail?" Judge Cocksucker said.

"No, I'm just objecting to that silly question."

"Did you go to law school?"

"No."

"Did you sit for the Maryland state bar exam?"

"No."

"Then you are not a lawyer. If you object again, I will throw you in jail for practicing law without a license. I'll put you in with the prisoners on death row, and I'll only release you when they have turned you inside out. Do you understand?"

I nodded.

Judge Cocksucker leaned over the bench to talk to the stenographer. "Remove that last comment from the record, sweetheart," he said.

You will not find that comment in the record. The stenographer did as she was instructed, and I do not blame her. As for the Marcus brothers, at the time I write this, Marcus (the fat one) is dead (heart failure) and hopefully rotting in hell with Peter John Darbin and Uncle Rob. Marcus (the short one) and O'Malley both grew fat themselves on vodka, bread and beef, then grew old. They are in their eighties now, both living in nursing homes outside Baltimore, swallowing pills the size of lentils throughout the day to address a litany of ailments (gout, high blood pressure, you name it), waiting for a nurse to change their soiled underwear.

Count those minutes now, boys!

Count them up good!

EXHIBIT O

— *The Allergic Boy* versus *The Left-Handed Girl*

TEXT

The Allergic Boy

Let me tell you about those stupid swimming lessons that I tricked Poppy into giving me. Sometimes, when you do sneaky stuff, it backfires on you, and this was definitely one of those times. First, I hadn't thought about the chlorine. The first time I stepped into the pool, I discovered that — surprise! surprise! — I was allergic. It made my eyes red and watery. I had to get out right away and have my mom take me to the doctor, and he gave me a bottle of pills.

I wish he hadn't. I wish he'd told me that I couldn't go swimming at all, because I hadn't foreseen the embarrassment of spending so much time flailing and flopping around in the water in front of Poppy. Boy did I ever feel like a major league jerk. She showed me what to do, and I tried like hell to copy her motions, but I just couldn't do it. I could feel myself making these really twisted faces,

The Left-Handed Girl

[A note to the editor: Pursuant to the "fair use doctrine," please insert here the entire fourth chapter of *The Left-Handed Girl*, which I am commenting upon and criticizing.]

and I kept hearing myself making these really goofy noises. Anyhow, I hate the goddam water, and the whole ordeal just made me realize once and for all that I wasn't some kind of genius. A genius would have considered the embarrassment. He really would have.

I don't know why I never learned to swim before. My father tried to teach me when I was just a kid, but I was as bad as when Poppy tried. He held my hands and asked me to blow bubbles in the water, but I never really got the hang of it. Don't even ask me how I was at floating, okay? I'm just not a swimmer. I'm a pretty good runner, though. I ran the mile at Highlands for four years. My best time was four minutes and 58 seconds, which really is pretty good for a high school kid. It really is. But I think what it is is that running and swimming use completely different muscles, or something like that. I think I heard that once on television. That could explain it.

Poppy did the same things that my father did. She held my hands and tried to get me to float, but I just wasn't catching on. I'd sink, and then I'd panic, and then I'd just start tossing my arms about like there was something wrong with me upstairs until I was standing again.

"Just relax," she'd say. She really was very nice about the whole thing. But it seemed that the more she said to relax, the less I did. You know how that is, don't you? Like if someone tells you not to think about something, there's absolutely no way *in the world* that you won't think about it. People really shouldn't tell you what to do — sometimes, it can really mess you up.

There were a bunch of five- and six-year-old kids swimming and playing games in the pool while Poppy held my face in the water and made me blow bubbles, and that just made me feel worse. It really did. Sometimes, kids bug the hell out of me, especially when they can do stuff that I can't.

"Keep your eyes open," she reminded me, "and inhale when you turn your head to the side." But right then, I did something really stupid — I swallowed about a hundred gallons of water and started choking and coughing all over the place like some kind of lunatic. Let me tell you, there's nothing better if you want to impress a girl than having drool all over your lousy face and coughing all over the place like one of those guys who smokes about a million cigarettes a day.

I turned my back to Poppy and moved a few steps away. I tried not to look at her, but when I did, she was laughing, and I laughed, too. She was pretty when she laughed, even prettier than usual. I don't mean to get sappy about stuff like that, but it's true.

"Can we stop this already?" I asked her. That lunatic coughing had stopped, and I was standing in water that was no higher than the bottom of my swim trunks, which wasn't very high at all because of my height. My hands were on my waist, and my chest was heaving as if I'd run about a dozen miles. It hurt like a son-of-a-bitch, too. I can't understand how people can smoke if it hurts anything like that. I really can't.

It'd been nearly two weeks since we'd started the lessons, and I'd made no progress whatsoever, though Poppy said otherwise. She was just being nice, though. People always do that when you really stink at something. They always tell you you're doing okay even though you stink.

"Sure, we can stop."

"I don't mean just for the afternoon." I was starting to get serious, and I'm not very good at doing that for long periods of time. "I mean for good. I don't ever want to come in here and make a fool of myself in front of you again."

She was still laughing. "Fine."

"I'm not kidding about this."

"Okay."

"I don't think you understand. I mean never. I am *never* coming in this pool again! I am *never* going to stick my stupid face in this stupid water again and blow bubbles like some kind of nut or something."

"Alright already," she said. She couldn't stop laughing, but I could tell that she was trying. She kept putting her hand over her mouth. "I believe you. I really do."

"So can we get out of here already?"

Poppy made her way over to me through the low water and put her arm around my shoulder, kind of like how your dad does when you've screwed up something pretty good, and he doesn't want you to go kill yourself over it. She patted the water with her free hand, looked at it, then at me. It really was low, believe me, and I was pretty embarrassed about that.

"Let's get out of here before you drown." She said it, and then she waited a moment before cracking up like some kind of crazy lady or something. She was laughing all over the place. She could be a regular card, let me tell you.

NO TRICKS

For many years after it was first stolen, then published, *The Left-Handed Girl* had something of a dual existence that was unique in the world of American letters. It was an enormously popular, well-reviewed, best-selling novel, translated into dozens of languages (including Swahili, for god sakes), converted into a popular (but execrable) Broadway play and an even more popular (equally execrable) movie, well-worn, yellow-highlighted paperback copies seemingly in every teenager's backpack or purse. It was as beloved by teenaged boys as the swimsuit issue of *Sports Illustrated*, and teenaged girls wrote endlessly in their diaries about their hope of finding a boy as rebellious and misunderstood as Allie, the main character, whom they would love and, little by little, change. At the very same time, though, the book was banned from many bookstores, libraries and schools in some jurisdictions and burned like kindling in others, mostly in the Deep South, where the notions of a boy mouthing off to adults and using vulgarities struck some as wrong, wrong, wrong.[88] So *The Left-Handed Girl* was, at once, revered and reviled. Its author — its *presumed* author who, in fact, was not its actual author — was saint and sinner, hero and villain.

As the author of *The Allergic Boy*, I must say I have very mixed emotions about all of that. I was proud that the book was much beloved, but angry and often distraught that the wrong man was the recipient of the accolades and wealth

---

88   The Deep South, of course, has a long, well-documented history of not being able to tell the difference between right and wrong. If you are unfamiliar with that, might I suggest a trip to your local library. There should be a wall of books devoted to the subject. That said, persons in the Deep South are known to be well read and will certainly enjoy this book, save perhaps for this particular footnote.

that followed, angry enough to go to court where no justice was found. As the author of *The Allergic Boy* (and now, this book), I was also troubled by the notion of anyone censoring an author's words or taking a match to them. Acknowledged or not, those were my words being burned, my story. But, but, but, if there has ever been a book that deserved to be burned, it is *The Left-Handed Girl*. It deserved to be burned in the same way that counterfeit currency must be set aflame.

Over time, gradually, very gradually, the bans and the burnings largely ended, the squalling and indignant protesters disappeared, and many high schools — including Theodore Roosevelt Regional High School! — began to include *The Left-Handed Girl* as part of their English curricula. Just like that, the book was transformed. It was no longer controversial. It was no longer something to be read by rebellious teenagers. It was no longer anti-establishment. No, now it was part of the establishment. But as anyone who has ever reared a teenager knows, once a parent approves of something a teenager enjoys, that something loses its allure to the teenager. There is probably a name for this phenomenon. When the box counter was fifteen and began to listen to loud, clunky music that had no melody, her black-haired, cornflower blue-eyed angel of a mother and I pretended to like the music ourselves. The box counter stopped listening to it within days. When she was seventeen and brought home a tattooed ne'er-do-well as her boyfriend (name: Rat), we did not protest. No, we sang his praises and greeted him enthusiastically whenever he visited ("Hello, Rat! Wonderful to see you!") until the visits stopped. In the same way, the acceptance of *The Left-Handed Girl* by many schools made the book less enjoyable and less interesting to the very people who should have enjoyed it and found it most interesting.

But that was not the only change that occurred. Years after it was first published, critics began to reassess the book. The same publications that had printed bold reviews proclaiming the book "mandatory reading for anyone who has ever been a teenager" (*The Cincinnati Observer*), describing Allie as "Every Teenager" (*The Washington Post*) and Peter as "a wordsmith to be reckoned with" (*The Providence Journal*), were now publishing articles stating that the book was "dated" and "rather quite silly" (*The New York Times*) or had been "wildly over-praised" (*The Los Angeles Times*), that Allie was, in fact, nothing more than a "whiny, dim brat" (*The New York Times* again) and that Peter's failure to author another book proved that he was no "writer to be reckoned with" but rather a "one-trick pony — and a pony that, upon closer inspection, has been painted in colors that fade over time and that has a bum leg" (*The Atlanta Journal-Constitution*).

Addressing only the description of Peter as a "one-trick pony," I must offer my full-throated objection. I must pound my fist on the desktop before me (bam! bam!) and say as forcefully as possible that it is completely and utterly unfair to call Peter John Darbin a "one-trick pony." He is a no-trick pony. He knows no tricks at all. None.

THE SHITTY MOVIE VERSION

You have seen the movie version of *The Left-Handed Girl*, have you not? If you are of a certain age, you likely saw it in the movie theater or at the drive-in, perhaps on a hot date. If you are of another age, you likely have seen it on television or videotape or whatever technology is available at the time you are reading this book.

Let me say this with no fear of contradiction: It's a piece of shit. In the movie version, poor Poppy Fahrenheit is played by a young, voluptuous red-haired actress given the name Allison Monroe by Hollywood producers (Allison Drumper by her actual producers). Only her hair color is true to the book (or to the other book). As anyone who has read the book knows, Poppy was not voluptuous. She was thin and practically flat-chested, and she normally wore a one-piece bathing suit to conceal her figure (or lack of a figure), not the revealing polka-dotted bikini bathing suits that Allison Monroe wears in the movie (and on the movie poster).

The shitty movie version also included a number of scenes found nowhere in the book (or in the other book), scenes not even hinted at. The scenes presumably were added by an ambitious, young Hollywood screenwriter trying to turn an admittedly slim novel into a full-length movie, not unlike the 98-pound weakling in the advertisement who turns himself into an oily, muscled hulk of a man through some body-building magic after the embarrassment of having sand kicked in his face by a bully at the beach.

There is a scene in the shitty movie version in which Poppy takes Allie to her home. She removes her flimsy blouse (pink, sleeveless), revealing her bra (white, lacy), then walks into her bedroom, turning and smiling over her freckled shoulder as a signal for him to follow in her wake. Allie, in fact, follows her and closes the door behind him, and behind those closed doors, Poppy and Allie presumably engage in carnal activities, the details of which are left to the viewer's imagination. But that never occurred in the book (or in the other book), nor did it occur in the relationship that inspired the book (me, Poppy Fowler). To put it more bluntly, Poppy Fowler and I never engaged in any carnal activities. There was no moaning to seep through the walls.

There is also a scene in the shitty movie version where Poppy strums a guitar on her marble stoop and sings a love song to a puppy named Plum. "Oh, my Plum," she sings, "will no man ever love me as purely as you do?" That never occurred in the book nor, to my knowledge, did it occur in fact. Poppy Fowler had no guitar. I never heard her sing (although, she once spoke of a desire to sing in nightclubs in Europe). And she did not own a puppy, named Plum or otherwise. If she had, I would have known. I would have sneezed.

The final scene of the shitty movie version, just before the credits roll, is the one in which Allie climbs into Poppy's hospital bed as she lays unconscious, drapes an arm across her waist and whispers, "I will always be here for you." But Allie Peller never climbed in Poppy Fahrenheit's hospital bed in the book *The Left-Handed Girl*. And Allie Hester never climbed in Poppy Fahrenberg's hospital bed in *The Allergic Boy*. And I never climbed in Poppy Fowler's hospital bed. And none of us, in fiction or fact, ever whispered, "I will always be here for you" to Poppy, or to Poppy, or to Poppy.

We should have, but we did not. Because boys are cowards.

EXHIBIT F

— The Allergic Boy versus The Left-Handed Girl

TEXT	
The Allergic Boy Actually, it's kind of odd that I couldn't get myself to learn how to swim because I'm usually something of a daredevil, and there's not too much that scares me. Like you know those haunted houses that they have at carnivals? Well, I can walk right through one of those like I was walking through my own goddam kitchen. And I've done some pretty wild things, too. Like once at a party, I drank some gasoline and pretended I was going to blow myself up by eating hot peppers. I don't know if I would've blown up, and it was only ginger ale that I drank anyhow, but boy was that ever a crazy thing to do. So right after I made a complete fool of myself for the last time at the pool, I decided to do something to show Poppy that I wasn't some weakling or something who's afraid of	*The Left-Handed Girl* [A note to the editor: Pursuant to the "fair use doctrine," please insert here the entire fifth chapter of *The Left-Handed Girl*, which I am commenting upon and criticizing.]

everything. I mean, if you're afraid
of the water, people think you're
probably afraid of everything,
like bugs and thunder and junk
like that. So on the way home,
I stopped at Adair's Pub and sat
in Adair's chair. Right in it. That
probably doesn't mean a lot to you,
but believe me, you'd think it was
a big deal if you lived in Darryton.
In Darryton, the absolute craziest
thing a person can do is sit in
Adair's chair. There's this whole
big story about Adair's chair that
I suppose would be pretty spooky
if you were a kid, but even the
grown-ups believed it. That ought
to tell you *how* corny our town was,
that everyone believed this spooky
story and everything. I didn't
believe it, though.

    You see, even when the bar
was really crowded, nobody would
sit in this one chair, Adair's chair,
and the reason hardly anyone
ever did was that whoever did
died. No kidding. They just died.
At least, according to the legend
or whatever it is you call it when
everyone believes something that's
completely stupid.

    There was this guy Adair who
was the original owner of the

place, and he had this favorite
chair of his that no one else was
allowed to sit in. Well, one day, he
was hit over the head with a bottle
of gin and died, and since he was
the only person who ever used
the chair, everyone in Darryton
started saying that whoever sat in
Adair's chair would die, just like
Adair had. I don't mean that they
would get hit over the head with a
bottle of gin and die, just that they
would die. I swear to God that I'm
not making this up — everyone
believes all of this junk. But if
you ask me, it's nothing but lousy
superstition. That's the word I was
trying to think of before.

The first one to die was Louise
Helman. Everyone knows her
name, almost like she was the
goddam president of the United
States. She ducked into the bar one
day because it was pouring out,
and besides, she wanted to rest
her stupid legs because she'd been
shopping all morning. So she sat in
Adair's chair. Seven years later, she
was dead. She got her hair caught
in a train door and was dragged for
six miles and died. Just like that.
I admit that that's sort of spooky,
but it was *seven* goddam years later.

Then there's this guy who was drinking a lot and got kind of groggy or something, so his friends told him to sit down. But being as he was drunk, he sat in the chair that's supposed to stay empty. Five years later, he was killed when he forgot to turn off his power lawnmower. The papers said it was an accident, but no one believed it. I wasn't even born yet, but if I had been, I would have believed it. I really would have.

One lady sat in the chair and died thirteen years later. *Thirteen goddam years!* She slipped on a slab of butter in the kitchen of her ninth-floor apartment and went *flying* out the window. She wasn't even in Darryton anymore — she was in goddam New York City. It's not like she died from the fall and splashed all over the pavement or anything like that, because she didn't. She landed in a big tree outside and was only hurt a little, but when a fireman came to get her out, she thought he looked just like her favorite movie actor, so she had a heart attack and died. *Thirteen goddam years later!*

One guy got killed on a rollercoaster four years after he sat in the chair, and there was a guy who drowned in his shower eight years after he sat in the chair, and one lady choked on her scarf two and a half years after she sat in Adair's chair. There are a bunch more, too. And everyone believed it was because of the stupid chair.

Do you want to know *how much* they believed it? Well, about a year before I sat in it, this guy from town named Mr. Kettles got in a fight with his wife at Adair's, and he got so mad that he picked her up and purposely put her in the chair. No kidding. He did it on purpose. That's no big deal, if you ask me, but everyone else thought it was. For about two months afterward, these policemen lived in their dining room and slept on their couches. They had a goddam warrant for Mr. Kettles' arrest for the murder of his wife. They were just waiting for her to die. Seriously.

I don't know about you, but I personally find all of this pretty corny. But like I said about a thousand times, everyone else in town believed this stuff, and Poppy thought I was an absolute madman for sitting in the chair. I just wanted to prove to her that I wasn't afraid of anything, and she thought I was an absolute, honest-to-God madman or something.

"I can't *believe* you just did that!" She was going crazy on me. Her face got all red, and her eyes bugged out, and her nostrils got really big. It wasn't a beautiful sight, let me tell you that. Poppy wasn't one of those girls who got pretty when she got mad, like they always say in the movies, because if she was, I would have tried to get her mad all the time.

She yanked me out of the chair and then out of the bar like I *was* her kid or something, and then she started yelling at me right out on the sidewalk. "I can't *believe* you just did that! What's wrong with you, Allie Hester? Are you crazy or something?"

I started laughing because I thought it was pretty funny that someone would get all mad at someone just because he sat in a chair. "Will you calm down?"

"I will not calm down. What's wrong with you?"

"You mean besides that I can't swim?"

"You know what I mean. What's wrong with you?"

"Nothing's wrong with me."

"Sure there is. You must be crazy or something!" She really was losing it, and I'm pretty sure that people were watching us by now.

"I'm not crazy. I'm just not afraid of anything." If I knew she was going to go nuts like that, I wouldn't have sat in the chair in the first place. I really wouldn't have. It wasn't worth it.

"That was positively crazy to sit in that chair!"

"Oh, that's just junk, Poppy. It's not true."

"Sure it's true. People *die* when they sit in that chair!"

"So I won't do it anymore, okay? Big deal."

"It doesn't matter. You only have to do it once."

You know, I have no idea why I did what I did after she said that, but I just did it. Sometimes, my mind goes so berserk that I can't stop it even if I want to. All of a sudden, I just picked her up — which was no little thing being as I'm so small — and I carried her back into Adair's. She was screaming and kicking and punching me on the back the whole time. Then I dropped her in the chair, just like Mr. Kettles.

"So we'll die together, okay?"

I really had pretty much had it with the whole stupid day, so I just turned around and started walking home. It's pretty beautiful when first you embarrass the hell out of yourself in front of a girl because you can't swim for the life of you, and then you have the most absolutely insane argument with her because you sat in a chair that she didn't think you should have sat in. What a splendid day. I'm being sarcastic if you haven't noticed. I hardly ever say "splendid" and mean it seriously.

But then, all of a sudden, Poppy was walking right next to me again. "Okay," she said.

"Okay what?"

"Okay, we can die together." I told you that sometimes she acted like she was right smack in the middle of a crumby movie. It was a pretty corny thing to say, but it was kind of nice, too. When you really like someone, it's alright if they say corny things every now and then. If you ask me, at least. It's like in the movies where the guy leaves an envelope on the girl's coffee table or something and says something like, "Here are tickets to New York. You can meet me at the airport if you want. If not, goodbye." And you absolutely *know* that she'll show up. And you absolutely *know* that she'll say something completely corny like, "You weren't going to leave without me, were you, mister?" Stuff like that breaks me up. Usually.

NOTES

Sometimes, when we were still married, my black-haired, cornflower blue-eyed angel of a wife would leave me notes around the house, reminders of certain tasks I had not yet completed.

"Remember to mow the lawn."

"Don't forget to pick Claire up from band practice." (She played the trombone. I am not sure what led her to choose that instrument. She could barely hold it.)

"Pick me up at 4 at the market."

Sometimes, now, my black-haired, cornflower blue-eyed angel of an ex-wife will come over to my apartment, bring me a hot meal (lasagna, fried chicken) and leave me notes around my apartment to remind me of what I should do.

"Don't forget to brush your teeth in the morning."

"Remember to make sure the oven is off before you go to bed."

"Did you turn the oven off?"

"Rent is due on Monday."

"The oven, Jimmy! Did you leave it on again?"

She is a good and kind woman. She always deserved better than me.

And this book may break her heart.

"Samantha," I say if she should read this, "I am sorry. I am so very, very sorry. Please forgive me."

I know she will.

EXHIBIT Q

— *The Allergic Boy* versus *The Left-Handed Girl*

TEXT

The Allergic Boy Poppy and I were in the kitchen when we heard about the fire. It was two days before she had to go back up to Elliot for school, and I wouldn't be kidding if I said I was in the rottenest mood of my whole lousy life. I really didn't want her to leave, but she was the captain of the swim team and everything, so she couldn't exactly not show up. Did I ever tell you about all of the medals she had? Well, she had a pile of them. Seriously. She was helping my mother clear off the dishes from supper, and I was telling the two of them all about the work I was going to do on my father's old pickup truck when Mr. Magruder knocked on the screen door. He was one of our neighbors, and he really was nice for an old guy. He wasn't always trying to give you some of his good old wisdom like most old	*The Left-Handed Girl* [A note to the editor: Pursuant to the "fair use doctrine," please insert here the entire sixth chapter of *The Left-Handed Girl*, which I am commenting upon and criticizing.]

guys do, and he kept coming to get me to do a bunch of father-and-son type things after my dad fell in the well. Mrs. Magruder, his wife, was a real looney, though. Not that it was his fault or anything. She was a real looney bird. Trust me.

"Hey, Allie, they've got sixteen engines going up to Long Bridge!"

Mr. Magruder came in, and he was about as excited as a little kid about seeing so many fire engines in one place. He really was, and it was kind of neat, if you know what I mean, to see an old guy get like that. Most old guys only get excited if they catch you on their lawn, and even then, it's not a good kind of excited.

"Do you two want to drive over with me and Mrs. Magruder to see it? It ought to be quite a sight." I looked at Poppy to see if she wanted to. Fires are the kind of things that guys like to watch but girls aren't too big on. Did you ever notice that? It's true. "It's just up in Long Bridge."

That really wasn't too far away. Long Bridge is about 20 miles from Darryton, just past Winchester Falls, and it wouldn't take much more than 40 minutes to get there.

"Sure," she said, "let's go." It was pretty surprising that she said that. It really was. I mean, I know that she didn't want to go at all, that she was just doing it to be nice. I don't mean that it was surprising for Poppy to be nice, because she was nice almost one hundred percent of the time. It's just that you never really get used to people doing nice things for you. At least I don't. I don't know about you.

Mr. Magruder ran out of the house, and we followed him. We kept pace with him as he ran down the street, which wasn't too hard at all because of his age and everything. Mrs. Magruder was already in the passenger seat of their car, looking considerably less enthusiastic than her husband, but she seemed really happy to see Poppy with us.

"Good," she said, "another woman. Now I'll have someone to talk to while these two are watching someone else's house burn down."

"It's not a house, dear." Mr. Magruder shook his head as he started his car up, then he headed out toward Route 11. "It's a factory. I told you that before."

"What difference does it make? It's still destruction. We're going to watch a house burn down to nothing ... "

"A factory, dear."

"We're going to watch a factory burn down to nothing when we could spend an evening in a museum looking at real beauty, looking at works of art, looking at colors and shapes and moods. That's what we should be doing tonight, looking at paintings and sculptures that people suffered and struggled to create." She was a weird one alright.

"Some people think fires are beautiful, dear."

The drive up to Long Bridge was a crazy one, believe me. The roads just rolled on and on like goddam waves or something, and if you thought about it hard enough, you could almost make yourself seasick. Really. And there weren't any lights on the road at all, except for the headlights of the cars and maybe a little from the moon if it was clear out, which made it kind of a spooky drive. And to top it all off, there were always these crazy cows and goats and stuff crossing the roads. That happened a lot because there were so many lousy farms around, and you'd figure that people would care enough about their cows and goats and stuff to make sure that they didn't get loose. But they always did, and you'd either have to honk your horn like a maniac or go out and shoo it to one side so you could drive by.

All of a sudden, when we reached the top of one of those monster hills, you could see this huge fire. It was enormous, and we still must have been three or four miles away. I swear, we really were that far away. So we'd go down one hill, and when we reached the top of the next, there it was again, only more gigantic. It looked like half the world was on fire. It was wild.

Anyway, just then, my mind decided to go berserk on me again. I really didn't want Poppy to go back to school. I think I told you that before. I'm not about to tell you all the corny stuff about how much I liked being with her or whether or not we fooled around or anything because it's none of your business. I just didn't want her to go, okay? If you've ever liked someone, you'd understand, anyway. So like I said, my mind went berserk on me, and I started thinking up some pretty sneaky stuff.

I've got this amazing criminal mind, and I could be a pretty incredible crook if that's what I wanted to do. Wait till I tell you what I did to Jeff Hill and how I didn't even get caught — boy will you ever get a kick out of that. Anyhow, what I started thinking I could do was that I could wait until three o'clock in the morning or something and then take my dad's pickup and drive up to Elliot. Then I could pour gasoline all over Poppy's school, set it on fire, hop in the pickup, and be back home and in bed before my mom even got up. I could even push the truck down the street when I left and start it up down there so she wouldn't wake up. So Poppy's school would get burnt down, and she wouldn't be able to go to school, and she'd have to stay. How's *that* for a criminal mind?

There were roadblocks up, so Mr. Magruder parked his car on the side of the road. We all got out and walked over to where a load of other people were standing.

They were mostly guys. We were still about a half-mile or so from the factory, but even from there, it was hot as hell. I'm not very good at judging temperatures or anything, so I can't tell you how hot it was in Fahrenheit or anything. But let me tell you this, I'll bet that if I'd have had a frankfurter with me, and I held it way up in the air, it would have cooked all the way through *right where we were standing.* That's how stinking hot it was.

And it was really bright, too. Poppy and I had to put our hands over our eyes, and I guess Mr. and Mrs. Magruder did the same even though I didn't look to see. It was like when an eye doctor takes one of those little lights and shines it right in your goddam eyeball, and you just can't see a thing for the life of you. That's a weird feeling, let me tell you.

The place was just crawling with fire engines, and there were firemen everywhere. There must have been about a thousand of them, firemen that is, and that's no exaggeration. They were all over the place. Some of them were on trucks, and some were on ladders, and some were spraying

water, and some were just
standing around talking. Probably
about the fire. I couldn't tell.

You know, I have a ton of
respect for firemen. I really do. I'd
rather be a fireman than a lawyer
any day of the week. Even though
I've never met one, they seem like
really good, honest people. For
instance, I heard about this one
in some city who ran into this
burning apartment building to
get this little boy out. He didn't
have to do it. He just did it. The
building was burning all over the
place, and this little kid was up
on the seventh floor. The seventh
goddam floor. So this fireman runs
all the way up the seven floors to
save the kid. I loved that. A lawyer
would have yelled up first to see if
the kid had any money. He really
would have, and even then, he still
might not do it.

After about a half-hour
Poppy asked if we could leave.
Mrs. Magruder wanted to get out
of there, too, so we did. I could
have stayed there for a really long
time, and I could tell old Mr.
Magruder wasn't ready to leave yet
either. But it's not worth arguing
over something like that.

Mr. Magruder let me drive his car home, which was nice of him. Most people don't trust you with their cars even if they're sitting right next to you. I'm an absolute lunatic about driving, and Mr. Magruder knew it. I swear I could drive anywhere even if it took me three days to get there, and I wouldn't even stop to rest. That's how much I like driving. I don't even have to be going really fast to enjoy it like a lot of people do.

Mr. and Mrs. Magruder both sat in the back so that Poppy could sit up front with me, but she was dead asleep within two minutes of being in the car. I'm not kidding. A lot of people get really tired out when they watch fires. I don't know why — it's not like you're doing anything. So every once in a while, I'd look over to take a look at Poppy. Her head was against the door, and her mouth was open just a little bit, and she looked real pretty. Some people don't look too beautiful when they sleep, you know. But Poppy did, and I'm not just saying that because I liked her.

There wasn't a radio in the car or anything, and even if there was, I wouldn't have turned it on

because Poppy was sleeping, so
I didn't have much to do while
I was driving. But then I started
looking in the rearview mirror at
Mrs. Magruder, and you'd better
believe that looking at that lady
a lot could really get your brain
going. She was a regular wreck.
She had this wild, grey hair
that was going in half-a-million
different directions, half of her
teeth were all dark and the other
half weren't even there in the
first place, and she had these big
wrinkles all over her face that
looked like they were nearly a foot
deep. I'd bet that if you took a hot
iron and pressed it right up against
her face, they still wouldn't come
out. Not that you'd ever want to
do that to anyone, even a looney
like Mrs. Magruder. But just
looking at her in the mirror was
scaring the hell out of me. I mean,
there was Mr. Magruder, who's a
really swell guy and everything,
and he's got to spend his whole
rotten life with someone who
looks like Mrs. Magruder. She
probably was okay when she was
younger, but she still ended up
looking like Mrs. Magruder. What
I want to know is how do you

know when you fall in love with
someone and marry her that when
she gets older, she won't wind
up looking like Mrs. Magruder?
And it's not just that, either. If
you ask me, I don't think any old
people look too gorgeous. Maybe
something happens to your mind
or something *when* you get old that
makes you think old people look
good, but all I know is that, right
now, I don't plan to spend a lot of
time with someone who looks like
an old lady. It's kind of spooky to
think that you'll fall in love with
someone, and then she'll end up
looking like an old lady, and then
you just might stop being in love
with her, isn't it? Do you know
what I mean? I hate thinking
about stuff like that. It depresses
me.

FAHRENHEIT

"You slipped up, didn't you, Mr. Nail?" another well-dressed, well-groomed New York attorney asked me. He had a deep, croaking voice. He spit out my name as if it were something unsavory he had discovered on the bottom of his shoe.

"Excuse me."

"You slipped up, didn't you, Mr. Nail?"

"I don't know what you mean."

"I'll play along with your game, Mr. Nail. It's your testimony that Mr. Darbin copied your book, correct?"

"Correct."

"And that he changed the name of Poppy Fahrenberg to Poppy Fahrenheit, correct?"

"Correct."

"And despite the testimony of Ginger Seel, who treated you when you suffered a severe head injury, it is your testimony that you did not copy a book written by Mr. Darbin, correct?"

"Correct."

"And you did not change the name of his character Poppy Fahrenberg to Poppy Fahrenheit, correct?"

"Yes, correct."

"If you'd transcribed Mr. Darbin's book as Mrs. Seel testified, then the name Fahrenheit would appear in your notebooks, correct?"

"Correct."

"And Mr. Nail, under penalty of perjury, it is your sworn testimony that the name Fahrenheit never appears in your notebooks?"

"Correct."

The attorney then bent his finger to his mouth, looking not like a man deep in thought but one who believed that such a gesture was the way to convey thoughtfulness. He handed me one of my notebooks and pointed to a line in the passage I have just shared with you. "Please read that sentence aloud," he instructed.

"But — "

"Just read what I've asked to you read, sir," he interrupted. He said "sir" as if it were a slur.

I looked at Judge Cocksucker, though I do not know why I thought he might assist me. I looked at my own attorneys, who were inspecting the ceiling again.

"Read it," Judge Cocksucker insisted.

I complied. "I'm not very good at judging temperatures or anything," I read aloud, "so I can't tell you how hot it is in Fahrenheit or anything."

The attorney cupped his ear and pretended he had not heard me. "I'm sorry, sir," he said, "but could you repeat that word that begins with a capital 'F.'"

"Fahrenheit."

"Again."

"Fahrenheit."

"Louder please."

"Fahrenheit!"

EXHIBIT R

— *The Allergic Boy* versus *The Left-Handed Girl*

TEXT

The Allergic Boy

We went to the movies the night before she left, Poppy and me, and saw this really terrific movie. I don't remember the name of it or who was in it or what it was about, but you've got to see it if you get a chance. You really should.

Anyway, there was this one scene where the lady says to the guy, "I'll stay with you come hell or high water." I remember that because it's such a corny thing to say to somebody.

But wouldn't you know it, Poppy said the *exact* same thing to me the next morning just before she got in her dad's car. "I'll stay with you come hell or high water." You know Poppy. So even though I was about to start bawling like a baby, I had to try not to start laughing, too. She could really break me up with that corny stuff, that's for sure. But even though it makes no logical sense whatsoever, I actually liked it that she sometimes said crazy things like that. I probably told you that before, didn't I?

The Left-Handed Girl

[A note to the editor: Pursuant to the "fair use doctrine," please insert here the entire seventh chapter of *The Left-Handed Girl*, which I am commenting upon and criticizing.]

I went back to my house, and like I said, I bawled like a little baby for most of the day. I really did. You know, I wasn't going to tell you that at first, but then I figured that if you think I'm creepy because I did that, then you're some kind of jerk or something. You really are.

The funny thing about that was that it was probably the first time I cried since I was a kid. When I say funny, I don't mean laugh-your-head-off funny, but peculiar-funny. You know, I didn't even cry at my father's funeral. I just didn't feel like it. Now you definitely think I'm a weird one, don't you? But sometimes, you just don't feel like crying even though you know that you're supposed to. I guess if I'd wanted to, I could have thought about something else really sad and made myself cry, but that would have been cheating. If you ask me, if you can't cry about something naturally, you just shouldn't cry at all. Period.

So Poppy was gone, but Lou was back, and that was good. Lou was Lou Hannah, my best friend, and I'd have mentioned him earlier except that he spent that whole summer at his grandmother's in Montana.

What a way to spend a summer, if you ask me. I'd rather spend a summer just about anywhere than with an old lady in stupid Montana. I really would. I mean, I know she's his grandmother and everything, but how much *fun* is it spending a couple of months with your grandmother? Very little, I'd bet.

Of course, I had to fill in old Lou on my whole crazy summer. His parents had written him all about my dad and the well and everything, so I didn't have to tell him much about that. You know, you're probably wondering what happened with that lousy well. Nothing happened to it, that's what happened to it. We just left it there. Who cares if you've got a big hole in your backyard? I certainly don't. I'm not one of those people who judges people by how their stupid backyard looks.

I told Lou all about Poppy, too. And wouldn't you know that all he wanted to hear about was the sexy stuff. He couldn't care less about her eyes or her crazy freckles or the corny things she said. All he was interested in was whether or not we fooled around, how much, and where. I told him because he was

my best friend and all, but I wish
that I hadn't. Once you tell someone
something like that, they just want
to hear more and more until that's
practically all they ever want to talk
about. Like we'd be talking about
the Baltimore Orioles, for instance,
and all of a sudden, he'd ask me
something about her body. As if it
had anything in the *world* to do with
the goddam Baltimore Orioles! I
swear, some people are so nosey.

NAIBLOW, NAIL, NAIMMEN

The used bookstore was the type of bookstore that smelled distinctly like used books and nothing else, and it could not possibly have been mistaken for any other store by a blind man. You know the scent. The scent of everything touched by readers' grubby fingers as they held their books before them, the scent of their breath as they breathed on the pages. Coffee, cigarettes, potato chips, chocolates, bologna sandwiches, tuna sandwiches, popcorn, tea, beer, wine, gin, bourbon, scotch. All of those odors clinging for dear life to the pages and the bindings and the dust jackets to produce a horrible scent, a wonderful scent.

The woman at the front desk eyed us suspiciously as we entered, the bell over the door announcing our arrival (ting! ting!), and I cannot say that I blamed her. I would have done the same. Poppy was wearing an enormous white sun hat that flopped over her ears on each side, along with her oversized bubble-gum-pink sunglasses and a polka-dot sundress that had been made for a woman constructed much differently than she; Poppy had safety pins fastened on both straps to gather the extra material. I was wearing shorts and a green polo shirt, which was not suspicious in itself, except that I may have stumbled more than a bit. I was drunk. I was a novice when it came to drinking beer. Poppy, my mentor, was an old pro. She could consume five or six beers in a sitting (always National Bohemian, which she called "Nattie Bo"), without any discernable change in her speech or manner except for an occasional belch or trip to the restroom.

"May I help you two kids with something?" the woman at the front desk asked. There were no other customers; we knew she was talking to us.

"No, we're fine," Poppy answered. She took me by the hand and pulled me deep into the store.

"Is there something in particular you're looking for?" the woman called from the front desk.

"Don't worry," Poppy said, "we're not going to rob you. We didn't bring our guns with us today."

I looked back at the woman and rearranged my face into an expression that I thought would approximate an apology.

The woman walked toward us. As she approached, she grew younger than I had first believed. She might have been my mother's age, but her dress was shorter than what my mother would wear, exposing the flesh above her knees.

"I didn't think you were going to rob me. Who on earth would rob a bookstore? It's just that I don't see kids in here very often."

"We're not kids," Poppy said firmly. "I'm 20 years old."

That could have been true. I never knew with Poppy.

"And he," Poppy said, shaking a finger at me, "is a famous author."

"Is that right?" the woman smiled.

I shook my head side to side, no, no, no.

"Maybe not yet, but he will be," Poppy said.

"Is that right?"

"Yes. He's writing his first novel right now, and he picked the most thrilling subject imaginable — *moi*."

The woman giggled and looked at me. I responded with a drunken nod.

"What is your novel called?" she asked.

"I don't know yet," I said. "I'll figure that out later, I suppose."

"And it's really about your friend here?" She gestured toward Poppy.

"Poppy?"

"It's about your friend Poppy?"

"I guess."

"Well, that's nice, isn't it?"

"It's not nice at all," Poppy interrupted. "It's actually very naughty. Very dirty. It's about how I surprise him and take his virginity."

The woman did not flinch. I am sure Poppy was expecting her to react with some display of outrage or embarrassment, but the woman simply pursed her lips and bobbed her head.

"I see," she said, "steamy and scandalous like *Lady Chatterley's Lover*, that kind of story?"

"I don't know that one," Poppy said. "Did it involve a stunning redheaded girl taking a boy's virginity in the back of a used bookstore?'"

"I don't think so," the woman smiled.

Poppy turned to me and said, "Don't worry, that's not going to be how it happens. It wouldn't be a surprise anymore if it was, would it?"

Poppy turned to the woman and said, "Can I show you both something?"

Before either of us had answered, Poppy begun to lead us through rows of bookshelves. She stopped at the section marked with a large red "N," then began to run her fingertips over the spines, finally stopping at the tiny gap between two books.

"There," she said.

"What?" the woman responded.

"There." Poppy pointed at the space between the books written by Howard Naiblow and Elaine Naimmen. "That is where you will find my friend's book, the book about *moi*."

The woman was amused.

"What's your last name?" she asked me.

"Nail," I said.

"N – A – I – L," she responded. "Like a hammer and nail?"

"More like a screw and a nail," Poppy said. "That's where you're going to find the book about how I took his virginity on top of a tractor-trailer while it was speeding down the highway."

I must have given her a look because she quickly added, "Jesus Christ, Jimmy Nail, I'm not going to take your virginity on top of a tractor-trailer on the highway. Get a sense of humor."

She looked at the woman and just said, "Boys," as if that word would explain everything. Apparently, it did.

"Tell her how we met," Poppy said.

"Why?"

"Because I asked, and because you think you love me."

"We met while I was delivering newspapers."

"That's not true," Poppy said.

"She saved me from a dog."

Poppy shook her head. "Tell her the truth, Jimmy Nail."

I inhaled. "She saved me from a tiger."

"A tiger?" the woman said.

"Yes," I answered, "a tiger loose on the streets of Baltimore. She kicked him in the guts, and he ran away crying like a baby."

The woman said, "That's a good story."

"Aha!" Poppy said, bringing her face close to mine, "I told you so."

"Is that in the book?" the woman asked.

"Not yet," I said.

"How much have you written so far?"

"I don't know. Ten or 20 pages."

"How does it start?"

"Aaaah-chooo!"

"What?"

"Aaaah-chooo! That's how it starts," I said. "You see, I have allergies."

"What are you allergic to?"

"Don't ask," Poppy interjected. "We'll be here all day."

"Hold on a moment," the woman said. She walked briskly to the front desk, gathered a few things, then returned. On a scrap of paper, the size my wife would someday use to remind me of things, the woman wrote, "RESERVED FOR NOVEL BY JIMMY NAIL," then taped it above the space between the Naiblow and Naimmen books.

Then she handed me another slip of paper and her pen.

"What's this for?" I asked.

"Your autograph."

I tried to pass them back, but she wouldn't accept them.

"What should I write?"

"Whatever you'd like. I'd like to be your first autograph."

I did not think for more than a moment before handing her a slip of paper on which I had written: "Aaaaa-chooo! Jimmy Nail"

She smiled — she might have winked — and said goodbye to us as we left the store (ting! ting!). When we were outside on the sidewalk, Poppy took my hand. She tickled my palm with her fingernail, and when I turned my head slightly toward her, she kissed me full on the lips. She pressed her lips against mine, then opened her mouth slightly and breathed into my mouth.

Although I have tried to locate it too many times to count, I do not recall the name of the bookstore in front of which we kissed for the first time, or even the town it was in. (It was outside of Baltimore, I know that.)

I do not recall the woman's name, and any description of her would be fabricated from whole cloth except for those I have already provided in this chapter (her age, the skin above her knees, etc.).

But the kiss?

That, I remember.

That, I have thought of every single day.

If you have ever been kissed like that, you will know precisely what I mean.

If you have not, you have my sympathy.

EXHIBIT S

— *The Allergic Boy* versus *The Left-Handed Girl*

TEXT	

The Allergic Boy
The night before Lou and I started school, I had him drive me up to Tariffville. I had been planning this for months, years maybe, and it would have been a hundred times better if I'd have done it myself without any help at all, but I couldn't get my dad's stupid pickup truck going. I called Lou and had him pick me up in front of my house, but I didn't tell him what we were going to do. If I had, he wouldn't have done it. That's the way Lou was — he wasn't a daredevil like me. Not at all.
 	
    "I want to know where we're going," he said when I got in the car.
    "Tariffville."
    "Why are we going up to Tariffville?"
    "Just take me, okay?"
    "Look, we're not going to take my car up to Tariffville unless I know what we're doing."
	The Left-Handed Girl
	[A note to the editor: Pursuant to the "fair use doctrine," please insert here the entire eighth chapter of *The Left-Handed Girl*, which I am commenting upon and criticizing.]

"In the first place, it's not your stupid car. It's your parents'. And in the second place, just do it, okay?"

"Why should I do it?"

"Because you're my friend, and that should be good enough." I absolutely *love* making people feel guilty like that. If you ever want someone to do something for you, just do what I did. Really. It'll shut them up in a second, if not faster. So good old Lou drove me up to Tariffville, and he didn't even ask me once why we were going.

Okay, so once we got up to Tariffville, I had him drop me off at this five-and-ten that they had up there. I just waited in front for a couple of minutes until some kid came by, then I gave him some money to buy me a can of orange paint. I'll explain in a little while why I didn't go in myself if you'll just wait a second. I had to give him some money for candy, too. Kids can be such mercenaries.

Then I ran over to Lou's car, and I told him to drive me over to Highlands.

"What for?"

I just looked at him, and he shut up.

Now, let me tell you what I did and why I did it. Remember before when I mentioned a guy by the name of Jeff Hill? Well, even if you don't, he was this guy I grew up with and who was in my class every year from kindergarten straight through to high school. Anyway, when we were in second grade, he took a baseball bat and belted me in the face for no reason at all. I swear that I must have stopped breathing for about a month. So when Lou took me up to Highlands, I painted "JEFF HILL IS A GODDAM ASSHOLE" right on the front of the school in letters that must have been a good 4-feet high. It was huge, and you could see it from a good distance. Probably from New England, that's how big it was.

This is where I'll show you what a great criminal mind I have. First of all, by driving all the way up to Tariffville, there was absolutely no way anyone could identify me as the guy who bought a load of orange paint. Besides, the kid was the one who actually bought it, and there's no way he'd ever remember what I looked like.

Kids don't remember stuff like that too well. And who's going to think that someone would wait *ten goddam years* to get even with someone because they hit him in the face with a bat? No one, that's who. I told you you'd get a kick out of this.

What happened next was even more gorgeous because I hadn't even planned it. I guess Mr. Ryan, our principal, saw it right away because when we got to school the next morning, there were already four guys with sandblasters going over and over the letters. The whole goddam building was shaking all over the place, and these guys were just going over and over the letters, trying to get rid of every last trace of the orange paint. And they did, too, only when they finished, "JEFF HILL IS A GODDAM ASSHOLE" was *engraved* right into the front of the building like a bunch of crazy Greek letters. It was beautiful, simply beautiful, and I'm not being sarcastic. In 20 years, these kids are going to show up for their first day of high school, and they're going to see that, and they're going to say, "Who the hell is Jeff Hill, and why is he an asshole?" Just thinking about that breaks me up. It really does.

THE KEY WITNESS

My lawsuit was not progressing as I had hoped. Far from it. Against the wishes of my lovely, reluctant, black-haired, cornflower blue-eyed angel of a wife, wishes she articulated unambiguously and often, we took a second mortgage on our home so I could continue to pay Marcus, Marcus and O'Malley to sit in the courtroom and inspect the ceiling, but even that small iceberg of money from the bank began to melt away under Judge Cocksucker's sun.

"You are going to lose," the fat Marcus brother said without a hint of emotion or regret.

"Your only chance," the other one, the short one, said, "is to produce Poppy Fahrenheit in the flesh."

Even my own convenience-store lawyers did not understand that there was no such person as Poppy Fahrenheit, or even Poppy Fahrenberg. There was only Poppy Fowler, who could have been anywhere in the world at that moment. She might not even be Poppy anymore. She might not even be Fowler. She could be using any name. She could be anyone in any phonebook in the world.

"Jesus fucking Christ," I said to fat Marcus and short Marcus, "I can't fucking believe this!"

It was then, invoking the words of my Army friend Frank Ditto, that a memory somehow returned to me, a memory that had been lost when I split my head open, a memory about which I have already told you: London!

I had known it all along but lost it in my sometimes-jumbled memory. But lost things and found things are always in the exact same place. And I had found it. I had found it!

"She's in London," I announced, as if I had just read that fact in an encyclopedia.

"What?" the Marcuses said, more or less in unison.

"She's in London," I said. Then I added, "Poppy is in England," as if it needed clarification.

"Why didn't you tell us before?" the fat Marcus said.

"That is a pretty important fact to conceal from us," the short one said.

"I didn't conceal it," I replied. "I just remembered it. I just remembered something that someone told me when I was in Vietnam. She's in London."

"Vietnam?" the fat one said. "That was more than a decade ago."

"I know, "I said. "I was there. I got a souvenir." I pointed to the fucking scar on the side of my fucking head.

"What makes you sure she's in London?"

"I'm not sure she's still there. But I know she was there before. I'm positive."

"What is she doing there?" the short one said.

"Working," I answered. I did not want to tell them that I believed she was a prostitute but knew I would have to someday. But first, I had to find her.

It was not long before I was at the airport with my passport and much of our family's remaining money, boarding first a jet from Baltimore to New York (one hour), then a much larger one from New York to London (10 hours). I had made no plans other than purchasing the airline tickets. I had made no hotel reservations in London. I had not even thought to buy a guidebook to London, although a guidebook likely would not have helped me with my search. I do not know of any guidebooks that would direct a reader to the whereabouts of a city's prostitutes.[89]

Hours after I had left Baltimore and with very little sleep on the way, I arrived at Heathrow Airport and passed through customs with just a small duffel bag containing a few changes of clothes (sweater, corduroy pants, underwear,

---

89   I have never looked. But still.

socks) and some toiletries (razor, shaving cream, toothbrush, toothpaste). I stopped briefly at a small glass booth in the terminal where a sleepy man converted my dollars to their pounds, then I walked outside to the cab stand to begin what I imagined would be a long and perhaps fruitless search for a redheaded girl I had once known, whom I had loved (despite her assurances that I did not), who had inspired me to hold a steak knife against the Adam's apple of one of her relatives. But I had not thought through my search as well as I should have, as well as a man who studied chess should have. A search for a single person in a large and unfamiliar city could be long and fruitless, yes, but a search for a redheaded prostitute with one arm?

Upon taking a seat in the back of the cab, I asked the driver to take me to the city's red-light district. He grinned at me in the rearview mirror. His teeth looked like a mutt's. I did not care enough to explain why I wanted to be chauffeured there. I pretended to study my used airline ticket as he drove.

The driver wound the car though the city, through neighborhoods I had never seen before and would only see once again, in reverse, several hours later on the drive back to the airport in a different cab piloted by a different driver with moderately better teeth. If I recalled the names of the streets or of the neighborhoods, I would gladly recite them here, but I do not, so I cannot. I imagine they were the names of deceased kings and queens and dukes.

After nearly 30 minutes, during which time no words whatsoever passed between us, the driver turned down a dark street, then a darker one, then one darker still, as if we had entered a cavern. There, on the sidewalks, were half a dozen young women, all dressed like superheroes — short, colorful skirts, tight tops, knee-high boots. Poppy was not there, I knew that instantly, but I asked the driver to drop me off nonetheless, paid him from the thin collection of paper currency handed to me by the sleepy man in the glass booth, then stepped onto the sidewalk, where the superheroes swarmed around, circling me.

"Hey, cutie-pie," one said. (Imagine she had a British accent, please.) She had white-blonde hair and a flat nose. "Are you looking for some fun?"

"Not really," I said. I hid my currency in one of my pants pockets.

Before I could explain, another said, "Oh, an American! I have a special for Americans!" (Imagine another British accent.)

"No, no," I said, holding up a hand beside my face as if taking an oath, a gesture I had recently perfected in a courtroom in my own country. "I'm looking for something in particular."

"Particular costs extra," one of the superheroes laughed. (British.)

"Particular is double," said another. (Irish perhaps?)

"I'm looking for one of you girls named Poppy," I said, interrupting.

There was no response at first, then one of the superheroes said brightly, "I'm Poppy." (British.)

Then another superhero said, "I'm Poppy, too." (Irish?)

Then another said, "I'm Poppy, three." (British.)

The superheroes all laughed, tipping their heads back slightly. One touched my shirt with her fingertips as if she were assessing the quality of the fabric. She was holding a book of poems in one hand. I could tell from the yellow sticker adhering to the spine that it was a book she had checked out of a library. It had a Dewey decimal number typed on it.[90]

---

90   Or whatever numbering system they used in libraries in England. It might not have been the Dewey decimal system.

"Maybe she uses another name," I said. "She's a redhead, about this tall" — I held a hand at my brow as if I were saluting — "and she's missing her right arm."

"Oh, you mean Dolly," one of the superheroes said. (British.)

"Dolly?" I said. "American?"

"As American as apple pie," the same superhero said.

So she was not Poppy anymore. Now she was Dolly. I would never have thought of searching for a Dolly. I was breathless in the very literal sense: I had no breath.

"Do you know where I can find her?" I managed to say.

The superhero held out her palm. It took me a moment to realize that she was requesting money. I took a slip of paper out of my wallet and handed it to her (a one-pound note?), and she pointed to a light that shined in the window of an apartment building a block or so away. Soon enough, I realized I was running in the brisk darkness toward the light, my duffel bag slung over my shoulder and thumping against my back. The light glowed in a window on the third floor. In the time it will take you to read this sentence, I bounded up the stairs and was standing in front of the door to the third-floor apartment. I knocked (knock-knock). There was no answer. I knocked again, harder (BAM! BAM! BAM!). There was still no answer.

"Poppy!" I yelled, before correcting myself. "Dolly! Dolly, open up!"

"I'm with someone, sweetheart," I heard through the door. (I had lost count of how many times she had called me "sweetheart." It was the first time in many, many years.) "Come back in 15 minutes."

"No," I said, "it can't wait!" I kept knocking. "I'll pay you! I have money! I'll pay you double!" Finally, I said, "It's me! It's Jimmy Nail!"

"Who?"

"Jimmy Nail."

"Who?"

"The allergic boy from Baltimore. You saved me from a tiger."

There was a pause.

"Hold on a second."

There were footsteps. They seemed as loud as my heartbeats. The door opened just a crack. I could not see anything more than a glimpse of her orange-red hair.

"A tiger?"

"Yes, a tiger. Remember? You saved me from a tiger when I was delivering newspapers in my wagon back in Baltimore. Remember?"

I could almost hear her thinking.

"Jimmy," she said, "you need to hold your horses. Everything will still be here in the same places in 15 minutes."

"Triple," I said, "I'll pay you triple, Poppy."

With that, she opened the door. Standing in front of me was a pretty red-haired woman, with freckles on her nose, clutching a bathrobe closed around her, a sleeve dangling empty. The left sleeve, not the right.

"Triple is intriguing," the woman said with a dirty grin.

It was not Poppy. It was a different pretty, one-armed, redheaded girl who surely had her own sad story, of which I had no interest at the moment (and still do not).

What did I do at that moment? I did something about which I shall always be ashamed, but I will tell you about it, nevertheless, because of our pact (truth, accuracy, etc., etc.).

I cried with disappointment upon discovering that the girl I had once loved was not a prostitute, and I fell to the dirty hallway floor where I was consoled by a one-armed woman in a shabby bathrobe, a tall, stoop-shouldered man with gray hair the color of a field mouse hovering naked behind her, his erect penis pointing at me like an accusing finger, a murderous look on his face.

"You said triple," Dolly reminded me when she released me, and I opened my wallet and gave her a good portion of our family's money, saving enough to be driven back to the airport by a cab driver with a decent mouthful of teeth.

The next day, my beautiful, black-haired, cornflower blue-eyed angel of a wife woke me up at midday. She had come from the bank. She had been told I had taken most of our money from our savings account.

"What did you do with that money?" she said. "It was for our mortgage fund. Our little girl."

"I went on a trip."

"Where?"

"To London."

"London, England?"

"Yes."

"You went to Europe?"

"Yes."

"Why on earth would you use our savings to go to London?"

"I had to see a prostitute," I said. I was half-awake, at best. Wide-awake, I might have phrased it differently. The next day, she was gone. She and the future box counter.

She left a note: "Get a lawyer."

But I already had a lawyer. I had three of them, and they were terrible.

EXHIBIT T

— *The Allergic Boy* versus *The Left-Handed Girl*

TEXT

The Allergic Boy

I don't know what to tell you about my year of being a senior except that it stunk to high hell like cheese someone left out in the sun. Everyone was really nice to me about my dad and everything, but it didn't help my grades at all. The principal even had to call me in to talk about my grades, that's how gruesome they were.

When I first heard that I was supposed to see him, I was positive that it was about the paint thing, and *I was* positive that Lou had told on me. That's the way Lou was. I mean, he never really told on you, he just gave you the *impression* that he could do it any second. Anyway, going down to Mr. Ryan's stupid office, I started to think up this incredible story to tell him. It was all about how Jeff Hill really had it in for me, and he painted the thing himself just to frame me so that I'd get in a pile of trouble. Then he threatened my best friend Lou and

The Left-Handed Girl

[A note to the editor: Pursuant to the "fair use doctrine," please insert here the entire ninth chapter of *The Left-Handed Girl*, which I am commenting upon and criticizing.]

told him he'd murder his whole goddam family in broad daylight if he didn't turn me in. So that's why Lou said that I'd done it — because he didn't want his whole family to be dead or anything. But like I said, he didn't want to talk to me about the paint thing, he wanted to talk about my grades. I'd almost rather he'd called me in about the paint. First off, I hate to waste a good story. Second off, I hate talking about how bad I am at school with people who obviously like school, because I obviously don't or I wouldn't be doing so bad in the first place.

"Son," Mr. Ryan said, "I think *we* have a bit of a problem here with our performance in school, now don't we?" Did I ever tell you how much I hate it when people call me "son"? Well, I hate it just as much when people refer to your problems as their problems. I really wanted to say, I don't know about *your* goddam performance, Mr. Ryan, but mine sure stinks alright. And I would have, too, if I didn't want to get stuck in detention hall. You know, being a principal must sure be tough because everyone you come in contact with absolutely hates your stupid guts. The

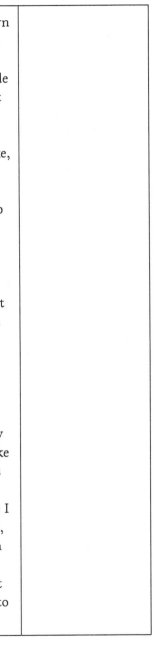

goody-goodies never get sent down to your office, so you never get to meet them, and they're probably the only ones with even an outside chance of liking you. You only get to see the ones who aren't doing too well, and sticking them in detention hall and saying stuff like, "We have a bit of a problem with our performance in school, now don't we?" sure isn't going to help make a kid like you.

"Yes, sir," I said. "I do seem to be having some difficulty this semester."

"Well, Allie, I understand that things didn't run too smoothly at home for you this summer, and of course, I offer my condolences about your father's untimely death."

That's an expression that always cracks me up — "untimely death." When you say that, it's like you're saying that there are times when it's *okay* for people to die. I'm just waiting for the first time I hear someone say about someone, "Yeah, it was a good time for him to die. Very timely." That'd be positively wild, but I'm not about to hold my breath waiting for it to happen.

"Thank you."

"And I understand that that must occupy your mind a great deal."

"Yes, it does." Now I know you're going to think I'm an absolutely *horrible* human being, but it didn't occupy my mind. Not at all. I could tell you that it did, and you'd think that I was a really swell guy and everything, but it didn't. I just didn't think about it too much, and it's stupid to make yourself think of something if your brain doesn't want to do it all by itself.

"All I can say, son, is that I sympathize with you. It's a terrible loss, but you've really got to move on. Your father would have wanted you to do well in school, wouldn't he?"

"Yes, I guess so. I mean, yes, he would have wanted me to do well."

"Then take what you feel, your anger or sadness or whatever, and turn it into something good. Don't jeopardize your whole future because of the way you feel. Take it and *turn* it around, *turn* it into something good. Make yourself work harder because of it."

He was getting cornier by the minute. He really was. I couldn't even listen to him because I was afraid I was going to laugh right in his goddam face. I was breaking my neck trying not to laugh. So I started nodding my head up and down and thinking about Poppy instead. I was thinking about her drowning. She jumped in some water, and it ended up being a lot deeper than she'd expected. Sometimes that happens to people — you jump in the water, and it ends up being deeper than you thought it was, and no matter how much you kick or how good a swimmer you are, you just can't get your stupid self out. It keeps pulling you back in, and you end up drowning to death. So there was Poppy drowning to death, and I was just standing there, and I couldn't do a goddam thing. This didn't really happen, of course, but I was just thinking what if it did.

"Well?" Mr. Ryan was looking right in my face, and I could tell that he'd asked me a question, probably about my stupid future, but I had no idea at all what he'd asked.

"I'm sorry, sir," I said. "My mind was wandering; I was thinking about my father again." If they had a contest for the sneakiest guy in North America, I would win hands down. I really would.

Poppy was sending me the craziest letters, incredibly long ones that told me everything that was going on in her life. Everything. We couldn't talk on the phone much. She didn't have one in her room, so she had to use a lousy pay phone out in the hall, and you know *how* it is trying to talk on the phone when you've got a million people all over the place. People just never shut up when you're on the phone. So Poppy wrote me these really long letters, maybe once or twice a week, and I wrote back, only not as often.

You know what's really stupid is how people think it's some kind of sign or something if you don't write them back right away, or if your letters are pretty short, or if they write twice as many letters as you do. Poppy didn't mind, but a lot of people would. It's like people measure how much you care about them by your goddam letters. That's absolutely asinine if you ask

me. It really is. I just wasn't much
of a letter writer, and that's all
there is to it. And if you're not a
good letter writer, people shouldn't
take it personally if they don't
get good letters from you. Do you
know what I mean?

I can't decide whether or
not I should show you a couple
of the letters she sent me. I still
have them. Really. At first, I
was definitely going to, because
there's no way in the world that
I can write as well as Poppy. Plus,
it would be kind of silly for me
to tell you what she said when
I could just show it to you. But
then I started thinking that that
would be kind of a crumby thing
to do, to show you Poppy's letters
and everything. When you write
someone a letter, you don't expect
them to let everybody in the world
read it, do you? I just made up my
mind — I'm not going to show
them to you. It wouldn't be right,
and Poppy would get mad. Sorry.

I hope you're not mad about
that. She just wrote me about the
girls at school and her classes and
the movies she'd seen and other
junk like that that would probably
bore you to death if you had to

read it. Boy did she ever have a crazy schedule, though, let me tell you that. She had to get up every morning at five o'clock and go to swim practice for two hours, and then they had two more hours of practice in the afternoon. This was every day, too, even on weekends. I don't know about you, but I could probably make myself get up at five o'clock once in a while, but not every goddam day, and *especially* not on weekends. That's absolutely insane. It really is.

If you're going to be an athlete, be on the track team. That what I say. Practices are 10 times easier than they are for swimmers, and you don't have to get up at five in the morning. At Highlands, track practice was right after the last class of the day, and all they ever had you do was run all over the place and do some exercises. And if you ever felt tired or just *wanted* to skip practice, all you had to do was tell the coach that you had a pulled muscle. He'd send you home every time. No kidding. Track coaches are more afraid of pulled muscles than of hydrogen bombs. They really are.

Anyway, I wanted to see Poppy race. She'd broken a couple of school records, which probably doesn't seem like that big a deal except that Elliot always gets the best swimmers in the whole state. The only real problem was that all of their swim meets were on Friday afternoons, and there was positively no way that I could get up there in time if I didn't take off school. So I decided to skip a day just to go up there, only that meant that I couldn't let Poppy know I was there. She'd absolutely kill me if she found out that I skipped out on school — she really took school seriously, believe me, and she thought that I did, too.

Now you're probably wondering why I didn't make up some story to explain to her why I wasn't in school. I thought about it some, let me tell you. First, I was going to tell her that it was some famous guy's birthday or something, and that's why we got the day off, only Poppy kept pretty up to date on famous guys. Then I thought about telling her that we were there in Elliot for a field trip, only then I would have had to bring my whole class with me, and

I really was in no mood for that.
Not that they'd have gone anyway.
So I just decided I'd go and watch,
and that'd be it. Besides, it's okay
to make up some kind of wild
story to tell someone who you
couldn't care less about, like your
principal or something, but it's
kind of rotten to do it to someone
you really like.

I'd bet a million dollars that
right now you're thinking that I
stopped being a sneaky guy and
everything just because of Poppy.
That happens to a lot of guys, you
know. They start out being really
tough guys, and then they meet a
girl or something, and then before
you know it, they're taking dance
lessons and shaving fifteen times
a day. They just stop being the
way they used to be. It happens
a lot in the movies. But it didn't
happen to me, because I could still
be as sneaky as the next guy, even
sneakier, any time I pleased.

I had to call up to school and
tell them why I wasn't going to be
there. You can't very well tell them
that you're going to watch some
girl swim, so when I called up the
secretary at the school, I disguised
my voice and pretended I was Dr.

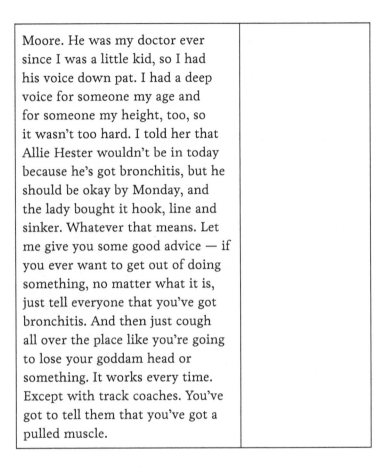

Moore. He was my doctor ever since I was a little kid, so I had his voice down pat. I had a deep voice for someone my age and for someone my height, too, so it wasn't too hard. I told her that Allie Hester wouldn't be in today because he's got bronchitis, but he should be okay by Monday, and the lady bought it hook, line and sinker. Whatever that means. Let me give you some good advice — if you ever want to get out of doing something, no matter what it is, just tell everyone that you've got bronchitis. And then just cough all over the place like you're going to lose your goddam head or something. It works every time. Except with track coaches. You've got to tell them that you've got a pulled muscle.

INTERROGATION

"Mr. Nail?"

"Yes?"

"Mr. Nail, you're perspiring."

"It's hot. I'm tired."

"Do you need to take a break?"

"No, I don't think so."

"Fine, I have just a few more questions. You promised to give me honest answers, didn't you?"

"Yes, I did."

"Have you done that?"

"Yes, I believe so."

"Do you know what the difference is between honesty and candor?"

"I believe so."

"Tell me what you understand the difference to be."

"Well, being honest is being truthful. Being candid is being frank or open."

"So you understand that it is possible to be honest without being candid?"

"Yes, I suppose so."

"Have you been honest with me?"

"Yes, I believe so."

"Have you been candid with me? Have you been frank and open?"

"I'm not sure I understand what you're driving at."

"Are there things you haven't told me?"

"There are many things I haven't told you. I haven't told you what size shoe I wear. I haven't told you my favorite color."

"Fair enough."

"I wear a size ten shoe. My favorite color is blue."

"Thank you."

"I've answered your questions. If you didn't ask me something, I didn't volunteer it."

"Okay. Then let me ask a few more questions, and then we'll be done. You're still perspiring."

"It's still hot."

"You have suffered some losses in your life, correct?"

"I suppose."

"Your wife divorced you?"

"I don't see how that is relevant to anything."

"But it's true, isn't it?"

"Yes."

"After you went to London to see a prostitute?"

"After I went to London to find a prostitute."

"There's a difference?"

"Absolutely."

"What's the difference?"

"Saying I went to see a prostitute implies that I went to engage in sexual activities with her."

"You were not interested in having sexual activities with the prostitute you were hoping to find?"

"No. I mean, not at that time. When I was younger maybe."

"You have suffered other losses, correct?"

"Yes, that's the nature of life. We all suffer losses."

"Your daughter does not speak to you."

"Sometimes she does."

"And sometimes she doesn't?"

"Correct. She's a teenager."

"She's a teenager whose father squandered the family's money, a teenager who lives in a small apartment with her mother because her father squandered their money?"

"It's a perfectly fine apartment. It's nicer than mine."

"But what I said is true?"

"Generally, yes."

"And her father is sometimes confused about things? He had a head injury in the war and sometimes gets confused?"

"Why are you referring to me in the third person as if I weren't here?"

"Does that upset you?"

"Upset me? No. Does it seem odd? Very."

"Fine. Sometimes, you confuse things. You had a head injury in Vietnam, and you sometimes get confused?"

"Sometimes."

"What day of the week is it, Mr. Nail?"

"What?"

"Today, sir. What day of the week is it?"

"Tuesday."

"Is that a guess?"

"No."

"Mr. Nail, we were talking about loss. Your parents are gone, is that right?"

"Yes, they died."

"You were upset about that?"

"Of course."

"You were close with your parents?"

"With my mother, yes. She was a saint. My father, not as much."

"And you have said you lost a friend during the war?"

"Yes."

"A dear friend?"

"Yes."

"Frank Ditto, correct?"

"Yes."

"Do you understand that you are the reason he is dead?"

"What?"

"Do you understand that you are the reason Frank Ditto is dead?"

"I don't understand what you are asking. He is dead because our country entered a war it had no right to be in and had no idea of how to get out. That's why he's dead."

"So it was President Nixon's fault?"

"Actually, it was President Eisenhower who promised that America would support South Vietnam and first began to send aid in the 1950s. And it was President Kennedy who first sent advisors to Vietnam, but from what I read, he also sent about 400 troops there covertly. Then after he was assassinated, President Johnson sent troops after what happened at the Gulf of Tonkin and just kept escalating it and escalating it. Nixon just inherited the mess."

"So it was President Eisenhower and President Kennedy and President Johnson who are to blame for Frank Ditto's death?"

"I don't know what you mean. They didn't start the war. The Viet Cong did."

"So you blame the Viet Cong for your friend's death?"

"I am not sure what you are driving at. I think you are looking for a simple answer, but I don't think it's simple."

"Okay, let me try again. You have allergies, correct?"

"Correct."

"You were on patrol in Vietnam with Mr. Ditto, correct?"

"Correct."

"It was night?"

"Yes."

"You sneezed, correct?"

"Correct."

"And Mr. Ditto was shot as a result, correct?"

"More or less, yes."

"Shot in the nose?"

"First in the leg."

"My apologies. First in the leg, then in the nose?"

"In the nose because he screamed, not because I sneezed."

"But he screamed because he had been shot in the leg?"

"Yes."

"And he was shot because you sneezed?"

"Probably, yes. He was shot the first time because I sneezed, and the second time because he screamed."

"So using basic logic, had you not sneezed, he would not have died that night?"

"Yes, using basic logic."

"So it is your fault he died?"

"Yes, I suppose. Mine, and the Viet Cong, and Eisenhower, and Kennedy, and Johnson."

"His nose landed on your chest?"

"Pieces of it, yes."

"The only reason you were in Vietnam in the first place, with all of your allergies, was because you lied about them, correct?"

"I wouldn't have been in Vietnam if it weren't for the Viet Cong and for our country getting involved and not knowing how to get the hell out."

"Yes, you've said that already. But you lied about your allergies in order to enlist, correct?"

"I'm not sure I lied."

"You know that your allergies would have disqualified you from service, correct?"

"Correct, but I wanted to serve my country."

"In a war you didn't think we should be in?"

"I didn't think that at the time."

"So to get into the Army, you lied about having allergies."

"I didn't lie. I told the doctor about them. The doctor agreed not to report them."

"However you want to characterize it, your dishonesty is what got you into the Army, correct?"

"I suppose so."

"And had you been honest, your friend would not have died?"

"He still could have died. Plenty of men died in Vietnam. He still could have died another day, another night."

"But not that day, correct? Not that night? And not the way he did, correct?"

"Correct."

"A bullet through the nose?"

"The leg first, then the nose."

"Now you have repeatedly referred to Mr. Ditto as your friend, correct?"

"Yes."

"A dear friend?"

"Yes."

"And that is how you refer to him to others, as your dear friend, correct?"

"Yes."

"Mr. Ditto couldn't stand you."

"Is that a question?"

"You are aware that Mr. Ditto couldn't stand you, aren't you?"

"I wouldn't say that."

"You're aware he called you a dumb fuck?"

"We all called each other that. It was a term of endearment."

"You are aware that he complained about you to the command sergeant major?"

"Yes."

"A formal complaint?"

"Are you asking if he was wearing a tuxedo when he filed it?"

"No. I'm asking whether he completed and submitted a complaint in writing to the command sergeant major?"

"He did."

"You are aware that he complained that he didn't want to go on patrols with you?"

"I had heard that."

"You are aware that he put in writing that he thought you were a fool, that he thought you were unstable and weak?"

"Yes."

"You cannot identify a single thing Mr. Ditto ever did to show that he liked or cared about you, can you? That he considered you a friend?"

"I would have to think about it."

"You were badly beaten by some of the men in your platoon, weren't you?"

"I sustained some injuries, yes."

"You refused to identify who the men were, didn't you?"

"I didn't identify anyone. There would have been no point. I'm not a rat."

"Mr. Ditto was one of the men who beat you, wasn't he?"

"I am sure he was."

"Mr. Nail?"

"Yes."

"Mr. Ditto was one of the men who beat you, wasn't he?"

"I believe so."

"With the heel of his boot?"

"I believe so."

"Do you need a break?"

"It's just sweat. I'm fine. Let's get this over with."

"So you were not honest about your allergies, and you were not honest about whether Mr. Ditto was your friend, correct?"

"If you say so."

"Let's talk about Poppy Fahrenheit."

"There is no Poppy Fahrenheit."

"Good. Now let's talk about Poppy Fahrenberg."

"There is no Poppy Fahrenberg."

"Very good. Now let's talk about Poppy Fowler."

"Okay."

"There never was a Poppy Fowler, either, was there? She has always been a figment of your imagination, correct? The broken skull. The head injury. The scar on the side of your head."

"No, that is not correct. That is decidedly incorrect."

"You are aware that there is no listing for a Poppy Fowler in any telephone directory anywhere in the United States of America?"

"I have heard that."

"How do you explain that?"

"She could have an unlisted telephone number. She could have gotten married and changed her last name. She could have moved to another country."

"England."

"Possibly."

"You looked there?"

"Not very thoroughly."

"She could have been a figment of your imagination?"

"No."

"Okay, then let me ask you this. Are you aware that we had an investigator review all of the high school yearbooks in the state of Maryland for a period of 10 years when Ms. Fowler could have been in high school, and they couldn't find anyone with the name 'Poppy Fowler'?"

"I wasn't aware of that."

"There was no Poppy Fowler at Elliot High School."

"So you say."

"Or in any other high school in the state of Maryland."

"So you say."

"How would you explain that?"

"Maybe she didn't go to the public high school. Maybe her school didn't have a yearbook. And 'Poppy' was a nickname."

"A nickname for what?"

"I don't know."

"This girl you cared about so much that you claim you wrote a book about her, who you cared about so much that you squandered your family's money, you don't even know her real first name?"

"No."

"Or where she went to high school?"

"No."

"That strikes me as very odd. Doesn't that strike you as odd, Mr. Nail?"

"Today, yes. At the time, no."

"What were her parents' names?"

"Stanley and Margaret Fowler."

"There are no records of any Stanley and Margaret Fowler ever owning property in Elliot, Maryland."

"Not everyone owns property. They could have rented their home. I rent the place I live in."

"What was her brother's name?"

"Scott Fowler."

"There's no such person who ever lived in Elliot."

"So you say."

"And where did you say he worked?"

"A grocery store. A grocery store called Kitchener's Market."

"There's no such place."

"So you say."

"What was her uncle's name?"

"Rob."

"His last name?"

"I don't know. I assume it was Fowler."

"We have checked the records. No one named Rob Fowler — or Robert Fowler — ever lived next door to your family."

"It was number 1336."

"No one."

"So you say."

"Would you like some water?"

"No, thank you."

"You waited for him in the alley behind your house one night?"

"Yes."

"What did you do?"

"I waited by the garbage cans. He was taking out the trash, and I had a kitchen knife — "

"From your home?"

"Yes, I snuck up behind him and pressed the knife against his throat."

"And?"

"And I said, 'If you ever touch her again, I will slice your head off.'"

"And?"

"And he said, 'Are you the grace-and-mercy guy? The guy who wrote a story for her?'"

"And?"

"And I confirmed I was."

"And?"

"And he promised me he would never hurt her again. He gave me his word of honor. Then he turned around."

"And?"

"And I saw that his nose was swollen the size of a piece of fruit and he had two black eyes."

"Were you the one who beat him?"

"No, of course not."

"Do you know who did?"

"It was either Sonny Liston or Poppy Fowler."

"Sonny Liston?"

"He was the heavyweight champion of the world."

"I'm aware of that, Mr. Nail. Do you believe that the heavyweight champion of the world traveled to Baltimore and beat your neighbor?"

"No, but it sure looked like that when Poppy Fowler got her hands on him."

"You find this amusing?"

"I'm laughing at myself."

"Why?"

"I don't know why I thought I needed to protect her. I forgot that I met her when she protected me."

"She protected you?"

"She saved me from a tiger."

"A tiger?"

"A dog."

"Do you not know the difference between a dog and a tiger?"

"I know that it's a better story if it was a tiger than if it was a dog."

"Mr. Nail, sir?"

"Yes?"

"Can we get back to the incident where you claim you held a knife to the throat of Poppy's uncle?"

"Of course."

"There is no police report of any such incident, is there?"

"I imagine not. To my knowledge, he did not file a report."

"Is there anyone who could verify this incident?"

"He could."

"Robert Fowler?"

"If that was his name, yes."

"He doesn't exist, does he?"

"He did then. He may not anymore."

"Anyone else?"

"Well, I told Poppy."

"And?"

"And she was upset with me. She said I didn't understand."

"So Poppy could confirm this event?"

"She didn't witness the event, but she could confirm I told her about it. I believe that's called hearsay."

"So once again, everything goes back to the elusive, red-haired Poppy Fahrenheit."

"The elusive, red-haired Poppy Fowler, not the elusive, red-haired Poppy Fahrenheit."

"Here is something else that is odd, Mr. Nail. The investigator who scoured through all of those old yearbooks looking for Poppy Fowler, do you know what they found?"

"I don't."

"They found a girl who went to your high school, who graduated a few years before you."

"Okay."

"Theodore Roosevelt Regional High School, right?"

"Right."

"Walk tall and carry a big stick?"

"Yes."

"You were on the chess team?"

"I was."

"The investigator found a girl with red hair who graduated a few years ahead of you."

"Okay."

"They found a red-headed girl named Ruth Nail."

AN EXPLANATION

Ruth Nail.

Of course, I know Ruth Nail.

She was my sister. My older sister. Her bedroom was next to mine. When she ran away for the last time, my parents emptied it out. My mother stored her sewing machine there, along with her sewing supplies. From the window of that room, from the right angle, you could see the stoop of the rowhouse next door.

If I had not mentioned Ruth before — I will have to review what I have already written to see if I did or not — it is only because she was not relevant to this book. There was no reason to drag her into this. She went through enough.

She is gone now. She stopped breathing and turned into a dead person. She is buried next to our parents, three headstones in a row that read "Nail," "Nail," "Nail."

If there is a heaven, I would assume the three of them are together. And if Peter James Darbin was somehow granted entry, I can count on Ruth to give him an earful for the rest of eternity. She was my sister. She was my best friend, for a bit.

A FURTHER INTERROGATION

"We have spent a great deal of time together the past few days, haven't we, Mr. Nail?"

"Yes, I agree."

"Somehow, you never once mentioned that you had an older sister named Ruth."

"It never came up."

"It never came up? You have talked endlessly about your childhood, about your parents, about this Poppy Fowler, yet not once did you think to mention your sister Ruth?"

"She had already left."

"Left where?"

"She'd already left our home. She'd already moved out of the house."

"Moved out?"

"Ran away."

"Where did she go?"

"Which time?"

"How many times did she run away?"

"I wasn't counting."

"Five, ten, a hundred?"

"Maybe."

"Where did she go these times she ran away?"

"Different places. Once, she went to Oklahoma. A couple times, she went to New York. She went to Florida. She went to Kentucky."

"Kentucky?"

"Yes, I think she wanted to see horses that time."

"Did you remain in touch with her after she left Baltimore for good?"

"Sometimes."

"Sometimes?"

"Yes, sometimes. She had more important things to deal with than her little brother. She had a hard life."

"Did you ever see her again after she left Baltimore the last time?"

"No."

"Not once?"

"No. She had a hard life. She died."

"I'm sorry. Did you get along with her?"

"Yes. I mean to say, sometimes we did, sometimes we didn't."

"Did you love your sister?"

"Yes. I mean sometimes yes, sometimes she was just the crazy girl who lived in the room next door."

"Mr. Nail, your sister was something of a free spirit, correct?"

"You could say that."

"She was wild, right?"

"Yes."

"Cigarettes?"

"Yes, Marlboros."

"Alcohol?"

"Yes, National Bohemian."

"Drugs?"

"Yes."

"What kind of drugs?"

"Marijuana, heroin."

"Heroin?"

"As I understand it, yes."

"You were sad when you learned she died?"

"Of course."

"Mr. Nail, I want you to take a breath. Okay? Take a deep breath."

"Okay."

"You served your country in Vietnam. You were injured. You suffered a head injury. Sometimes, your thoughts get a bit scrambled. I understand that."

"Okay."

"I've read the reports from Dr. Dodd and Dr. Pellicane and Dr. Taffy. You know them?"

"Yes. Three jackasses."

"You know what they said about you?"

"I do. They had no business saying anything to my black-haired, cornflower blue-eyed angel of a wife, though. There's something called doctor-patient confidentiality."

"Nevertheless, you acknowledge that your thoughts can get scrambled?"

"I acknowledge there have been times when people believed I forgot things or got them confused."

"Who?"

"Well, my black-haired, cornflower blue-eyed angel of a wife for one."

"Anyone else?"

"My daughter, the box counter."

"The box counter?"

"Yes, she's responsible for keeping the inventory at a foam insulation company. She counts boxes. One, two, three, four."

"Boxes?"

"Five, six, seven, eight."

"Anyone else who thought you got things scrambled in your mind?"

"Some people I worked for. My convenience-store lawyers."

"Your lawyers work in a convenience store?"

"No, above one. That's what I call them so I don't get confused. If you repeat something, you remember it."

"Do you recall my name?"

"I'm afraid not. I'm sorry."

"I want to propose something, sir, and I'd like you to consider it carefully. Can you do that?"

"Yes."

"Your mind created someone named Poppy Fowler. No, no, don't say anything yet, let me finish. Your mind created Poppy Fowler. You made her up. You took parts of a character from a book you read called *The Left-Handed Girl*, and you added some of your sister's qualities to it. That's what happened, isn't it? It was nothing nefarious. You had a head injury. You were lonely. You were confused. You were in a foreign country. You were serving your country. You were a hero. You read a book you liked; you were sad about your sister; and before you knew it, your brain had created this entirely new person named Poppy Fowler, who has never walked this earth, who exists only in your mind. You created someone you could love. You created someone else who could care about you. That's what happened, isn't it?"

"No."

"Mr. Nail, it's okay. If you can just admit that's what happened, we can move on, and I can help you. That's why the Veterans Administration sent me to talk to you, to help you. Once you can admit that, we can start getting you healthy again."

"I am healthy."

"Are you ready to admit that's what happened?"

"No."

"Mr. Nail?"

"No! Get the fuck out of my apartment! And don't ever talk to me again about Poppy Fowler! And don't ever talk to me again about my sister! Do you understand? Do you fucking understand, you motherfucking fuck?"[91]

---

91   I warned you about the cursing a couple hundred pages ago. Don't say I fucking didn't.

EXHIBIT U

— *The Allergic Boy* versus *The Left-Handed Girl*

TEXT	
The Allergic Boy	*The Left-Handed Girl*
Here's what my biggest problem was — the goddam pickup truck. Sometimes it ran, and sometimes it didn't, and it usually didn't just when I really wanted it to. I'm not making this up. Like if my mom wanted me to drive over to Kitchener's to pick up some milk, it'd work like a goddam charm. But if I ever had to drive to Baltimore, to save the stupid country or something important like that, there's no way in the world that it'd ever start up. Absolutely no way. So I called up Lou and made him skip school, too, so he could drive me up to Elliot.	[A note to the editor: Pursuant to the "fair use doctrine," please insert here the entire 10th chapter of *The Left-Handed Girl*, which I am commenting upon and criticizing.]
It was easy to get Lou to do stuff like that. A regular piece of cake. All I had to do was ask him, and he'd do it, even though I had to put up with his complaining for a while. You see, I was pretty much Lou's	

only friend in Darryton and maybe in the whole world, unless you count his lousy grandmother out in Montana, which I don't think you should do. It's not that Lou wasn't a good guy, because he was. He was a *terrific* guy, a million times better than most of the creeps up at Highlands, except only I knew that.

You know what the problem is with living in a small town — if you do something dumb when you're just a kid, everyone remembers it even when you're practically grown up, and they never let you forget it even though you're not a kid anymore. Like if you threw up on the school bus in third grade, you can pretty much forget about getting a date even when you're in high school. You'd probably brushed your goddam teeth close to a million times since you threw up, and still, no girl is ever going to let you kiss her. You'd have to move out of town if you ever wanted a stupid date just because of something you did when you were a kid. Sometimes, people make absolutely no sense to me. None at all.

That's pretty much what happened to Lou, and that's pretty much why I positively loathed most of the kids at Highlands. When we were in grammar school, second or third grade maybe, Lou used to do this wild trick for everyone during recess. He used to put a marble in one nostril and blow it out the other. I swear to God he did. No one could figure out how Lou did it, a reasonable guess being that he stuck an identical marble in his other nostril before he went to school in the morning, and he wouldn't even tell me. Admittedly, it wasn't too gorgeous, especially during cold and flu season, but that's the kind of stuff you get a kick out of when you're a kid, and everyone loved it. But then when everyone got a little older, they realized that it was a pretty gross thing for someone to do. And even though he'd stopped doing it, they all began acting like he was absolutely the most disgusting person they'd ever met. They acted like he was the goddam dog-faced boy. You've heard of him — he's the one in the circus with the hair all over his face. Anyway, it was a rotten thing to do to Lou being as he was such a great guy. You can't help what you do as a kid. You really can't.

So Lou drove me up to Elliot,
and we stopped at a diner on the
way to get some lunch. I bought
him a hamburger and a chocolate
soda, which I wouldn't normally
have done except that I'd just
been thinking about all that stuff
I just told you about. Sometimes,
you've got to do something nice
for someone when you realize how
rotten their life is.

Poppy's swim meet started
at four o'clock, and Lou and I got
there almost an hour before that.
We could have had the best seats
in the whole place if we'd wanted,
but we didn't want her to see us,
so we waited for a crowd of people
to come and kind of blended in
with them. Then we sat all the
way at the top of the stands. We
must have been a goddam mile
from the pool. No kidding. You
had to sit all the way at the end of
your seat and squint just to see the
stupid pool, which meant it was
next to impossible to see Poppy all
the way down there. And the fact
that all the swimmers from Elliot
wore identical bathing suits and
caps didn't make things any easier,
believe me. I had to listen to the

lousy PA announcer just to find out what lane she was in. Anyhow, she won three races, each of them by a mile, and I was going positively nuts inside. It's absolutely fantastic when your girlfriend is an incredible swimmer. I guess you'll have to trust me on that one unless you've got a girlfriend who's an incredible swimmer because then you'd know it already.

So like I said, I was going positively nuts inside, and I was in an amazing good mood, and I wasn't worried in the least about getting in trouble for skipping out on school, and I was even planning on buying Lou another hamburger at the diner for being such a good friend and everything. But then something happened while we were leaving that I hadn't planned on at all, because if I had planned on it, I definitely would have handled it a hundred times better. I really would have. It's just that my crazy mind usually needs some warning before it goes into action, and this time, it didn't have close to enough warning.

"Well, son, it's quite a surprise to see you here." It was Mr. Fahrenberg, Poppy's goddam father.

"Hello, Mr. Fahrenberg. It's very nice to see you." Was that ever a lie. I introduced him to Lou to buy some time, but I couldn't get my mind going right.

"Shouldn't you two be in school now?"

"No, sir. School got out at three o'clock."

"Yes, but how did you two get here in time for the meet?"

I couldn't get my mind settled down on a good story because I kept thinking of how I had to stop Mr. Fahrenberg from telling Poppy that he'd seen us. She'd murder me if she found out that I skipped school.

"What?"

"I said, how did you ever get here in time for the meet?"

"We flew." Sometimes, I absolutely *hate* my mind. It can come up with some pretty outrageous things, let me tell you.

"You flew?"

I'd already said it, so I figured I might as well stick with it. You can't go back on something like that because then you just end up looking like twice as big a dope than if you'd just stuck with it. "Yes, sir. We flew here. Lou is actually quite a good pilot, and his father owns a small aircraft. A two-seater. So we flew here right after our last class."

"You don't say."

This is when Lou decided to jump in. "Well, I haven't been flying that long, sir. I just got my license last week, and my dad would absolutely kill me if he ever found out that I borrowed the plane." Sometimes, Lou was the most terrific guy in the world.

"And I wouldn't want Poppy to know that we flew here," I said. "She doesn't like me flying, and there's no need to get her all upset, is there?"

"No, there's no need to get her upset." Mr. Fahrenberg took off, and I could tell that he probably didn't believe us, but then it hit me that it really didn't matter. I mean, who cares if your girlfriend's father thinks you're an absolute nutcase anyway? I sure don't.

On the way home, I made Lou stop at a restaurant in Abercrombie. Not a diner, but a real, honest-to-God restaurant with tablecloths and everything. Then I bought Lou a goddam steak and a baked potato. It's nice to do something like that when someone tries to bail you out of a jam, even if they don't bail you out completely. If you ask me, that is.

NOBODY DIES

Dearest Claire,

Have I mentioned lately that you are the joy of my life? Oh, I have? Well, well. Let's mention it again because it cannot be said too often: You are the joy of my life.

I know — I hope — that someday you will read this book, and when you do, you will understand your father better than you had before, that you will know that he was no madman, that he was a man of letters. A wordsmith, if you will, despite the stupid scar on the side of my stupid head.

But I also know you will read that next-to-last section and say aloud, "What the hell? I had an Aunt Ruth?" Or you will believe I fabricated Poppy Fowler. Because you had never heard of either one.

Please, hear me out. I am the boy of your life, remember. Remember?

About Poppy Fowler, how could I tell you about a girl I loved more than your black-haired, cornflower blue-eyed angel of a mother? How could I?

And technically, you never had an Aunt Ruth. She was gone before you arrived. But I am splitting hairs.

I had a sister named Ruth. I do not speak of her. I do not speak of her because it breaks my heart in half to try.

Next Sunday will mark the sad anniversary of my sister Ruth's death. I quite literally would not be alive but for her saving me from drowning in an accident back when we were children, and I would not have had my black-haired, cornflower blue-eyed angel of a wife (now ex-wife), or you, the box counter, the joy of my life, or much of anything else, to be truthful, but for her.

It is a story not many people know, even our closest friends. Poppy knew; I told her once when she was teaching me to drive her uncle's car, and she pulled over and hugged me, and I smelled the strawberry shampoo in her hair when she did, and then we kissed and kissed and kissed because it seemed like the right thing to do at the time but seemed entirely wrong afterward considering the circumstances.

By the time I joined Ruth at Theodore Roosevelt Regional High School as a coughing, wheezing, sneezing freshman, she and I could barely stand each other. Siblings can be like that. We could not have been more different, and candidly, we were embarrassments to each other. She was the girl in the leather jacket who smoked Marlboro cigarettes out on the wall, and I was the boy in the chess club who studied too hard and was largely friendless. We would not even acknowledge each other if we passed in the hallways at school, and barely did so at home.

The summer after my freshman year, our father (your grandpa) entrusted the barber shop to his only employee (George Leafe), and our family took a trip to Lake George in New York. The drive was long and dull. We listened to the radio, and it was in that boredom that I stumbled upon a copy of a war novel called "All Quiet on the Western Front," which turned me into a reader, a writer, and later, a soldier who would kill no North Vietnamese persons.

On one of the very dull, hot days at the lake — it felt like someone had left an oven door open — Ruth was playing around in a crappy little sailboat by the dock. I believe it was called a Sunfish. (I suppose I could look it up to try to find the name, but I have never wanted to see a picture of it.)

I had nothing else to do, and our father (your grandpa) convinced me to go sailing with her. Neither of us was happy about it. We had no interest in spending any time together and nothing to talk about. And we had no idea how to sail a sailboat and no life jackets. You are an avid reader; you may have guessed already where this is heading.

Despite Ruth's efforts, our sailboat kept drifting further and further north until we could no longer see the dock. That is how big that fucker of a lake was. We drifted and drifted, and then it began to drizzle. Then the sky turned dark and a heavy storm hit. Rain, thunder, etc., etc. You know storms. We drifted further and further, and the boat began to take on water like a tub.

Ruth and I started cursing at each other, blaming each other not just for the sinking boat but for everything else, and we tried to bail the water out of the boat with our hands, but the storm was incredible. The choppy water kept splashing into the boat faster than we could empty it. It sank beneath us. The entire boat sank. And there we were, in the middle of that huge fucker of a lake, the sky dark, the rain coming down as heavy as I have ever seen it.

We treaded water near the spot where the boat had been and kept cursing each other. But if you have ever treaded water for even a few minutes, you know how tiring it can become. It was even more tiring as we were fighting wave after wave.

Eventually, we each kicked off our sneakers, which helped some but not much. We reassured each other that someone would find us soon, but we could barely see the shore and saw no one else out on the lake. We were alone. Trying to swim got us nowhere. It only made us weak, and one of us started out each day weak enough as it was.

After 30 minutes or so of treading water, we started to joke about what the headlines would read in the *Sun* if we both drowned. "Chess Club Vice President Dies Tragically. Promiscuous Sister, Too." Or "High School Beauty Dies. Egghead Also." Those are the only two I still remember. I know there were others.

Then we could not keep treading water. Ruth went under the waves a few times, and I pulled her up and tried to keep her head above the water. Then I went under, and she did the same for me. For years afterward, I could close my eyes and still taste that water. I cannot anymore. I forget things.

And then we concluded that no one was going to find us.

"We really are going to die, aren't we?" Ruth asked.

And I confirmed that. It had been an hour, or close to it, if I had to estimate. We saw no one else on the lake. There were no boats speeding toward us. We were goners.

We traded off trying to rest or float. We held each other up. Then like a miracle, a rowboat appeared beside us. The rain was coming down so hard that we had not seen it approaching. A Japanese man and his young Japanese son had been out on the water, too, and they had spotted us somehow. I have always assumed they saw Ruth's red hair and rowed toward it.

There was no room in the boat for Ruth or me, but one of us could hang onto the side while the other tried to swim beside the boat. We switched off doing that and somehow, eventually, reached the shore about a mile north of the cabins where we were staying.

Not thinking straight at all, I left Ruth with the Japanese man and his Japanese son, then ran along the gravel shoulder of the two-lane road to get back to the cabins to let our parents know we were safe, that they could stop worrying about us. It was still pouring, and it never occurred to me to flag down one of the passing cars. Instead, I kept running, the little rocks tearing at the bottoms of my feet. They are still scarred today. Maybe only I can see it.

When I finally arrived at the cabins, beside a little general store, it was only to learn that no one had looked for us. Two teenagers with no sailing experience or life jackets, lost in a heavy storm for nearly two hours (if I had to esti-mate), and no one had even looked for us. Our father (your grandpa) was in the phone booth outside the general store. He must have been on the phone with the Coast Guard or whatever the authorities would be to help him locate two children missing on the lake in a storm. I pounded on the glass to let him know that we were safe, that there was no need to worry. He opened the glass door, his face as red as if he were sunburned, and before I could move, he had slapped me across the face.

"Can't you see I'm on the phone with George," he said. "He can't work the fucking cash register." He closed the glass door of the phone booth behind him. It might be a better story if he had been drunk, but I do not believe he was at that moment.

A car pulled up to the general store with Ruth a few minutes later. Someone had given her a plaid blanket that she had wrapped around herself. She was shivering. Her red hair looked black. She put her head on my shoulder and began to cry when she realized that no one had looked for us.

After all of these years, that remains remarkable to me. It should be to you, too, Claire. "Nobody Dies. Nobody, Too" would have been the headline in the *Sun*. Ruth and I were nobodies. No one cared enough to look for us, and now we knew it.

It would be nice to say that Ruth and I became closer after our experience at the lake, which is true, but there was always a dark cloud of sadness over it, always the reminder that no one had cared enough to look for us while we were trying to stay alive. Who wants to be reminded of that?

Ruth and I were no longer embarrassed by each other. I told Poppy that. What I did not tell Poppy, but will tell you, is that when Ruth got her driver's license, she would steal our father's car from the garage, and we would go driving at night. She would get our father's car up over 100 miles per hour on the highway headed out of Baltimore, then turn off the lights. I never knew if she was trying to crash or just did not care if she did, but I was the one who got in the car with her willingly. Please make of that what you want.

It is hard to be a nobody, Claire. People deal with it differently, I suppose. Ruth ran away from home five, ten or a hundred times. She ran away for good a week before she was to graduate from Theodore Roosevelt Regional High School, got married, too young and to the wrong person — a guy who worked as a landscaper and hated women, blacks, Asians and Puerto Ricans. She was happy for a time, I suppose. I ran off to college (New York University), then came back (horse racing, alcohol, no more need be said), worked in a variety of jobs (delicatessen, movie theater), then joined the Army so I could kill some North Vietnamese (but did not do so), and returned with a scar on my head and more blood on my hands than I earlier admitted to you (a man who loathed me named Frank Ditto). Ruth moved all around the country; we never saw each other, not once. A few times, when she called on the phone (collect), we would talk about the lake, and once or twice actually thanked each other. We never spoke of the fact that no one had looked for us. I'm 52 years old as I write this sentence, and I have not spoken of it until now, except to Poppy. I told her when we were driving, and she pulled over and hugged me, and her hair smelled of shampoo. Have I mentioned that already? Yes, yes, I did.

We each made more than a few bad decisions after the accident. You know many of mine; they are in this book. Somehow, I was able to get past them, more or less, to find jobs, to find a wife (your black-haired, cornflower blue-eyed angel of a mother), to have a child (you, the joy of my life), even if P.J. Darbin and Judge Cocksucker conspired to make my life less than it should have been. And somehow, Ruth's bad decisions accumulated, one leading to another, and so on. She wanted so badly to be loved. She wanted so badly to be someone people would look for on a lake in the middle of a storm.

There are people who will tell you that the person who called herself Ruth for the last few years of her life, the person who inhabited her skin, was not the Ruth they knew. I would be one of those people. She left her husband and children and, we were told, lived on the streets in San Francisco and Seattle. She made a half-hearted suicide attempt just before my black-haired, cornflower blue-eyed angel of a girlfriend (then wife, now ex-wife) and I got married. I called her in the hospital, told her that she had to get better and get on a plane back to Baltimore because I could get married without our father but not her. She did not show up. You will not find her in any of our wedding pictures.

Her bad decisions continued, I am sorry to say. She spent time with people who should never have been in her life. She tried heroin, and apparently, she liked it enough to use it again and again. And then she died, alone, in a tiny little apartment in Newark, New Jersey that looked like it was made out of chocolate pudding and twigs. After a short investigation, the Newark, New Jersey police concluded that her death was an accident, the result of the interaction of painkillers and alcohol. What the police report did not mention was that the man she was dating at the time had left her there to die in her bed, in her pudding-and-twigs apartment. He did not call an ambulance for her. We never heard from him. He never contacted our family and did not even come to Ruth's funeral.

The *Sun* did not even run an obituary. They did not run obituaries for nobodies, and to most of the world, Ruth's death was the death of a nobody. But she was not a nobody. She was a troubled person, true, but she was not a nobody. She was, literally, the girl who saved my life in a storm on a lake. That is not a nobody.

A QUESTION OR TWO FOR MY DAUGHTER

You cannot question that of which you are sure.

Can you?

What happens if you do?

My head hurts, Claire. There is a storm inside it. Thunder. Lightning. Old Testament rains.

Can you fix it, Claire?

Have you finished medical school yet?

Did you do well in your brain surgery classes?

EXHIBIT V

— *The Allergic Boy* versus *The Left-Handed Girl*

TEXT

The Allergic Boy

Poppy came home only once all year, at Christmastime, and she had to spend most of her time with her family. I could've gone over to her house as much as I'd wanted to, but I wasn't exactly overly excited about seeing Mr. Fahrenberg again, if you know what I mean. I only got to see her one night the whole time she was home, and that's when we exchanged Christmas presents. I got her a stuffed animal that I found in a store in Howard Lakes, and she got me this really great wooden heart, which is about a million times more romantic than a stuffed animal, if you ask me. I'm just not very good at stuff like that. Some people aren't any good at picking out presents for people, and I'm definitely one of them.

It was late at night, and Poppy and I were just walking around looking in all of the shop windows

The Left-Handed Girl

[A note to the editor: Pursuant to the "fair use doctrine," please insert here the entire 11th chapter of *The Left-Handed Girl*, which I am commenting upon and criticizing.]

even though all the shops were closed. If you ever want a girl to like you, pretend you like looking at things in shop windows, because all of them like to do that. Seriously. All of them.

For no reason at all, I decided to tell her about how we'd gone to see her swim. She wasn't mad at all about me not going to school.

"Why would I be mad?"

"I don't know. I just figured that you'd think that I should have been at school or something."

"No, not at all. That was very sweet of you to come. You should have come to talk to me."

"Well, I would have if I didn't think you'd be mad at me."

"I wouldn't have been mad. Really. I would have absolutely *loved* to see you."

"Now you tell me."

I didn't tell her about us running into her father, though. It's better just to leave stuff like that alone. So there we were, looking in a bunch of windows like a couple of morons, and all of a sudden, she told me about the scholarship she'd been offered by Texas A&M. It was a swimming scholarship. I told you she was good, but it really made me sad to hear that. I mean, I'm always sad around Christmastime anyway because that's when I think about how I just wasted another year being a jerk, but that made me even sadder. It really did. In case you don't know it, Texas A&M is approximately a million miles from Maryland, or something like that. No kidding. It really is far away.

I tried to act like I was really happy for her because you're supposed to do that when something good happens to someone, even if you don't personally think it's all that hot. But Poppy could tell that I wasn't all that thrilled to hear that she'd be in stupid Texas, and she knew why, too.

"Allie, it's only Texas."

"It's halfway across the stupid country."

"I know."

"So I'll never get to see you."

"Sure you will. I'll be home for the summers, and I'll be home for Christmas."

"But I was hoping I'd see you more than that. I was hoping we'd be together for a while." Boy was I ever making myself depressed.

First, I was thinking about missing her, and then I started thinking about her meeting someone who was better looking than me, which wouldn't be that hard to do. Honestly, it wouldn't.

"Allie, I can't *not* go. Everything will be okay. I promise." Then out of nowhere, my mind got way ahead of me, and I said, "I love you, Poppy Fahrenberg." I really said that without even knowing that I was going to do it. Does that ever happen to you — your mind goes ahead and says something before you even have any idea that you might say it, and then you have to think about whether you really wanted to say it in the first place or if your crazy mind is just being a goddam pain-in-the-ass. Anyhow, I thought about it some, and I wasn't mad at myself for saying it. It's kind of strange to tell someone that you love them, though, I mean other than your parents or something. Do you know what I mean?

Poppy gave me a kiss. "I've told you before — I'll stay with you come hell or high water, Allie Hester." That's the same corny thing that she said to me before she went up to school, remember? But I guess it's not any cornier than telling a girl that you love her. Or at least, not by much.

MY COMPUTER

Several years ago (five? ten?), the box counter gave me a computer for one of my birthdays. I do not recall which (52? 58?). She is as sweet as cake batter, my little girl, who is no longer little and no longer a girl. Many years ago, she married a good man who sells appliances for a living (Tim), and they had three children of their own (Lizzie, Lucy and Scott), each of whom I adore as only a grandfather can. (One plays the piano at her church! And the boy can sink a basketball like a champ!) The box counter has never forgiven me for squandering our finances and her future as I suppose I never forgave my father for doing the same a generation before.

The box counter taught me how to use the computer to search for information — or in my case, to search for a person — by pushing certain keys on the keyboard. For years and years, I searched for Poppy on that computer, pushing at different keys in the hopes of locating her after the last series of key pushes had failed. As you will see if you conduct your own computer search for "Poppy Fowler," you will find no such person anywhere on this planet. Instead, you will receive a message in bold letters that reads, **"Do you mean Poppy Fahrenheit?"**

No, I do not mean Poppy Fahrenheit! I have never meant Poppy Fahrenheit! Poppy Fahrenheit is a fiction based on a fiction, a copy of a copy. And anyone who has ever photocopied a copy knows the result is something different, something dimmer.

EXHIBIT W

— *The Allergic Boy* versus *The Left-Handed Girl*

TEXT	
The Allergic Boy Some pretty weird things happened towards the end of the year. My year, not the normal one. Do you ever notice that when weird things happen, it's always a bunch of them at once? Like you could go a whole goddam decade without anything weird happening to you, and then, all of a sudden, you get about a hundred-and-one of them in one week. Well, it's true. First of all, my mom started doing something really crazy. She chipped one of her front teeth with a fork, and she had to go to the dentist to get it fixed. Then she began using chopsticks to eat. You know what they are — they're those wooden sticks that they give you at Chinese restaurants except that you never use them because you keep dropping stuff all over your goddam clothes and everything. She said she wasn't ever going to use silverware again, that it was dangerous, so she used the chopsticks	*The Left-Handed Girl* [A note to the editor: Pursuant to the "fair use doctrine," please insert here the entire 12th chapter of *The Left-Handed Girl*, which I am commenting upon and criticizing.]

for everything. Let me tell you this, it's corny as all hell to watch someone eat cereal or something with some stupid sticks. And it's even cornier when your mom's the one who's doing it. Believe me.

Then I ran my fastest time in the mile which, in case you don't remember, was four minutes and 58 seconds. That probably doesn't seem really weird to you, but it was because it was a full 16 seconds faster than I'd ever run before. That's a big difference. No kidding. Anyway, it was pouring like mad out, and the track was practically flooded with water. But even though the footing was horrible, I was having a great time, and I felt like I could run forever. The rain was really cool, my hair and my uniform were soaking wet, and it was just like sloshing around in the water like a little kid or something. You know how kids are, always jumping in stupid puddles and stuff. Well, that's how it was. It was fun as hell.

Want to hear something you'll never believe? I got an A in English. How's that for weird? It was all because of this poem I wrote for class. Mrs. Engelbart made us each write a poem for class, and I wrote mine in homeroom because I'd completely forgotten about it. Lou reminded me, and I whipped out this really corny thing about how beautiful the beach is in about three and a half minutes. Old Mrs. Engelbart said it was fabulous, simply fabulous. How's that for a laugh?

And the absolute strangest thing happened one morning when I was walking up to school. A lot of the neighbors were hanging out in the middle of the street, and Mr. Winston was holding one of those green plastic garbage bags. Mr. Winston's this guy who lived down on the corner who I didn't know really well. Mrs. Corrigan and Mrs. Magruder were standing there, too, and because she's a hundred times more normal than Mrs. Magruder, I asked Mrs. Corrigan what was up.

"The baker's dog is dead, and someone will have to tell the baker," she said. That ought to tell you something about how friendly everyone was to the baker — he lived on our street ever since I was little, and still, no one ever called him by his name. I think that was partly because he was pretty nasty and partly because he had one of those Italian last names with about a dozen vowels in it. Even so, you should try to call a guy by his name. It's extremely rude not to.

The reason that this was such a big deal and that everyone was in the road talking about it was that this wasn't the first time the baker's dog died. The last time, the baker was so upset that he couldn't think straight at all. He put chocolate in the meringue and yeast in the Napoleons, neither of which you're supposed to do, and he left the crescent rolls in the oven so long that the entire bakery nearly burnt down. Engines came from as far as Harper's Square to put out the fire. It was absolutely unbelievable — you know how I am about fires. But of course, the baker's stupid dog wasn't really dead then. He was just sleeping, and when the ground where he was buried started barking all over the place, the baker ran out with his shovel to dig him out. But this time, the trash collector said he definitely was dead, and Mrs. Magruder was certain as well. She said that that was exactly what her dog looked like when it died. So someone had to tell the baker.

"I can't do it," Mr. Winston finally said. "I'm already half an hour late for work as it is." He passed the bag with the dog in it to Mrs. Magruder. What a chicken. It's hard to like a guy when he's a chicken, if you ask me.

"Well, I certainly can't do it. I hardly even know the baker. He never comes to my Christmas parties, and he doesn't even call to say he's not coming even though it specifically says to R.S.V.P. right on the invitation." She gave the bag to Mr. Scottsdale.

"I'd rather not do it," he said. I swear, our block was absolutely lousy with chickens. It really was. "I might say something wrong. Honey, why don't you do it? You're good with people." He handed the bag over to his wife.

"Not as good as Allie, though, and the baker likes him so much." Before I knew it, I was holding the goddam bag. I *hate* it when adults try to trick you into doing something they don't want to do just because you're a kid. I absolutely hate it. The baker hardly even knew me, and there's Mrs. Scottsdale pretending we were buddies or something.

So there I was, standing there like a jerk, holding a stupid plastic bag. Mr. Kilkenny, Mrs. Corrigan, Mr. and Mrs. Billingham, and the postman were left, and I was trying to figure out which one to give the bag to because I didn't want to be late for school. Really, that's why. But all of a sudden, the bag started twisting and shaking all over the place, and everyone was watching. I put the bag down on the road, and the baker's dog jumped out. No kidding. All of the neighbors were mad. They were positively furious.

"Next time, we're not going to listen to Mrs. Magruder," someone said.

"Next time, we'll get a doctor's opinion," someone else said.

I was kind of mad, too, and I started heading up to school again except that I heard someone crying, so I turned around. It was Mrs. Magruder. She was sitting on a rock by her mailbox just crying and crying like one of those ladies in the movies whose son got shot up in the war or something. I went back and asked her what's the matter.

"Maybe my dog wasn't dead," she said.

I told you she was a fruitcake.

NO CREDIT

Everyone tells stories. Me and you and you and you.

We tell stories about ourselves, and maybe we exaggerate, and maybe we change the details a bit here or there, but it is those stories we tell that people remember about us just as much as they remember the color of our hair, the sound of our voices or other such things.

Poppy liked to tell stories, and for the best of them, she would occasionally point at me and say, "You really should be writing this down, Jimmy Nail. You're going to want to use this story someday. Just make sure to give me credit. Don't be a piece of shit and pretend you made it up yourself, okay?"

There was one story she told about getting her fingers caught in a pop-up toaster. Her parents rushed her to the hospital, and (she claimed) the doctor considered amputating her fingers before (she claimed) a nurse thought to pour melted butter onto the slots to free her fingers. "If it weren't for that nurse," she said, "I'd be right-handed."

Poppy told another story about the time her family went horseback riding and (she claimed) her horse bolted away and ran for 20 miles before it stopped at a gas station, with Poppy yelling, "Stop, you motherfucker!" the entire way. Do I believe the horse ran for 20 miles? Of course not. But it would have been a funny story even if it ran 100 yards. And a pretty red-haired girl yelling, "Stop, you motherfucker!" is funny at any distance.

There was another story about her next-door neighbors who liked to walk around naked in their backyard. They raked leaves naked (she claimed), they mowed the lawn naked (she claimed), you name it, they were naked.

"The first time I ever saw a man naked," she said, "he was on his hands and knees pulling weeds."

One time, when we were walking back to our homes after getting ice cream sundaes at the shop down the street (Smoothy's Ice Cream Shop), Poppy told me this story:

"When I was a junior in high school, it was getting close to the junior prom. We had an English teacher who was a complete shitheel. Mr. Montabello. What a shitheel. He was always picking on me and asking me questions he knew I didn't know the answers to.

"So just before the junior prom, in front of the entire English class, Mr. Montabello said, 'Hey, Poppy, has anyone asked you to the junior prom yet?' I said, 'No,' and everyone had a good laugh. I was humiliated, but fortunately, he just left it alone.

"Toward the end of class, he asked if someone would take a note down to the boys' gym teacher, another shitheel named Mr. Greggs. No one volunteered, so Mr. Montabello called me to the front of the classroom, handed me the note, and told me to run it down to the boys' gym and give it to Mr. Greggs. He told me to wait to get a response from Mr. Greggs and to bring that back to him. Fine, no biggie.

"When I got to the boys' gym, all of the boys were lined up for some kind of athletic shit, jumping jacks or some other bullshit, and Mr. Greggs was standing in front of them. I handed him the note, he opened it up, and he started laughing. I could tell something was up, so I began to walk away, but he grabbed me by the elbow and told me to stay.

"'Boys,' he said, 'I just got a note from Mr. Montabello. Apparently, this girl here needs a prom date. Will any of you take her to the prom?'

"They all started laughing and yelling and calling me names — 'slut' and 'whore' and 'bitch' — and when I was finally able to twist my arm free, I ran away crying. I never went back to Mr. Montabello's class. He ended up giving me an F for the year.

"But here's the epilogue. A few months later, I was walking home late at night from a party or something, and who should pull his car up beside me but Mr. Montabello. He asked me if I wanted a ride home, and I said no. He asked me if I'd been sick or something, and I said no. He asked if I would be taking his class again senior year, and I said I didn't think so. Then he said, 'Listen Poppy, I'm sure you could use some money. How about I give you a couple of dollars to help me out here.' I looked into his car window, and his wrinkly little cock was sticking out of his pants. 'You have to use that pretty mouth, though, okay?' I told him to screw off, and when he drove away, he called me a whore.

"That's a true story, Jimmy Nail, every word of it. A true story about how terrible people can be. How mean. I think about that all the time. I think about how, if those two grown men hadn't done something so cruel to a teenage girl, maybe I'd have gone to college, or maybe I'd have a nice job as a secretary or something, instead of living in my uncle's house and doing whatever it is I'm doing with my life, which is nothing really.

"You really should be writing this down, Jimmy Nail. You're going to want to use this story someday. Just make sure to give me credit. Don't be a piece of shit and pretend you made it up yourself, okay?"

I said, "Okay."

That was Poppy Fowler's story that I just told you. It is not a story about grace and mercy. Quite the opposite, really.

And I take no credit for it. None at all.

EXHIBIT X

— *The Allergic Boy* versus *The Left-Handed Girl*

TEXT

The Allergic Boy

I told you that bit with the baker's dog was the weirdest thing that happened that year, didn't I? Well, I was wrong. I completely forgot something. You'd never in your wildest imagination guess the absolute weirdest thing that happened. Mrs. Kettles died. Do you remember her? She's the one whose husband put her in that stupid chair over at Adair's Pub. She got pneumonia or something, and then she just died. You're crazy if you think that I told Poppy.

Want to know what my favorite movie of all time is? "Too Late for London." Do you remember that one? It was great. Mick Dewhurst was in it, and Sandra Carter was in it, and that guy who was in all of those corny musicals where everyone just starts singing for no reason at all was in it, except that I can't remember his name right now. I'll think of it later. Anyway, what

The Left-Handed Girl

[A note to the editor: Pursuant to the "fair use doctrine," please insert here the entire 13th chapter of *The Left-Handed Girl*, which I am commenting upon and criticizing.]

happened in it was that Mick
Dewhurst and Sandra Carter fall
in love and everything, except
this gigantic company that she
works for transfers her to England
right when they're still in love.
But Mick Dewhurst can't go with
her because he's got a job, and his
father's this old guy who's sick and
alone and everything. So they're
crying all over the place and saying
goodbye and saying how much
they're going to miss each other,
but when they get to the airport,
she's already missed her plane. They
start hugging and kissing and stuff,
and the movie ends right there, and
even though she could've got on
the next flight, you know that she's
going to stay. I really got a kick out
of that. I don't know what made me
think of telling you that.

Graduation was a regular bore,
and I probably wouldn't even
have shown up myself if my mom
didn't think it was such a big deal.
Sometimes, you do stuff for your
parents you really don't want to do
because they pay for your food and
clothes and everything, so that's
why I went. It really was corny, and
I didn't pay much attention to all of
the speeches everyone was giving. I

did listen to Mr. Ryan's for a while, though, and right when he got to the part about how we'd all matured and everything, one of the guys who was graduating with us set off a cherry bomb. Those are like little dynamite things, and it was pretty ironic that he did it right then, if you ask me. I mean, setting off a cherry bomb right smack in the middle of graduation isn't exactly the most mature thing in the world to do, if you know what I mean.

You know what I was thinking about the whole time I was sitting at graduation — I was thinking about whether or not Jeff Hill's parents were embarrassed because of what it said on the building. Everyone had to pass right by it when they went into the school to go to the auditorium. I was getting pretty upset about it. I mean, I didn't want to make their lives any lousier, just their kid's. He really shouldn't have belted me in the face with a bat, you know. When you do something like that, you deserve that something rotten should happen to you. You really do.

Lou and I both got jobs at Kitchener's Market for the summer doing the exact same stuff that I

did the summer before. It's funny
that I would go back there because
I already told you what a crumby
job it was, but I did because it was
easier than going around looking
for another job. Do you ever do
that, do something that you're
really not too hot on just because
it's the easiest thing to do? Well,
that's the way I am. I told you
about that doctor who said I was
an underachiever, didn't I? Yeah,
I guess I did. So I went back to
Kitchener's because they already
knew me and everything.

EXHIBIT WHATEVER

— WHAT EXHIBIT ARE WE UP TO?

There is no movie called "Too Late for London." There is no actor named Mick Dewhurst. They are fictional. I made them up.

But anyone could have made them up, you say.

Well, I suppose that is true.

Except I have proof: a short story I wrote for Poppy that used the same movie title and the same name for the movie actor.[92]

---

92   A note to the editor: Please have someone type up "Too Late for London" from my notebooks and insert it here. I am too old and tired to type up all of those words. Some of them are very long, like "lugubrious." It means "looking or sounding sad or dismal."

THE END

ON WE GO

It would be nice if the book ended right there, right?

It would be nice if all three books ended there.

The Allergic Boy.

The Left-Handed Girl.

This book.

But they do not end there, and if you have read *The Left-Handed Girl* (or seen the shitty movie version), you know that they do not end there. There is more to come. So on we go, as we must.

ABOUT THE GIRL

"Mr. Nail, let me ask you a provocative question. Do you mind?"

"No."

"You contend you wrote a book called *The Allergic Boy*, correct?"

"Correct."

"And you are aware that Mr. Darbin published a book called *The Left-Handed Girl*, correct?

"Correct."

"And you called your book *The Allergic Boy* because you believed the book to be about the boy?"

"I suppose."

"And Mr. Darbin called the book *The Left-Handed Girl* because he perceived the book to be about the girl, correct?"

"I don't know. You would have to ask him."

"I have, and that is what he said."

"So you say."

"Now, Mr. Nail, I ask you under penalty of perjury, who is the protagonist in this book, who is the hero — the boy or the girl?"

I paused. I had taken an oath to tell the truth, not unlike the one I took in the "Introduction" of this book. "The girl," I said.

"I'm sorry, I can't hear you," he said, feigning deafness once again.

"You heard me," I said. "The girl."

"Who?"

"The girl."

"Which girl?"

"The left-handed girl, is that what you want me to say?"

EXHIBIT Y

— *The Allergic Boy* versus *The Left-Handed Girl*

TEXT	
The Allergic Boy	*The Left-Handed Girl*
Poppy didn't return to Darryton until the beginning of July because her school ended later than Highlands did, and this time around, I made sure that I didn't have to spend the Fourth of July in a stupid supermarket. I told one of the managers that I had bronchitis, but I really didn't. I really wanted to take Poppy up to Winchester Falls to see their fireworks. Every year, they have this huge fireworks show up there on the high school football field, and that's a pretty romantic way to spend an evening with a girl you're nuts about, if you ask me that is. So I told her to meet me over at my house so we could drive up.	[A note to the editor: Pursuant to the "fair use doctrine," please insert here the entire 14th chapter of *The Left-Handed Girl*, which I am commenting upon and criticizing.]
Boy was I ever nervous about seeing Poppy again, let me tell you that. I mean, I hadn't seen her since Christmas or anything, and it's a pretty long time between Christmas and the Fourth of July. If you want,	

you can figure out the exact number
of days. I sure don't feel like doing
it. Anyway, like I said, it was a long
time, and I really had no idea what
I was supposed to say to her when I
first saw her. I could be really smooth
and yawn or something like it was
no big deal that she was back, or I
could get all mushy and everything.
They do both of them in the movies.
As it was, I just said the first thing
that popped into my crazy mind
when I saw her — "I really missed
you, Poppy" — and it ended up being
the perfect thing to say. Sometimes,
you've got to trust your mind. Even if
it's a crazy one like the one I've got.

We talked some with my mother,
just the stupid stuff you talk about
with your parents, and then we
headed out to the backyard to get in
the pickup. And being as this was
something really important to me
— taking Poppy up to Winchester
Falls, that is — the lousy pickup
wouldn't start. I *knew* that was going
to happen, but just because you know
something rotten is going to happen,
doesn't mean that you're going to be
any less angry about it. Do you know
what I mean?

"Allie, it's okay. We don't have to
go."

"I really wanted to go, though."

"We could just stay and talk. We haven't talked in a long time."

She was being as understanding as hell about the whole thing, and that just made me want to take her to see the fireworks even more. It really did. And then it hit me to give good old Lou a call and see if he wanted to go with us. I mean, it wasn't nice not to have asked him to go in the first place being as we were best friends and being as he'd never met Poppy. Besides, he could get his parents' car practically any time he wanted.

By the time Lou came to get us, we were already late for the fireworks. I introduced him to Poppy, and I could tell right away that Lou was really impressed that my girlfriend was so pretty and everything. That's a real crazy feeling when someone thinks your girlfriend is pretty. It really is. I let Poppy sit in the front seat because that's the polite thing to do, and I sat in the back by myself. Poppy knelt on the front seat and turned so she could talk to me while we drove.

Lou got out on Route 11, and we must have been the only car on the road. No kidding. Everybody else was already up at Winchester Falls, and as we drove on those wavy roads, we were headed right toward the fireworks. They were exploding all over the place in front of us, and even though we were pretty far away, you could see them really well, particularly if you turned off your headlights, which we did.

The fireworks were fantastic. They had some of those that explode into three or four different colors, one right after the other, which I could never figure out how they did that. Do you know what I'm talking about? Like first, there are all these red sparkles, and then all these white ones, and then all these blue ones, and I could never figure out why it didn't just come out as a mush of red, white and blue ones. Not that I exactly broke my neck thinking about it or anything.

Well, anyhow, I was half listening to Poppy and Lou and halftrying to keep track of how many fireworks we'd missed since we were so late. And then when we started coming down one of those crazy hills, there was a goddam cow right in the middle of the road, which meant we'd be even later because we'd have to get it out of the way. Things were really going pretty rotten, let me tell you, and they just got more rotten because Lou didn't even see the stupid cow, and not just because the headlights were still off. Lou could be a real creep sometimes, and he was being very sneaky about looking at Poppy's chest. You had to be another guy to even tell that he was doing it because all guys have that sneaky look mastered. You know what I'm talking about, where they look at parts of a girl's body and stuff and make it look like they're not looking.

I yelled something out so Lou would stop before we plowed into the cow, but he hit the brakes too late to stop from hitting the thing or to stop from throwing Poppy right through the goddam window. I'd never seen that happen before — someone going right through a windshield, I mean — and trust me when I tell you that it's nothing you'd want to see. Poppy was lying on the ground about 10 feet from the cow, and I got out of the car as fast as I could to see if she was okay. She was crying all over the place, and she just kept yelling my name over and over again like she couldn't say anything else. The whole thing was strange as hell, believe me.

Lou jumped out of the car, too, and he ran over to us. "I'm sorry. I didn't mean it. I really didn't. I'm

sorry. Poppy, I'm sorry." He was
apologizing nonstop, and it was
driving me absolutely crazy, so I just
told him to shut the hell up and get
the car going again so we could get
Poppy over to a hospital. The only
problem was that the car was wedged
right in the stupid cow, and the
stupid cow was still lying there half-
alive or something, and we couldn't
figure out how to get the car out. It
wasn't a lovely sight, let me tell you.

Poppy was still screaming, and
since there was no way that anyone
would come by, since everybody
was up at the football field, I just
picked her up from the ground, slung
her over my shoulder, and started
running towards Winchester Falls.
It was still about three or four miles
away, and I just kept getting madder
and madder because the fireworks
didn't seem to be getting much closer.
You know how it is when you don't
feel like you're getting anywhere at
all. And those crazy hills were a real
pain-in-the-ass. You go up one hill
and your legs are all tired, and then
when you go down, you feel like
you're going to lose your balance and
fall right on your face like a moron.

I kept talking to Poppy while I
was running, telling her about the

stupid fireworks and about Kitchener's and about this idea I had for a movie and about a bunch of other things I can't even think of now. I kept saying, "Everything's going to be alright, Poppy," which is a pretty corny thing to say unless you're a doctor or something and know for sure that everything is going to be okay.

Remember before when I told you about how the summers started getting pretty hot after the one where my father fell in the well? Well, this one was a real son-of-a-bitch. It was so hot and muggy out, and I was sweating like crazy. The sweat from my hair kept running down into my eyeballs, and that stung like hell, so I kept wiping off my forehead with my hand. The back of my neck was damp, too, and when I went to wipe that off, I found that it was Poppy's blood that had soaked my collar. That was scary as all hell. You probably thought that junk like that only happens in the movies. Well, you're wrong.

There was blood all over my shirt, and my mind wouldn't go berserk on me. I mean, I was trying as hard as I could to make my mind go berserk on me so that I could think up what to do, but it just wouldn't do it. Boy did that ever make me angry, because it

usually just goes berserk whenever
it wants, for no reason at all, but
just when I need it to go berserk,
just when I really need it to think
up something good for me, it won't
work. I couldn't think of *anything*.
Minds are a lot like pickup trucks,
you know. They really are.

So I just ran like an absolute
madman towards the fireworks,
and I knew at that moment that
everything I would ever become,
for better or worse, I would owe to
Poppy Fahrenberg. I was going so
fast that I couldn't believe it. I'd bet
that even with Poppy on me I was
running about four minutes and 30
seconds per mile. And not just for
one mile either, but for two or three
in a row, which is next to impossible
to do unless you're in the Olympics
or something. No kidding. I wish I'd
have had a stopwatch with me.

When I was just a kid, sixth
grade I think, we had to read this
poem for school that was called "The
Human Body" or "A Man's Body" or
something like that. I'm not one of
those people who memorizes poems
or anything, mostly because I can't
stand them, but for some reason, I
remember the last line in that one: "A
man without love wouldn't miss the
human body." I think the title comes
from that line. Anyway, you see, the

whole poem was about people missing things. Like a guy who loses his arms is going to miss holding his wife. And a guy who loses his legs is going to miss dancing with his wife. And a guy who loses his eyesight is going to miss seeing his wife. There were a couple others, too, about guys and hearing and smelling and other junk like that. So I guess what the guy who wrote it was probably trying to say was that if you're married or something and you lose a part of yourself, you can get pretty depressed and ornery and stuff. There was this man in our town who lived over the luncheonette who was missing his left leg. He was really mean to everyone, and he used to scare kids practically to death on purpose. But he was like that before the accident, so I don't think the poem is about someone like him. But I've told you about how terrific Poppy was and everything, and she wasn't so terrific after she lost her right arm.

Want to know why she lost her right arm — because I'm an idiot, that's why. An absolute, goddam, stupid idiot. I mean, I ran like a lunatic until we found someone with a car to drive her the rest of the way to the hospital, but not once the whole time did I even think of

putting a goddam tourniquet on.
She was bleeding all over the place,
and I didn't even think of putting a
tourniquet on to stop it even though
they must have taught us how to do
it about a million times in school
— you know, with a piece of cloth
and a stick or a twig or something.
Sometimes, I can be the biggest idiot
in the whole world.

    Well, you don't have to be a
genius or something to know that
she couldn't swim anymore with
only one arm, so Poppy didn't get
her scholarship and ended up staying
in Darryton. I know you're probably
thinking that I had this whole thing
planned out in my mind just to make
her stay because I already told you
how sneaky I can be, but I didn't. You
know something, you're an out-and-
out jerk if you think I'd do something
like that to Poppy. You really are.

    I wouldn't be lying if I said that
Poppy wasn't too thrilled with me
when they had to amputate her
arm. I never asked her about it, but
I'm pretty sure she blamed me for
the accident and for not putting a
tourniquet on, and she was probably
right to. I mean, it was my fault
for not fixing up the pickup, and
for making her go even though she
probably didn't even want to, and for
calling Lou, and for making her

sit up front. You could probably
think up a few others if you tried.
Anyway, I went to see her when
she was still in the hospital, and she
didn't really want to talk to me, and
I wasn't really too big on seeing her
on account of I was feeling so lousy
about the whole thing.

THE DIFFERENCE IS IN THE DETAILS

A story twice told will test any reader. But a story told *three* times? I will not subject you to that. Instead, let me just say that what happened to Poppy Fahrenberg and Poppy Fahrenheit in fiction is, more or less, what happened to Poppy Fowler in fact. A dark night, a boy and a girl in a car (there was no friend with us), the headlights turned off (a trick the boy had learned from his sister), a cow in the road, a collision, a panicked boy who forgot what he had learned about tourniquets in health class, a pretty red-haired girl losing her right arm at the shoulder as a result. It is only in the details that fiction and fact differ.

Poppy and I had driven to the beach for the day. Ocean City to be specific. We had taken my father's car, the make and model of which are of no import, because her uncle the homosexual had driven off on some business trip in his convertible. We swam, we drank beer, we bought salt water taffy that tasted exactly like watermelon, we ate warm sandwiches we had made ourselves, and as Poppy relaxed on a blanket, I read her the first chapter of a book I had started to write for her but would not finish until I had gotten to college. It started like this: "Aaaah-chooo!"

When the sun sank, we packed our blanket and books into her oversized bag, left the beach, and visited several seaside bars where the bartenders were all too happy to ignore the fact that I was only sixteen if that meant that Poppy (bare-armed, bare-legged, tanned, smiling, a flash of a black brassiere) would remain. I understood what they were thinking. I understood their envy when they did their romantic calculus and concluded, half-wrong, that she was mine, all mine. I did not mind that they thought that, and I encouraged the thought by occasionally slipping my arm around her slender waist or whispering something in her ear or kissing her full on the lips. When the bars finally closed their doors for the night, I, the now-drunken son of the long-drunken barber began to drive the long-drunken barber's car back to Baltimore with Poppy asleep in the passenger seat. Only the angels who watch over eager, young boys were not watching over me that night.

A dark country road.

The car's headlights turned off because, well, just because.

A drunken glance at a pretty girl's tanned legs while she slept.

A cow appearing in the middle of the road.

A collision.

Glass.

Blood.

Panic.

Suddenly, it was very cold, as cold as if the blankets had been pulled off of us on a January night. I swear I could see my own breath for a moment.

I remember all of this clearly, too clearly, even after getting injured in the service of my country, even after being left with booming headaches and a fucking scar on the side of my fucking head. I remember it the way you remember a scene from a movie you have watched too often.

Hours later, I sat alone in the hospital waiting room, my clothes as discolored as a thundercloud from my perspiration and from the dried blood, the sun beginning to rise warmly through the enormous window over my shoulder. The town was called Tariffville, a name you should recognize from *The Left-Handed Girl*, where the entire town was picked up and transported from Maryland to Virginia by a thief. The hospital was known as the Tariffville General Hospital.

It was not long before a short, dark-haired surgeon with a German surname (Schulz) joined me in the waiting room, a surgical mask dangling from his neck like a scarf, specks of fresh blood on his surgical gown. His eyes were like seeds. His face was wet and speckled, like a trout pulled from water. Perhaps he was just tired.

"I'm sorry," he said, "but we couldn't save the arm. We tried, but there was too much damage. The nerves, the muscles, they were all severed."

"What?" I said.

"The arm. We couldn't save it."

"I screwed up," I said. I may have been crying. Correction: I was crying. "I didn't see the cow. I didn't think of making a tourniquet."

"That might not have helped," he said. Years later, in Vietnam, I remembered to apply a tourniquet to Frank Ditto's leg. That did not help him, either: A bullet had already gone through his nose; I was wrapping the leg of a corpse who despised me.

"Can you tell me the boy's name?" the surgeon said.

"What?"

"We need to call his family. I need to know his name."

I was confused. Or Schulz was. For an instant, I was certain he was talking about another patient, a boy who, as coincidence would have it, had also injured his arm badly. In that instant, that seemed a reasonable thought.

"I'm here with the girl who was in the car accident. Her name is Poppy Fowler. She's my neighbor. She lives with her homosexual Uncle Rob. She saved me from a tiger."

The surgeon's mouth fell slack.

"Are you trying to be funny?" he asked.

"No. Of course not. No."

"A tiger?"

"A dog. It's something we joke about. But I brought a girl in. She has red hair. Poppy Fowler."

Not Fahrenberg.

And not Fahrenheit.

"There's only one emergency patient tonight, the one from the car accident. The one you brought in."

I am sure I said something, but I do not know what.

Schulz looked left, then right, as if he had heard sharp, sudden sounds from opposite directions, before pointing firmly at the doors that led to the emergency room. You could not miss the sign: EMERGENCY ROOM STAFF ONLY, in glowing red letters the color of Twizzlers.

"That's a boy that I just operated on," he said, talking to the air. "The boy you brought in, the one with the long red hair. I had to cut a lot of his hair to get the glass out of his scalp. But it'll grow back."

TWO QUESTIONS

"Want to see my dictation pad?"
"Want to touch my ascot?"

TODAY

My head feels fine today. No volcanic eruptions.

Tonight, the box counter called, and I had a delightful conversation with my grandchildren. They are wonderful. I wish you could meet them. The oldest (Lizzie) is going to be the president someday! Mark my words!

I found a note on my desk near the computer. I read: "Did you turn off the oven?"

I do not know who it is from.

MY DEFENSE

I have turned things over in my mind hundreds, perhaps thousands of times. There had been hints all along, I suppose. The occasional disapproving glances from older men who examined Poppy with the glare of county fair judges eyeballing a sorry calf. The occasional affections of other men whose smiles always seemed to betray something lurid or forbidden. The too-large shirts. The one-piece bathing suits. The strong, toned arms. The heavyweight beating she had given Uncle Rob.

Perhaps you already figured it out yourself. I asked the publisher to use large print so you could read between the lines.

In turning things over in my mind, I wish I had responded differently than I had that morning in the Tariffville General Hospital, frightened not by the disappearance of one appendage but by the appearance of another. A boy had just lost his arm. He was drugged, and when he finally awoke, he was certainly in great pain, lonely, angry, sick. You can list the adjectives as well as I can. His hair was shorn to nubs; that would be the least of his worries. There should have been someone sitting on the edge of the bed, reassuring him. There should have been someone to say, "I will always be here for you." Instead, he likely awoke alone. If he was very, very lucky, he awoke to the half-smile of a kind nurse, who read to him and brought him bologna sandwiches. Not everyone is that lucky.

He should have awakened to see me, I know that, and you know that, and so do you and you and you. In my defense, I was a teenager and behaved like one. And further in my defense, I was in love. Yes, my notebooks were filled with stories I had written, stories of cowboys and ghosts

and mysteries solved. But my notebooks from that particular summer were also filled with the same words written
over and over for pages: "I love Poppy Fowler! I love Poppy
Fowler! I love Poppy Fowler! I love Poppy Fowler!" And one
notebook was filled with the first chapter of a novel that
began, "Aaaa-chooo!"

I wish I could say that I returned to Poppy's hospital room
when I came to my senses and hugged him to me until he
awoke, that I consoled him, that I apologized for my role in the
accident that left him with one arm, that I told him everything
would be okay even when I knew it would not and could not
be okay. That, after all, is what happened in that shitty movie
version of *The Left-Handed Girl*. But I promised you accuracy.
I made a commitment, and I will not dishonor that now. It
is a horrible man who is the villain in his autobiography. It is
someone altogether worse who lies in that autobiography.

The truth is that I left the hospital and never returned. I
did not even look back. I walked to the Tariffville bus station
(four miles) and took a bus back to Baltimore (65 more).
It was only when I was home that I noticed the tiny frag-
ments of windshield glass embedded in my legs, twinkling
like diamonds in the kitchen lights. My mother removed
them with tweezers and rubbed my wounds with alcohol, my
hands flapping in front of me like I'd eaten a jalapeno as she
did. Soon I was asleep. I awoke late and was greeted by angry
neighbors when their morning newspapers were delivered
after lunch. Days passed, maybe weeks. I never saw Poppy
Fowler again. Faster than a rumor, Uncle Rob (whom I now
understood to be Poppy's lover, not her uncle, a conclusion
you likely reached 200 pages ago) vacated the row house next
to ours. From a bedroom window that had once belonged to
my sister, I saw him on the sidewalk as he pushed suitcases
into the backseat of his car. He looked up and glared at me.
I glared back at him. We should have fought, but I am not
much of a fighter, as the Viet Cong could attest. After I had

pressed a knife against his Adam's apple, he had never struck Poppy again (to my knowledge). He should have been pressing a knife against my Adam's apple now after what I had done, maybe even draw a little blood, but he did not. He drove off into the sunset, like people do at the end of a silly movie.

Another family of unremarkable So-and-sos moved into 1336 within days. We heard them singing "Happy Birthday" to one of the children on their first night living there. It did not wash away the sounds left by Rob and Poppy. Once, I had tried to scrub those sounds from my memory, but after discovering that half of them belonged to Poppy, I found myself trying to recall them, trying to picture her face as she contributed her part, her lips, her eyes.

Soon, school started, my senior year at Theodore Roosevelt Regional High School. I remember little of it and will not waste your time with what I do recall. I went to classes. I played chess. I wrote stories (boo! bang!). I did not go to football games or pep rallies. I graduated. You can fill in the blanks if you are so inclined.

There was another summer, and then I was off to New York University, where a clown-haired writing professor (Stephen Duncan) would tell me to write about what I know. And so I did. I retrieved the book I had started to write for Poppy, the one that began, "Aaaa-chooo!" I wrote about love. I wrote about grace and mercy. I did not have a scar on the side of my head or else I would have written about that, too.

I loved a boy who dressed like a girl and called himself Poppy.

I can say that now.

I loved him, even if he did not think so.

I have thought about all of this so often, but even now, so many years later, the earth having spun on its axis thousands of times, the words in this section poured out of me as slowly as the venom from a rattlesnake.

AN APOLOGY

In the last chapter, I referred to Poppy as "he" and "him" and as a "boy." I apologize if that caused any confusion, and I apologize to Poppy and to anyone else like her who would prefer to be referred to as "she" and "her" and as a "girl" (or "woman"), which is how I will refer to her for the remainder of the book you are holding. I hope you will understand why I used those terms in that last chapter and forgive me if you do or do not.

My point, if I was not clear, is that he or she, boy or girl, it did not matter to me.

"Love is love," someone once said. "You can't control who you love."

Who said that?

The answer is blowing in the wind.

EXHIBIT Z

— *The Allergic Boy* versus *The Left-Handed Girl*

TEXT	
The Allergic Boy	*The Left-Handed Girl*
That was pretty much it for me and Poppy Fahrenberg. It's funny how quickly some things end, and you can't even stop them if you try because you have no idea that they're about to end in the first place. I don't mean laugh-your-head-off funny, either. I saw her a couple more times when she got home, but we didn't get along too great after all that. We just sat around mostly. And if you think Mr. Fahrenberg was pleased as punch to see me, then you're out of your mind. I'll bet you're thinking that I'm a real big creep for not dating Poppy anymore. But if a girl doesn't want to see you, there's not much you can do about it. And if you feel rotten every time you see her, there's not much you can do about that either. Can you understand that? I'd really rather not talk about Poppy anymore, okay? It's starting to bug me.	[A note to the editor: Pursuant to the "fair use doctrine," please insert here the entire 15th chapter of *The Left-Handed Girl*, which I am commenting upon and criticizing.]

Anyway, that summer didn't get much better. I ended up quitting work at Kitchener's. Again. Boy, I'll bet those guys over there must've really loved me. I'm being sarcastic. I mean, every summer I worked for a couple weeks and just wound up quitting on them. If anyone ever did that to me, they wouldn't exactly be my favorite person in the world anymore, do you know what I mean?

Lou went back to his grandmother's after the car wreck, and I'm not too sure I would've wanted to hang out with him much after it anyway. Mr. Magruder kept trying to do those father-and-son things to cheer me up because I was really in the dumps about ruining Poppy's life and everything. He took me camping up in the mountains one weekend, but it ended up raining the whole time, and I ended up being as sick as a dog. Have you ever had it where your goddam nose is running all over the place, and you start thinking that maybe the only way to get it to stop is to stand on your stupid head or something? Well, that's how bad it was. My nose just wouldn't stop running, and I was sneezing constantly.

Mr. Magruder drove me up to Baltimore to see a baseball game, too. It was the Baltimore Orioles playing the Cleveland Indians, but I didn't pay attention much because I find baseball pretty boring, even though that's how I got my stupid nickname and everything. I mean, I always pretended I liked baseball — everyone *pretends* they like baseball — but when you get right down to it, it's just a bunch of guys standing around, and a bunch of guys standing around doesn't excite me too much. He bought me a beer at the game, though, which is a neat thing for an old guy to do for a kid, if you ask me at least, and then he took me to go look at a load of old buildings in the city. Boy did he ever get a bang out of looking at old buildings. I personally don't see anything too interesting in them. I don't buy it that things are interesting just because they're old. They have to be interesting *on top of* being old.

Anyway, it was really nice of Mr. Magruder to do all that stuff with me, even if it didn't cheer me up much. If you're not in the mood to be cheered up, a guy could break his neck trying to cheer you up and still not even come close to doing it. But it was nice of him to try. I really mean that.

Mr. Magruder really was an alright guy in my book. He just married wrong, and you can't blame a guy too much for the way his wife turns out.

Just before I went up to college, my mom got me a dog to take up with me. I was just going upstate about 50 miles, but she thought I'd like some company, so she got me this raggedy, black mutt that was pretty cute except for I had to teach it to go to the bathroom outside. I called the dog Dewhurst after Mick Dewhurst, my favorite actor. He was the guy who was in "Too Late for London," remember? That was my favorite. I saw it seven times.

Believe it or not, I was actually looking forward to going to college. Really, I almost couldn't wait for it to start, and I had the pickup loaded with all of my things about a week before I was even supposed to leave. I know you think I'm making this up because I told you how much I hate school, but I'm not. And if someone ever told me that I'd *want* to go to school, I probably would've told the guy to go get himself checked into one of those insane asylums. But it's true. The way I figure it, when your summers start being even lousier than your years, it's easy to start looking forward to school.

And the way I figure it, everything I would ever become, for better or worse, I would owe to Poppy Fahrenberg or whatever I would remember of her. That was a pretty corny thing to say, wasn't it? I thought so. I can be the corniest guy in the world if I feel like it. And some days, I feel like it.	
AUTHENTICITY	
Authentic!	Fraud!

I KNOW

This morning, just hours ago, a speck of time really, I sat in front of my computer terminal again, the one the brain surgeon gave me for my birthday. I pushed at different keys this time, and this time, my key pushes yielded something entirely new. No, I did not search for "Poppy Fowler." Instead, as I have done many, many times, I searched for "red hair," "woman," "one arm," and "64," which would be Poppy's age if she were still among the living (and if she had told me her true age when I knew her which is, well, questionable).

This time, an article flashed on my computer screen from a website for a small-town newspaper in the state of Oregon called *The Agazola Bugle:* "Transgendered Woman Organizes Neighborhood Crime Watch." The article included the woman's full name, which I will not share here, but which any reader can discover with a computer and a modicum of effort. Let me just say that the name was not "Poppy Fowler" (or "Poppy Fahrenberg" or "Poppy Fahrenheit," an absurd name for any person, real or imagined). Another series of key pushes led to another website, and I was looking at the woman's telephone number on my computer screen.

Without giving any thought at all to what I would say, I dialed that telephone number immediately, and a woman answered after the second or third ring.

"Hello," I said as matter-of-factly as I had intended. "I am not sure if you will remember me. I'm calling from Baltimore, Maryland. I was looking — "

"Hello, Jimmy Nail," she interrupted. I recognized her voice in an instant.

"Hello, Poppy."

Neither of us spoke for several moments, as quiet as if we were in church. My heart was racing. I cannot speak for hers. But still.

"You recognized my voice?" I asked.

"I have caller identification on my phone," she laughed. "Your name and number popped up. I'm looking at them right now."

"Oh."

"Don't you have that on your phone?"

"No," I said.

"But it's nice to hear your voice," she said, "regardless."

"Yours, too."

We spoke for a bit, talking about nothing particularly significant before I said, "May I ask a question?"

"Of course, sweetheart. Ask away."

"Did you ever make it to Europe?"

"No. Not even close."

"You never made it to England?"

"I made it to New England. Does that count?"

"Probably not."

"May I ask another question?"

"Of course, sweetheart."

"What have you been doing? I mean, for work?"

"Nothing glamorous. I worked in a supermarket for a bit. I did the books for a company that sold cement."

"Oh."

"You sound like you're disappointed."

"No, no. I was just curious."

"It's okay if you're disappointed. I am, too, if I think of it. Do you think any little girl ever said, 'Mommy, when I grow up, I want to do the books for a cement company?'"

I let out a laugh. "Probably not, but you never know."

"How about you," she said. "What have you done?"

"Nothing special. A bunch of jobs with no meaning. I was married for many years, but we divorced."

"I'm sorry."

"Thanks, but it's fine."

"Children?"

"Yes, one. My daughter, Claire."

"That's a lovely name. What does she do?"

"She's a brain surgeon," I said after having to think about it.

"Wow. Very impressive."

"Yes," I said. "She's a very smart girl."

"My turn to ask you a question, Jimmy Nail."

"Do you still scream like a girl?" she asked. I could hear her smiling. I could see her grape-green eyes.

"I hope not," I answered, in as deep a voice as I could muster, and now I was smiling, too.

Again, we did not speak for several moments, and my smile evaporated as I remembered the last time I had seen her.

"Poppy," I said, clearing my throat for effect. "I want to tell you how very, very sorry I am for the way I behaved. I was a kid."

"I know, Jimmy," she said sweetly. "I saw the movie."

"That movie was so shitty!"

"I know!"

"I almost walked out."

"Me, too! Where did they get the part about her singing that song to that stupid dog?"

"Plum?"

"Yes, Plum! Who sings a love song to a dog?"

"It was ridiculous."

"I've seen it at least a hundred times, Jimmy."

"Me too," I admitted. After a moment, I finally asked her, "Did you read the book?"

"Yes."

The silence returned, except for the dim and pleasing sound of her breathing.

"Jimmy?" she finally said.

"Yes."

"It wasn't a very good book. I mean, it was better than the shitty movie version, but still."

I heard myself laugh. It took a moment to realize that the sound had come from within me; I do not laugh often or well. "I know," I said, "I know. It's a terrible little book, isn't it? But it's mine."

"Fine," she said. "Jimmy?"

"Yes?" I licked my lips.

"How soon can you get here?"

"I'll be there Saturday," I said. I do not know why I picked that day, but I did, and I stuck with it because you should stick with your commitments, which is why they call them that in the first place. I looked up at the calendar taped to the wall above my desk beside a painting of a girl. I looked at a colorful map of Oregon on my computer screen. I would fly into the airport in Portland, Oregon, rent a car, then drive 60 or so miles to Agazola, if my measurements were right (one inch equals 15 miles), then she would be in my arms and perhaps (fingers crossed) her lips would be on my lips.

"Yes," I said confidently, aware of the loud beating of my heart that threatened to drown out my voice. "Saturday."

Until then, I will count the days. One day, two days, three. Four days, five days. Soon, it will be Saturday. Just not soon enough.

A FAIR REQUEST

If you are the owner of this book, kindly clip the cover below from this page and glue it over the existing cover of your copy of *The Left-Handed Girl*.

✂ CLIP HERE

THE ALLERGIC BOY

A novel

By Jimmy Nail

The following should be glued onto the back of the book jacket.

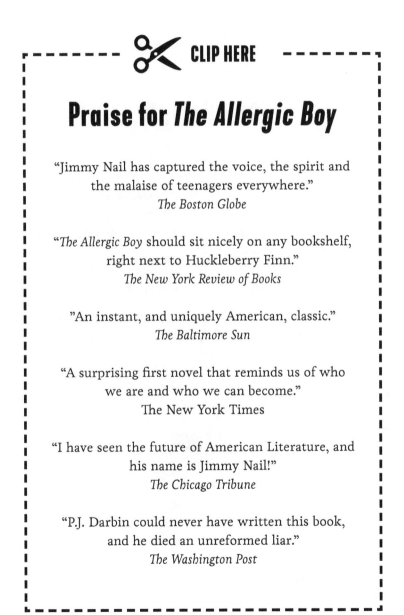

✂ **CLIP HERE**

Praise for *The Allergic Boy*

"Jimmy Nail has captured the voice, the spirit and the malaise of teenagers everywhere."
The Boston Globe

"*The Allergic Boy* should sit nicely on any bookshelf, right next to Huckleberry Finn."
The New York Review of Books

"An instant, and uniquely American, classic."
The Baltimore Sun

"A surprising first novel that reminds us of who we are and who we can become."
The New York Times

"I have seen the future of American Literature, and his name is Jimmy Nail!"
The Chicago Tribune

"P.J. Darbin could never have written this book, and he died an unreformed liar."
The Washington Post

DEDICATION

Please use a thick, black felt-tip marker to cross out the dedication that appears after the title page in *The Left-Handed Girl*. In its place, please insert the following words in your best penmanship: **This book is dedicated to Poppy Fowler, with grace and mercy.**

Be careful not to press too hard or the ink may seep through to the first page. Then it will dry like blood.

THE END

About the Author

Michael Kun is the author of works of fiction and non-fiction. Among other recognitions, his novel *You Poor Monster* was a Barnes and Noble "Discover Great New Writers" selection and was chosen as "Book of the Year" by *Baltimore* magazine. His novel *The Locklear Letters* was adapted for a movie entitled "Eat Wheaties!" starring Tony Hale, Elisha Cuthbert and Paul Walter Hauser and is being reprinted with that title in connection with the release of the movie.

About the Publisher

The Sager Group was founded in 1984. In 2012, it was chartered as a multimedia content brand, with the intention of empowering those who create art—an umbrella beneath which makers can pursue, and profit from, their craft directly, without gatekeepers. TSG publishes books; ministers to artists and provides modest grants; designs logos, products and packaging, and produces documentary, feature, and commercial films. By harnessing the means of production, The Sager Group helps artists help themselves. For more information, visit TheSagerGroup.net

More Books from The Sager Group

Mandela was Late: Odd Things & Essays From the Seinfeld Writer Who Coined Yada, Yada and Made Spongeworthy a Compliment
by Peter Mehlman

#MeAsWell, A Novel
by Peter Mehlman

The Orphan's Daughter, A Novel
by Jan Cherubin

Words to Repair the World:
Stories of Life, Humor and Everyday Miracles
by Mike Levine

Miss Havilland, A Novel by Gay Daly

Revenge of the Donut Boys:
True Stories of Lust, Fame, Survival and Multiple Personality
By Mike Sager

Lifeboat No. 8: Surviving the Titanic
by Elizabeth Kaye

See our entire library at TheSagerGroup.net

Artifex Te Adiuva

CPSIA information can be obtained
at www.ICGtesting.com
Printed in the USA
BVHW082154291121
622844BV00016B/412